Grace Restored Series, Book 5:

Forever Fall

C.J. Peterson

Texas Sisters Press, LLC

ISBN: 978-1-952041-11-2

Published by Texas Sisters Press, LLC. Lufkin, TX U.S.A.

Texas Sisters Press, LLC.
2020

Second Edition

This book is dedicated to my loving husband and dear family who love and support me. You all mean more to me than you will ever know. Thank you! I love you!

A portion of the proceeds will be donated to Hope's Door, whose mission is to offer intervention and prevention services to individuals and families affected by domestic violence and to provide education programs that enhance the community's capacity to respond. To learn more about them, check out their webpage: http://www.hopesdoorinc.org/

To learn more about C.J. Peterson, you can find her online at: http://cjpetersonwrites.com
'While the stories are fiction, the journey is real!'

<u>Summary</u>

Forever Fall, is the final installment of the Grace Restored Series. The direction of Katie MacKenna's life has made a drastic change. In order to escape the heavy hands of Lucca and Joey Rossi, Nick came up with a plan to fake their deaths. With Nick and Katie's identity changed, it allows them to start over with a new life in Australia. Getting married upon their arrival, they plan on living life to the fullest as husband and wife, but have all loose ends been tied? Did Lucca and Joey believe the reports? What about Nate, Nick's twin brother? If he shows up, he could expose them, therefore putting Nick and Katie in danger again. And then there's Dominic Cook. In a memorial to Katie, he gets on a plane to Australia using the photos Katie posted from her first Australia trip to plan his travels. Does he find more than he bargained for once in Cairns? Will Nick and Katie ever be able to get their happily ever after?

Daniel 2:20-22:

20 "Praise be to the name of God for ever and ever; wisdom and power are His. **21** He changes times and seasons; He deposes kings and raises up others. He gives wisdom to the wise and knowledge to the discerning. **22** He reveals deep and hidden things; He knows what lies in darkness, and light dwells with Him.

Table of Contents

Preface - Scenes from Book 4 of the Grace Restored Series:
SUMMER SECRETS 9

Chapter 1 - Into Each Life A Little "Fall" Must Rain 17

Chapter 2 - Autumn Memories 35

Chapter 3 - Indian Summer...55

Chapter 4 - And the Leaves Came Tumbling Down 71

Chapter 5 - Shades of Autumn..85

Chapter 6 - As Autumn Leaves Turn..109

Chapter 7 - A Harvest of Memories..133

Chapter 8 - Autumn Blessings 149

Chapter 9 - Harvest Delights 165

Chapter 10 - Cutest Little Pumpkins in the Patch........................185

Chapter 11 - Harvest Moon 247

Chapter 12 - Golden Days of Fall...261

Chapter 13 - Forever Fall..283

Preface

Scenes from Book 4 of the Grace Restored Series:

SUMMER SECRETS

"GO!" Seth roared before firing off a couple more rounds. Changing the magazine, he shouted, "Don't make me tell you again! GO!"

Nick floored the vehicle, leaving Seth behind. "Katie, love, are you hit?"

"No," she said weakly.

"Can you come up here?"

As she made her way to the front of the Explorer with blown out windows, her body was trembling. "I can't stop shaking."

"I know, just get your seat belt on," he said, fishing his cell phone out from his pocket. When she was settled, he asked, "Katie, do you love me?"

"Of course I do! Why would you ask?"

"Do you want to be with me for the rest of our lives?"

"For however long it is, yes."

"Do you trust me?"

"With my life."

"Then know that I've already got a plan in place that I need to activate."

"What does that mean?" Katie asked, her heart racing out of control.

"We need to go under. There's no escaping Lucca and Joey Rossi, unless we're dead."

"But –"

"Dial Sandy," he said into his phone, cutting her off.

"Hey, Nick. What's up, buttercup?" Sandy answered her phone.

"Sandy, do you have what I asked you to find about three weeks ago?"

Sandy's tone immediately shifted as she asked, "This isn't a social call, is it?"

"Did you do what I asked?"

"Yes."

"Can you meet me at the Cleveland Marriot?"

"The one near City Hall?"

"Yep."

"Yes."

"Bring the envelope I gave you from Damian, along with the little bag," he said before he hung up.

"What did Damian give you?" Katie asked, her nerves raw from the day's events.

"I had him get a hold of one of his contacts who created fake paperwork for us."

"For *what*?" Katie asked, stunned by what she was hearing. "How did you know to plan this?"

"I've had this set up for some time. Actually, since I found out that Rossi was the one who was hunting you down. The only people I have included in the scheme are Sandy and Damian."

"And the bag?" Katie asked.

"It's hair color for me. I'll need to change my hair color to brown."

"Okay," Katie said, taking a deep breath. "And, what *exactly* is the plan?"

"Sandy's found a cadaver to represent both me and you. This took a bit, but she obviously was able to find them. In the meantime, I had Damian get our paperwork."

"What are our new names?"

"Well, I hope you don't mind that I took liberties with your name. Mine is going to be Nicolas Zachariah Sullivan, having people call me 'Nico' – using my dad's first name as my middle, and Nana's maiden name as our last name. Yours, I had changed to Kathryn Megan Sullivan. Megan is for your mother, and I used Kathryn, as a form of Katie."

*   *   *

The next morning Katie groaned when the sun pierced through the curtains of their room on the station in Australia, right into her eyes. With memories of the wedding and the honeymoon night flooding her mind, she turned to her husband and brushed her fingers on his cheek. "Morning, sunshine," she said when his eyes fluttered open.

He grinned. "Morning, Mrs. Sullivan."

"I like that. Kathryn Sullivan," she said, dreamily. "It's pretty, but," she crinkled her nose, "I don't think I like being called Kathryn. It sounds so formal."

"What about Kit, for Kit-Kat? Like my favorite candy bar, since you're so sweet," he said, with a wink.

"I like Kit. That'll work. Not sure about the Nico thing either."

"It's as close as I dare go to my real name. I figured it was close enough to our real names that we'll be comfortable in using them. Also, if we happen to mess up, we can quickly fix it."

"Got it. That makes sense."

"Can you handle the name changes?"

"You gave me your heart, my mom's name, and your grandmother's name. Of course I can handle a name change. It will just take a bit of getting used to."

"Your words touch my heart. You know that?"

"And your heart touches my soul."

He pulled her down to him, and they reignited the passion that started the night before. Showing each other how deeply they felt for the other, they enjoyed their time in the room, undisturbed.

*   *   *

"So," Seth said, as he and Nico still sat on the bench on the station, where he had been filling Seth in, "you're telling me that you and Katie, I mean, Kit, are married?"

"Yep."

"And that you're about to take over this station?"

"Yep."

"And that I *shouldn't* kill you for putting me through this mess?"

Nico chuckled nervously, realizing how deeply it hurt Seth. "I know you're hurt, and I get that, but I needed it to look real and sincere. I know a lot of people were hurt because of this, but at least you now have the knowledge that we're safe and sound."

"What would have happened had I not brought your body here?"

"Sandy said she would make you do it. I'm pretty sure she didn't give you a choice in the matter."

"Not really."

Nico sighed. "I miss her. She had a way of putting things into perspective."

"Trust me. I know. What I *don't* know is what I'm going to do."

"What do you mean?"

"I have to go back knowing you're alive. You're my best friend. How can I go back, supposedly after your funeral, and act like you're dead? How can I go back at all? You don't understand. Your desk just sits there...empty. We've been brothers for too long to leave here knowing you're alive. I can't do it."

"Can't go back, or go back to work?"

Dropping his head into his hands, he sighed. "I don't know."

"Just take some time here to relax and breathe. My funeral is set for tomorrow."

"*What*?" Seth asked, stunned. "You're still going through with it?"

"Yep. According to everyone here, I'm dead. I may look like me, but most of my family resembles everyone else, so I look like a cousin. As a matter of fact, anyone from here who introduces me to anyone, calls me a cousin from the Sullivan side."

"I can't believe you colored your hair," Seth grumbled, ruffling Nico's now dark brown hair.

"That helps remind the guys to call me Nico instead of Nick. Also, if Nate shows his ugly mug around here, they'll know which one is which."

"What are you going to do about that? What *if* Nate shows up? He could blow this wide open."

*   *   *

Dominic Cook couldn't believe what he was reading from those on his social media page about Katie. They were words of memorial. Looking up on the internet about her, he discovered that she and Nick died in a car bomb, and Joey Rossi was wanted for questioning in regards to the incident.

"Katie," he breathed out, tears crawling down his cheeks. "I can't believe she's dead."

Going over to his desk, he pulled out his new identity papers that he got about a month into his move to Canada. Deciding against going to Oklahoma, because he was wanted in the United States, he decided to follow the photos of her trip in Australia as a memorial to her. He had always wanted to visit Australia, this was a good reason, and he felt it was a fitting way to say goodbye to her.

After printing out the photos, he applied for his visa. As soon as it was cleared, he would buy his ticket.

*   *   *

The day Dominic got his visa to visit Australia, he bought his ticket. Picking up the photos Katie posted on her social media, along with his passport and bag, he said, "Well, Michael Esposito, looks like you're going to Australia," he said, referring to his new identity.

Chapter 1

Into Each Life A Little "Fall" Must Rain

"Breathe, Kit! Don't push!" Nico encouraged. "The ambulance will be here shortly."

"Nooo!" Kit growled.

"No, what?"

"No! I can't wait! I neeeeeee –!" she screamed as another contraction immediately spiked, making it difficult to talk.

"Need what?" Nico asked.

Glaring at Nico, Kit breathed as quickly as she could until the contraction would slow down enough to talk again.

"What does she need?" Nico asked Pete.

"She's not talking when the baby comes, because it's too painful, mate," Pete explained, as he and a neighbor, Andi O'Leary from Koala Pass Station, worked to get ready for the delivery if the ambulance didn't make it in time.

Nico furrowed his brow. "What do ya mean?"

"He *means* that when you have a baby, it's like your lower parts are ripping in two," Andi explained. "Give her a few."

"But…she's in so much pain. Isn't there something you can do?"

"SHUT UP!" Kit growled when the contraction finally slowed enough for her to talk.

Looking at her, upset by her reaction, Nico apologized, "I'm sorry."

"You don't understand," Kit groaned. "Pete, is it supposed to hurt this…Ahhheeee!" she screeched.

Pete spun around in alarm. "Kit?"

Tears poured down her cheeks. No longer in labor pain, it was a sharp, searing pain.

Pete and Andi were immediately to her side. "Kit?" Pete asked. "What is it? This is more."

Feeling warm liquid pouring out of her, out of breath, Kit whispered, "Blood."

"What? Where?"

Nodding toward her legs, Kit did her best to control the pulsating pain that pounded through her body.

When Andi and Pete looked under the blanket, Andi's face went pale. "Go get Nana," she ordered.

"Is she going to be okay?" Nico asked.

"Go get Nana," Andi ordered again.

Nico ran down the stairs and out the door. "Nana, Pete and Andi need you."

"Me?" she asked, dread written all over her body. "Pete and Andi asked for *me*?"

"Yes. Please hurry."

"What is it?"

"Kit's hurt, and there's a lot of blood."

"Oh, dear Lord!" Nana jumped up. With Nico on her heels, they took the stairs two-by-two. By the time they reached the top of the stairs, the room was deathly silent.

Nico ran to her side. "Kit?"

"I'm sorry, mate." Pete put his hand on Nico's shoulder. "There was nothing I could do. It was too much."

"What are you…*what*?" Dropping to his hands and knees, shaking, he looked at Kit's lifeless body. Then he turned to Pete and weakly asked, "Both of them?"

"All three of them."

*   *   *

Kit sat upright in bed with tears streaming down her face. "Kit? What's wrong?" Nico asked. Glancing at the clock, he groaned. "It's three o'clock in the mornin', love. We don't have t' get up for another two hours. You've had us up through the night every day this week."

"I'm…." She sniffed, wiping her eyes. "I'm sorry. I'll go sleep in another area, so you can get some rest."

"If anythin', I'd sleep in the other bed in Flynn's room, but I enjoy sleepin' with my wife. What's going on? These dreams are gettin' stronger."

"I don't know what to do about them."

"What was this one?"

"I go into labor. The babies were twins. We were up in this room, but I didn't make it. Neither did the babies."

"The other one had you kidnapped, right?"

Dropping her head into her hands, she sighed. "Yeah. Then there was the one where I found a dead child face down near the north field. Ya know, I'm fixin' to turn into an insomniac here if this doesn't stop."

"No." He sat up and hugged her. "You need sleep. I would miss cuddlin' with you if you didn't sleep with me."

Kit growled. "I'm just tired of these dreams. They're strong. With Shawn not coming back after the couple of days that Danny promised, I'm really concerned for all of their safety. There's no one to ask."

"We're going t' have t' wait on God for any news on them. In the meantime, I'm prayin' over the field in the mornin' after breakfast an' at night. I've banned the use of it, too. They've been ordered t' use the other three fields an' t' stay away from that one. Nana's not too happy, but she's been a nervous wreck since Shawn didn't come back as well."

"How do we get a hold of them?"

"We don't. We trust God an' let Him have control of the situation."

"Another lesson in trust, huh?"

"Yep. Can ya handle it?"

"I don't think I have a choice. I'll just have to take each day as it comes."

"Good, because we have a funeral t' go to t'day."

"Whose?"

"Mine. You slept all last night. Seth brought my, um, doppelganger here yesterday."

"Oh yeah? How'd *that* go over when he saw you?"

"It was rough at the start, but he's better now."

"Did he forgive you?"

"After a while. I told him everythin'."

"Good. That's one less person who I feel we've lied to."

"Just relax. We did this for safety. I would be willin' t' bet that anyone who finds out about it would just be happy we're safe."

"You don't think they'll be angry with us for not trusting them?"

"Kit, just relax," Nico said, pulling her down to him. As she cuddled in, he sighed. "I know this is where we're supposed t' be."

"I do too. It's just a little frustrating that I won't be able to talk to anyone anymore. Are you sure I can't even log onto my computer to see what's going on via social media?"

"Nope. I'm pretty sure yer profile's been tagged. If so, they'll know as soon as you log in. If it's any consolation, I can't do it either."

"Not really. I *am* glad we still get to be in contact with part of your family, though. I miss everyone."

"I miss them too, but you'll get sucked into life on the station soon enough. Then you won't have time t' check social media."

"That busy?"

"Yep. Now, we need t' eat breakkie with the rest of the group this mornin'. Seth wasn't happy when he didn't see ya for himself last night."

"Okay."

"I have a skeleton crew workin' t'day durin' the funeral. When we get back, we'll have a lot t' catch up on around the station."

"Well, you've jumped right on into this boss roll, haven't ya?" Kit smiled as she nudged him. "It fits you well."

"Thanks. I've been doing the orders through Nana for the moment, so the blokes on the station don't think I'm comin' in here actin' like his nibs."

"Meaning?"

"Meaning, comin' here actin' like a know it all – bossy."

"Got it."

"I think she has me in the sheep area this week, lettin' the blokes out there teach me what they know, even though I could do it with my eyes closed. Next week I move t' cattle. Then the week after, I go t' the barn with Pete. While those who knew me growin' up know it's a pretense, others are takin' t' the idea a little better knowin' they have input. It's tedious, but it will help in the long run."

"Um, Nico?"

"Yes, my love?" he asked, looking down at her.

"Ya know we still have over an hour and a half until we have to get up, right?"

"Right."

"Um, we could fill that up with some bonding time?" she suggested.

"Really? You wanna bond, huh?"

"Well, if you're fixin' t' be buried later, I'd better enjoy you while you still have life in ya, Nicholas Scott Locke," she said with a smile, tracing the lines on his chest with her finger.

"Well, unfortunately, Katie Marie MacKenna is already dead an' buried."

"Yeah, but you have her new and improved clone, Kit."

"This is true. She's full of life an' looks a lot more healthy."

"Really? You little bugger," she said, and started tickling him.

"Not fair!" he objected. Grabbing her wrists, he flipped her over before he leaned down, kissing her neck.

"Now *that's* not fair," she breathed out as tingles flooded her body. "Not fair at all."

*   *   *

When they walked into the dining room for breakfast that morning, Seth looked up, stunned. "Kit? You look great! A little sleepy, but *much* better than I have seen you in a long time." When he hugged her, he said near her ear, "And, I forgive you for this ruse as well. As long as you guys are safe, I feel much better."

Hugging him one more time before letting him go, she said, "Thank you."

"So, you're Kit?" one of the ranch hands, Liam, asked, looking her up and down.

"Mind yerself," Nana cautioned. "She's his," she said, nodding toward Nico.

"I get that. Just a little admiration."

"If he doesn't rip yer arm off an' beat ya with the messy end, *she* will," Nana warned.

"She doesn't look like she could pull skin off a custard."

"Oh, she can beat you within an inch of your life," Seth spoke up. "I know who trained her."

"What are you goin' on about, ya bloody seppo?"

"That's enough!" Nico snapped. "You've offended my wife, me, *an'* my cousin's best friend, *an'* we haven't even sat down t' eat breakkie. I know y'er new here, so I'm cuttin' you a break…this time. I want everyone t' hear this: I *do not* want t' hear the term 'seppo' on this station again, *ever*! Have I made myself clear?"

"Crystal," Liam mumbled before picking up the plate of bread to pass around.

"Not so fast." Nico stopped him. "You owe both of them an apology."

"Technically he owes all three of ya an apology," Nana pointed out. "Unless ya wanna work with Pete in the barn all day shovelin' horse –?"

"Nana!" Nico cut her off.

"Pucky," Nana finished.

Nico took a deep breath before he explained, "We need t' clean some a' the language around here too. In the long term, if we have any ankle biters runnin' around here, I don't want 'em havin' mouths worse than dock workers."

"Seriously?" Liam shook his head. "We can't even talk normal? What kind of station is this?"

"One that takes care of their people like family," Barwon explained. "I don't mind watchin' my tongue t' get treated equal t' family. That don't happen on many stations."

"I know, but havin' rules on what we can say an' what we can't?"

Nico gestured. "You know where the door is."

"Y'er bloody serious?"

"Watch it, Liam," Nana warned. When he looked at her stunned, she said, "*He's* the boss."

"No, he's not. *You* are."

"Nope. He's been givin' the orders for quite some time. I've only been handin' 'em out. Y'er lookin' at his nibs over there. An' personally? I wouldn't wanna go against 'im. He's kinda big."

"I see that, but can he hold 'is own?"

Nico burst out in laughter. When Liam raised an eyebrow, Nico suggested, "We could go a couple a' rounds if ya think you can handle it?"

"No," Nana said sternly. "No fightin'."

Liam sighed. "Fine. I'll go along with yer rules."

"Right-oh," Nico said, sitting down at the table, as Kit sat down between him and Seth. "So, where am I t'day?" he asked Nana, changing the subject.

"Sheep," Nana said. "Cattle starts next week."

"Why is he doin' that? Has he never been on a station?" Liam asked.

"Wow, y'er really pushin' it, aren't ya?" Nana snapped.

"Well, if he's the boss, why is he doin' the circuit?"

"Because he wants input from all y'all," Kit explained.

"You don't have a say in any a' this," Liam scoffed. Then under his breath, he added, "Bloody seppo."

"That's it!" Nico growled as he stood, slamming his hands on the table. "You got one more shot an' y'er outta here!"

"Nico?" Nana questioned.

"He just slammed *my wife*! *No one* will slam her on this station…*ever*! This is hers just as much as it is mine."

"From what I hear, she can't even ride a horse. How is she supposed t' run a station?" Liam challenged.

Barwon leaned over and turned Liam by his chin so he was looking at him. "If ya got a problem with Kit, then ya can take it up with *me*. She is part a' the station. Whether she can ride or not, does not make or break whether it's hers. Now, ya got somethin' else t' add, *mate*?"

Liam looked at him wide-eyed. Barwon's size was intimidating at best. "Uh, no. I'm done."

"Good. If *I* hear one more objection from that big mouth a' yers, we're gonna take a walk t' the road and sort this out. At that point we'll be off the station, so Nana can't object," he said glancing at Nana. When Nana nodded, he said, "See?"

"I get it," Liam growled.

"Good. Now that that's settled, how about –" Nico was cut off by a flash of blinding light that lit up the entire house as the barn roof blew out. "Get t' the horses!" Nico shouted while a sudden rush of rain poured from the sky like a waterfall, and debris blew all over the ground from the strike.

"Good heavens!" Nana exclaimed, as everyone ran outside. "The barn's gonna burn t' the ground!"

Kit ran into the kitchen and called Tommy and Andi O'Leary, from Koala Pass Station, the station adjacent to theirs.

"Hello?" Andi answered.

"Andi!"

"Kit? What's wrong?" she asked, hearing the panic in her voice.

"Barn's on fire!"

"We're comin'," Andi said and hung up.

Seeing portions of the barn in flames despite the rain, the flashes sent Kit back to the warehouse and car explosions. Rocking on her feet as she crouched on the ground, she covered her ears from all of the shouts of the men and sounds of the animals, as the flashes of the last year flew through her mind at an alarming rate.

"Kit?" Pete ran up to her, while Nico was in the barn doing his best to release the horses from their stalls. "Are you okay?" When she didn't answer, Pete shook her. "Kit! I need ya t' focus!"

"Flashbacks," she squeaked out, as the thunder rolled and lightening continued to flash around them.

"Take deep breaths an' get them under control," Pete ordered, holding her arms. When they locked eyes, he explained, "You need t' help get the horses out of the barn. They won't come out if they're scared. They need you. Do your best t' get t' Star an' Jumbunna."

Taking a deep breath, she slowly let it out. "I-I think I can."

"I *know* you can. C'mon. You need t' focus for me."

"I-I'm okay," she said, getting her emotions under control.

Pulling her up, he dragged her to the barn. "Good. Let's go."

The smoke from the burning wood and hay instantly stung her eyes as they neared the barn. Inside of the barn suffocated her, but she did her best to keep up with Pete. Coughing, she struggled to get air while grasping the reigns Pete shoved into her hands from Star.

She wanted to get out of the barn, but Pete pulled her to Jumbunna's stall. As she stumbled behind him dragging Star with her, Pete left her at the stall door to retrieve Jumbunna. Quickly returning, he thrust the reigns into Kit's other hand. Covering the horse's eyes with a cloth so they didn't see the fire and refuse to leave, Pete shouted, "Get them out a' here!"

Squinting to protect her burning eyes from the fumes, Kit barely made the outline of the door of the barn twenty feet away. The horses pulled and tugged as she walked backward toward the doorway, fighting the horses every step of the way. "For crying out loud!" Kit said before she coughed. "Just come with me! I'm trying to save your behinds!"

Struggling to yank the horses out of the barn, Kit continued to look over her shoulder toward the door, praying with everything in her to keep everyone safe.

"Get out of here!" Liam shouted, grabbing Jumbunna's reigns. "I have this one. You get Star!"

The only thing Kit could do was nod as she used her arm to cover her mouth. The air was saturated with the stench of burning wood and hay making the air heavy. *Would she be able to do this? Could she really help run this station with Nico?*

As she and Liam finally made it outside, she heard Pete yell to Nico, "What do we do with the barn itself?"

"Let it burn."

"*What?*" Nana asked, stunned, as she carried a saddle over the pile of equipment already rescued that was near the main house.

"Nana, at this point the integrity of the structure is in trouble," he explained, tossing a handful of equipment onto the pile. "It's better t' rebuild it from the ground."

Nana dropped her head and sighed. "Y'er right."

Kit's heart broke. Understanding the amount of work that would have to go into rebuilding a barn, she shook her head while tying Star to the rail.

"Probably a wise idea," Liam remarked, tying Jumbunna to the railing next to Star. "We'll be lucky t' keep the shell. The bigger concern at this point is the hay. We lose that, we could be in trouble for the winter."

The group from Koala Pass pulled in as Kit finished tying Star. While the two truckloads of men got out and ran to help the others, Tommy and Andi went over to Nana and Nico, who were still standing by the main house. "Are ya lettin' it go?" Tommy asked.

"Yeah. We need a new one anyway. There's no savin' it," Nana pointed out. "It was too far gone by the time we got everythin' out of the horse barn."

"Thanks for yer help," Nico added. "We're doin' our best t' save the sheep barn an' keeping the hay clear. That's where our concentration is focused at the moment."

As she stood in the pouring rain that had since slowed to a steady flow from the initial burst, Andi and Tommy's fifteen-year-old daughter, Anna, walked over to Kit. "Y'er lookin' a little pale. Are ya okay?" she asked.

"I'm fine. That was just scary. It shook the house."

"I'll bet. We've seen some big ones out here," Anna commented. "One even took out the main house before. Now *that* was scary."

"I would imagine. How old were you?"

"Seven."

"Were y'all able to save any of it?"

"Thanks t' Serenity Wells we were. Nana brought her crew an' they helped. It took hours t' make sure it was all the way out, but they did it. They also helped rebuild the portion that got burnt. Mum an' Dad were grateful. Our two stations work t'gether very well. Not too sure about that Akoonah Station, though." Anna shuddered. "That place gives me the creeps."

"G'day, Anna." One of Serenity Wells Station's ranch hands named Alec smiled at her. "Thank you for yer help."

Grinning ear-to-ear, Anna said, "Our pleasure."

As Alec walked away to continue clearing the sheep barn, Kit observed, "So, you like Alec?"

Anna looked at her, panic in her eyes. "What?"

"How long?"

"How long, what?"

"How long have you two been together?"

"We haven't…yet. My brothers would kill him," she said, upset, referring to her five older brothers.

"I'll bet! He's three years older than you."

"Technically he's only two an' a half. It's just how our birthdays fall. He just turned eighteen."

"Is that justification? Or are you trying to convince yourself that it's okay?"

"I don't know. Is it even possible t' have a successful relationship with an older guy? How many years are between you an' Nico?"

"There are seven, but we met when we were older. Right now you both are in very different phases of life. Keep in mind that after college, age isn't so much an issue. Until you turn eighteen, though, age will be a *very big* issue," Kit said sternly. "Your parents would have a conniption if they even had a clue the two of you were seeing each other."

Watching him work, Anna dreamily sighed. "He's very handsome. Sweet too."

"Is he a Christian? I know y'all go to church."

"Not sure," she admitted. Then she turned to Kit and asked, "Are you guys comin' t' church on Sunday?"

"I believe we are. Unfortunately, we have to bury Nico's cousin here in a couple of hours. Although, if this weather keeps up, we may have to switch that to tomorrow."

"That's a shame. I heard he was a great guy."

Adam, one of Anna's brothers, took a bottle of water from the cooler Kit had set out, and asked, "Who?"

"Nick."

"Nick Locke?"

"Yeah."

"Nick's blood was worth bottlin'! It was a real shame the way he went. Wish I could a' known 'im better. My brother Alex had nothin' but nice things t' say about him," Adam said. "He knew Nick before he moved to The States. They were about the same age."

"Better get the lead out. Looks like the fire's hit the hay bales," Anna pointed out.

"Crikey!" Adam exclaimed before he ran back toward the barn.

"If the hay's on fire, we're not having a funeral today," Kit decided. "I need to go see what Nico and Nana want to do."

"Okay. I'll keep the water bottles stocked."

"Actually, if you want to help your mum with making sandwiches, that would be great. *Then* you can come back out and admire Alec," Kit said with a knowing smile.

"Got it," Anna said, and disappeared into the house.

As she made her way over to Nico, Kit couldn't help but enjoy the camaraderie she felt between the two stations. She hoped with every bone in her body that the peace would continue, and that things with Akoonah would continue to stay calm.

Chapter 2

Autumn Memories

Standing in the shower the next morning, Nico couldn't believe it took them the rest of the day, along with the entire night to get all of the fires under control. Exhausted was a mild term for how he felt, but there were family and friends coming in from all over the territory for Nick's funeral. While the funeral was going on, he already scheduled a skeleton crew for the station to keep things in order, along with four guys watching the hay bales since they were still smoldering.

After his shower, Nico fumbled with the colored contacts that turned his blue eyes to dark-brown. He got them only for today, knowing people he knew growing up in Cairns were going to be there. He prayed his brother would not be attending, but knowing him, he would just to cause problems for the family.

Trimming his beard and mustache that he had grown out since his arrival; he shook his head at the difference in his appearance. He would be more than happy to shave it off the next morning. Looking in the mirror, to him lately, was like looking at a total stranger.

Getting dressed in his dress shirt, pants, and tie, he admitted to Kit, "I'm kinda nervous." Bungling his tie for the third time, he whipped it off and started over again.

"What? Going to your own funeral? Could be interesting. Have to say not many people get to experience that," Kit said, zipping her skirt before slipping into her white silk top.

"Should I wear a jacket?"

"Depends."

"On what?"

"On whether you want to have heat stroke or not. Pretty sure a short sleeve dress shirt is more appropriate for this area. Besides, your pants and shoes are black. That should be enough."

"Right-oh. Grrr!" He growled as the knot came out wrong again.

"What's wrong?"

"I can't get this. I don't understand what the problem is."

Kit went over to him and fixed his tie. "Could be nerves. Just relax. You're not fixin' to say anything, are you?"

He nervously chuckled. "No. Nana didn't think it was a good idea."

"Do you know who all will be there?"

"Quite a bit from Cairns an' the territory from what I understand. Then there'll be an open house here for a couple a' hours before people have t' head back home after the funeral."

"Think you can play Nico that long?"

"What do ya mean?"

"Nico, let's get serious here for a moment. You're supposedly his cousin. I'm supposedly your wife. Now, not many people saw me at your parents bar-b-que, but Nate should easily recognize me."

"Hmmm. Good point. What do ya want t' do?"

"Well, I've already thought about that. Your mum's on the way with the answer."

"What did you do?"

"A simple solution for today, but we have to come up with a more permanent solution."

"What did you do?" he asked again, his heart racing. "You're not supposed t' make major changes without checkin' with me first. That could put us all in trouble."

Hearing a light knock on the door, Kit asked, "Who is it?"

"It's me," they heard Nico's mom's voice.

When Kit opened the door, Paige threw her arms around her, not wanting to let her go. "You have *no idea* how hard it's been not comin' here, knowin' you two were here."

"I know. I'm sorry. Did you bring it?"

"Yep. Here ya go," she said, passing the bag to Kit, who took off for the bathroom, before she ran over and hugged Nico. "Don't *ever* give me heart failure like that again."

"I'm sorry," he apologized. "The only one who knew here was Nana. The less people who knew, the better."

"I know. She finally told me after all the ruckus cleared. Yer dad is ready t' kill ya himself…if ya weren't already dead, so t' speak."

Nico chuckled. This situation would be awkward at best.

When Kit walked back in from the bathroom, he was stunned to see her wearing a shoulder-length dark-auburn wig. "What? A wig?"

"Yep. I'll cut it and color it later," she explained, showing him the two boxes of hair color.

"Who's gonna cut yer hair? *Why* are ya gonna cut yer hair?"

"Because I need to. In order to keep us safe, I need to make sure that I don't look exactly like me."

"Here are yer color contacts," Paige said, handing her dark-brown contacts. "We still have a couple of hours. Want t' cut yer hair now? I can do it. It's a straight cut. Right?"

"If you cut it off, I can layer it," Kit agreed. "Then I can color it without changing my hair twice. I'll put my contacts in after we finish cutting my hair."

"Okay. Change into shorts an' a tank top, an' I'll be right back," Paige said before taking off for a towel, broom, and a pair of scissors.

"Are ya sure? You've given up so much. I really didn't want t' make ya do that too."

"I know. And I appreciate it," Kit said, as she quickly changed. Laying her clothes neatly on the bed, she explained, "I have to do it."

By the time Paige got back upstairs from talking to Nana, Kit was sitting in a chair in the middle of the bedroom with her hair wet.

"Okay, these are t' cut with, an' this is t' clean. Nico, that's gonna be yer job," Paige explained, handing the broom to Nico. "Not too bad. It's close enough t' yer name that I can deal with it. By the way, Nana said it was a smart move."

After Kit combed her hair out, Paige cut a strand of about two feet. Nico just about had heart failure. "We're savin' those big cuts," he insisted, scooping it up before Paige cut again. As she cut, he held onto it, and then set it on the dresser until he could get a bag to put it in.

"You *could* donate most of it t' canter patients, since ya won't be needin' it," Paige suggested. "They make wigs out of donated hair."

"That sounds like a great idea!" Kit exclaimed.

"How about I keep this section?" Nico held it up. "You know, t' remember. I'll put it in yer memory box. Then I'll secure the rest for Mum t' take into town when she goes."

"That will work," Kit agreed.

When she finished the initial cuts, she made sure it was all the same length. Then Kit used the mirror in the bedroom to layer her hair before she disappeared into the bathroom.

"What do ya think?" Paige asked, while Nico bagged Kit's long hair and then cleaned the mess off the hardwood floor.

"I think I'll feel like I'm sleepin' with a stranger. She has *always* had long hair. I didn't want her t' have t' do that."

"She'll look good either way. Her heart's still the same. It's just her hair. Besides, how do ya think *she* feels wakin' up t' a brunette instead of a blond?"

"Point taken."

"Just so ya know, that's a smarter idea than ya think."

"Oh yeah? Why?"

"Because yer brother's supposed t' be comin' t' the funeral."

"*What*? You were supposed t' talk him out of that!"

"We tried, but he can be a stubborn bugger. If he gets out a' line, Nana'll shoot him."

"This is true," he said, sitting next to his mom on the bed with the bag of Kit's hair in his hand. "If we need t' start over, then we need t' do it right. So far she's been sheltered here. If we can pull this off, then it should be smooth sailin' from this point forward."

"Too true. That's the spirit." Paige put her arm around him. "After t'day, it'll be a piece a' cake."

"Sure. Famous last words."

*   *   *

After Kit washed the color out and dried her hair, she was stunned by the difference a haircut and color made. Even her head felt lighter. This was the shortest her hair had ever been for as long as she could remember. She liked the new color. It was just different.

"Well?" Kit asked, walking into the room with her hair styled and her contacts in.

Nico and Paige stood, jaws dropped. "Bloody hell!" Paige whispered.

Nico was too stunned to reprimand his mom. "You look so different, yet the same."

"Is that good or bad."

"Neither. Just different," Nico explained.

"Hmm, kind of like *you*," Kit hinted. "You went from blonde hair and blue eyes, to dark-brown hair and dark-brown eyes...*and* a beard and mustache," she said, rubbing his beard.

"Yeah, but this way Nate shouldn't recognize you," Paige pointed out.

"Nate's going to be there?" Kit squeaked out, her face draining of color.

"Now, love," Paige said, resting her hands on Kit's shoulders, "you can't be actin' like that when ya see him or he'll suspect somethin'. Right now, you look different enough that you should be able t' pull it off."

Kit took a deep breath and slowly let it out. "You sure?"

"Yep. So, get dressed an' meet us downstairs. I'll give ya two a few minutes t' talk, but we have t' leave here in ten minutes max."

"Yes, ma'am."

"Y'er gonna have t' call me Paige. Maybe later you can be my adopted daughter, but for now y'er supposed t' be related by blood as Nana's brother's son's wife. Good heavens! That's a mouthful."

"Or, you could just call me cousin." Nico smirked. "At least on paper, that's who I am."

"What if Nana's brother comes?" Paige asked, as the thought struck her.

"Nana's already talked t' him," he dismissed her concern. "He doesn't mind havin' a son, so t' speak. Actually, since he never married he's all over it."

"At least she picked a good great-uncle for you t' belong to. I like Zack's Uncle Fletcher. He's a good guy now, but wasn't in his younger years. He was a bit of a player. When Jasper got killed, Fletcher just about lost it. Jasper was Fletcher's favorite of all the nieces an' nephews. Nana said they were thick as thieves."

"I see," Kit said, following the story as she changed into her skirt and dress shirt again.

"If anyone asks you, Kit, Fletcher is Nico's dad. He'll be your father-in-law."

"Got it. Are we fixin' to pull him aside as soon as he gets here?"

"No worries. He'll be up here in a few minutes t' let us know it's time t' go," Paige explained. "He an' Nana are talkin' right now."

"I see," Kit said, slipping on her shoes just as there was a knock on the door.

Paige got up and opened the door. "Speakin' a' Fletch."

Kit watched Fletcher take a really hard look at Nico before he turned to Kit. His build was quite a bit like Nico's, but he had dark-brown hair and dark-brown eyes, same as Nico at the time, thanks to his disguise. "Crikey! Ya could definitely pass as one a' my own!" the six-foot-five Fletcher remarked. "An' ya got yerself a beauty!"

"Thanks, mate," Nico said before going over to his great-uncle, giving him a hug.

"Are ya sure you can pull this off?"

"Yep. Y'er from Perth, right?"

"Yep. An' you two need t' be from there too."

"Actually, accordin' t' the story, I grew up in Perth with you since my real mum supposedly died in a car accident. Once I graduated, I supposedly went t' a friend of Nana's station in Alice Springs area. Then I met Kit when she an' some friends came t' Alice on a college graduation trip. We ran into each other at Red Rock, an' we've been inseparable from that point forward. I followed her back t' The States, an' we were in Texas for a bit before Nana called about poor Nick, an' wanted t' know if my wife an' I wanted the station so it would stay in the family."

"Got it," Fletcher agreed. He went over and gave Kit a hug. "Nice t' meet ya, Kit." Then he looked up at Nico and asked, "What are ya goin' t' call me?"

"Would Dad or ol' man work?" Nico asked.

"Sure." Then he turned to Kit and said, "An', you can call me Dad or Fletcher."

Kit nervously tucked her hair behind her ear. "This is still kind of new to me. What about Fletcher?"

"That'll work. When y'er comfortable, you can call me Dad. Until then, Fletcher will be just fine. Just don't call me a nasty name, an' Bob's yer uncle." He smirked. "I've been called some colorful names in my day."

"I'll bet!" Paige jumped into the conversation. "Pretty sure they weren't anywhere near as nice either."

"Ya know, I *used* t' like you," Fletcher said, giving her a gentle nudge.

"Ya still do, an' ya know it."

"I do," he admitted. "Well, Charlotte said t' get our bums down there. It's time t' load up."

"Right-oh. Let's get t' my funeral." Nico sighed. "Should be interestin' at best."

*   *   *

When Kit walked downstairs, some of the guys who knew her had a stunned look on their faces. She shrugged it off and told them with the hotter weather coming in that she wanted a new look.

As they drove the half-mile down the road, Seth asked, "Why is it so far from the main house?"

"The station is 650-acres, a little over a square mile," Nico explained. "When the family settled, they allocated a portion away from the house where it's peaceful, quiet, an' surrounded by trees. Havin' it down the road, allows the graveyard an' the main part of the station t' have some distance, givin' those grievin' some privacy."

"I see. So, what's with the red hair? And, why did you cut it off?" Seth asked Kit.

"I figured if he has to change his appearance, so should I," Kit explained. "The contacts we're wearing are just for today, since some people may recognize us from Cairns. We'll only have to wear them if we go back into Cairns. What do you think?"

"Definitely different. Not in a bad way, just different."

"I know."

"As Mum put it, while she looks different on the outside, her heart is still the same," Nico added.

"It's nice. When the sun hits it, the red pops. When you're not in the sun, it's more of a dark-red, kind of like an auburn," Seth added.

Changing the subject, Nico asked, "Are ya ready t' say a few words at my funeral?"

"Shut up!" Seth snapped. "This is confusing at best. I don't know how I should feel."

"Just keep the feelings you've had this past week an' pour yer heart out."

"Going to have to be convincing since you're brother's coming."

"Who told you?"

"Nana. She said not to look dumbfounded, because he really *is* your doppelganger."

"In pretty much every sense of the word. He's the only one who could blow this sky high."

"Then you had better keep your temperament in check, or he'll spot it a mile away," Kit pointed out. "He knows how to get to you. He may test you if he suspects."

"This is our lives, here," Nico said, pulling up next to Nana and Pop's truck. "I will *not* slip up. There's nothin' he could say that would trigger me enough t' tip him off."

"Keep that thought in mind," Seth said as they got out of the car. "Seems he's making a beeline for you."

Sure enough, Nate, who had been standing in a crowd, headed straight for them as soon as they stepped out of the truck.

"Wow!" Nico exclaimed when Nate walked over to them. "It's incredible. My ol' man said you looked exactly like him, but I didn't believe him." Taking Nate by surprise, Nico hugged him. "It's so good t' finally meet you. Wish it were under better circumstances, but a pleasure nonetheless."

Nate took a step back and studied Nico and Kit for a few moments. "It's uncanny. You an' Uncle Fletch look a lot alike. And, who's the sheila?"

"This is my trouble an' strife, Kit," Nico introduced them. "She's from Texas."

"Really? How did the two a' ya meet then? An', do ya have any sisters?"

Kit giggled before she pulled the deepest Texan accent she could, "No, I don't. I have two brothers, but no sisters, so I don't think they'd be interested. And, we met when some friends and I came here for vacation."

"Shame." Nate clicked his tongue. "Anyway, they've set up over there. Nana got plenty a' beer back at the station for when this is over?"

"Really?" Seth asked, taken aback. "Is that what you're concerned about? Not that your *twin brother* is dead, but about beer?"

"Haven't met you yet," Nate said, sticking his hand out. "I'm Nate."

"I know exactly who you are." Seth crossed his arms, refusing the handshake. "I now have a much better understanding as to why you and Nick didn't get along."

"Oh yeah? Enlighten me, please." Nate crossed his arms in response. "I'm curious t' see what tales the golden boy had spun."

"Nate," Nana groaned, walking over to the group. "You've barely met yer cousin, an' y'er already startin' somethin'? If it wasn't for Nick's funeral, yer sorry bum wouldn't be welcomed here at all. At least show some respect an' keep yer tongue in check t'day. Not everythin' is about you."

"Nice t' see you too," Nate quipped.

"Go find yer ol' man. He's the only one who can tolerate you."

"Who says I'm *not* keepin' my tongue in check?" Nate asked, offended.

"The looks on their faces tell me all I need t' know. Now, are ya gonna listen, or am I gonna have t' kick ya off my land?" Nana asked sternly.

"From what *I* hear, it's *his* land," he said, pointing to Nico.

"Not until I sign it over t' him. Right now, it's still mine."

"Well, wouldn't want t' mess up my brother's last day on this planet. Oh wait! Actually, he's already gone. Guess I can't mess up anythin' for him now, can I? Seems he already messed up himself. That's what got him into the position he's in now." Gesturing toward where the casket was resting over an open hole, he added, "Can't get anymore gone than dead."

Nico grabbed Kit's arm when she went to jump, and she froze. Nate was pushing with everything he had.

"Seems he was *such* a wonderful FBI agent, that he even got his girlfriend killed," Nate pushed. "Yep, pretty sure I can't do any worse than that."

"Go-find-yer-dad!" Nana growled.

"Ya may wanna calm down. That high blood pressure ya got goin' on could kill ya, an' then you'll end up right next t' yer favorite grandson," he said and he left.

"He's a piece of work," Seth said under his breath when Nate was out of earshot.

"Very much so," Nico said, still holding Kit's arm. "If I had t' hold on any tighter t' Kit's arm, I'd probably bruise it."

Kit whipped her arm back and crossed her arms in a huff. "I know who *I* would like to bruise."

"Easy on," Nana warned. "He's got that anger that spreads like wildfire. Keep yerself in check."

"No worries, Nana. I won't let him get t' me," Nico said confidently.

"You either," she warned Kit.

"I won't," Kit promised.

"We can't afford any more death or destruction."

*   *   *

Pastor Paul Peters got up to say a few words before he called if anyone wanted to say anything. Several ranch hands, and many old friends of Nick's from his school days spoke before Seth got up for his turn. When Seth stood beside Nick's casket, he rested a white rose on top and said, "Nick Locke was an amazing Special Agent for the FBI. His concern was for those he worked with and those he loved. It was an honor to call him friend and to stand beside him in the field. He never thought twice about giving himself for another. He was everything that the FBI stands for – patriotic, kind, protective, and full of integrity and fortitude. Every day we go to work, there is a chance we won't make it home. Nick knew the risks, but he did it anyway. On the day he passed, he was with his love, Katie. I have the comfort of knowing that in the end, they were together…and are still together today." He paused a moment. "What can you say about a best friend? Nick was on my unit as soon as he graduated from the FBI academy. We were partners from that day on. He had my back and I had his. Even on his last day, I ordered him to get he and Katie out while I put down cover fire." He shook his head. "And, in the days following, all that was left of him was an empty desk. His playfulness will be missed in the building, and his strength of character and heart can never be replaced. He was a good man." He sighed. "What am I going to do without you? Bringing him home was the hardest thing I have ever had to do. Knowing his lifeless body was below me so I could bring him to you was heart wrenching." Looking toward the sky, he took a deep breath before he continued, "Life is an interesting thing. Nick lived every day as his last. He was strong in heart, soul, mind, and body." As a tear slid down his cheek, he admitted, "The man could be a pain in the behind, but there was no one else I would rather have by my side. Knowing I'll never have him beside me each day is breaking my heart." He sighed. "I'll miss you, Nick. Today the world lost a hero and Heaven gained one. You will never be forgotten, my friend."

Taking the folded American flag to Nick's mother that he brought with him, Seth presented it to her, and said, "the American people thank you for raising such a brave man, and allowing him to serve our country."

"Thank you," Paige said, accepting the flag as she wiped the tears from her eyes.

Afterward, he went and stood by Nana, who held his hand. Pastor called for Paige to come up next. "My boy," she sighed, placing a red rose on his casket while she clutched the flag with her other hand. "He was one in a million. Who knew just how much life would change when we sent him t' The States? When he came back several months ago, I was thrilled. He had gone from a boy, t' a man, t' now…" she gulped, glancing at the casket. Looking toward Zack, she whispered, "I can't," and ran to the car in tears.

Pastor got up and asked, "Is there anyone else who would like t' say a few words?"

Zack placed a red rose on the casket as he wiped his eyes. Without a word, he shoved his hands in his pockets before heading for Paige.

Noticing no one else moving, Pastor said, "While there are many joys in bein' a pastor, this is not one of them. It's durin' this time, we continuously ask 'why?' Why does a parent have t' bury a child? Why would such a strong young man, with excellent morals an' integrity get taken from us so soon? John 15:13 tells us, 'There is no greater love than to lay down one's life for one's friends.' Nick did that every day he went t' work. He worked t' keep his country, his family an' friends, an' his love, safe. That's not a job a lot of people are cut out for, but he did it with everythin' he had in him. A man like that is rare. Most importantly, though, he was a strong Christian. I got the chance t' talk t' him when he an' Katie were here this past summer. He knew the Word. He had a strong relationship with Jesus. He knew if somethin' happened, that he would be able t' run into the Father's arms…to safety. Well, friend," he said, setting his hand on Nick's casket, "now that you've made everyone you could safe, it's yer time t' rest in peace. May God continue t' bless yer legacy as you live on in the hearts of others," Pastor said before bowing his head in prayer. "Father, we thank You for the life of Nicholas Scott Locke. We thank You for all the lives this young man has touched. We thank You for keepin' him safe for as long as You did, an' only ask that many blessed things may come from this life taken too soon.

Thank You, Father, for the knowledge of knowin' when things don't make sense, that You have it all under control. Please bless this family an' keep them safe an' sound. In Jesus' most precious name I pray, Amen."

When he finished he added, "It is my understandin' that we are t' go back t' the main house for some time of sharin' stories about Nick. I would also like t' extend a message of gratitude from the Locke an' Sullivan families for yer attendance today, along with the part you played in Nick's life. Each one of you meant a lot t' him. May God bless you as you continue t' live your life, sharin' whatever gift Nick gave you."

As everyone dispersed, they said their condolences to the family. Getting back into the vehicle, Seth commented, "That was awkward."

"That was sweet," Kit countered.

"Yeah. That was nice of ya," Nick agreed.

"I meant it. I would have probably said more, but trying to pull feelings was difficult knowing you were standing right there," Seth explained.

"Pretty sure that's why Paige left," Kit pointed out

Starting back to the house, Nico said, "I really felt for my Mum. I wish I could have gone t' her, but I am supposed t' be a distant cousin."

"Your brother is the one who acts like a distant cousin, six times removed. Callous thing, isn't he?" Seth huffed.

"Yes. Keep yer distance," Nico warned. "There's a family curse that has attached itself t' him. If you noticed, he has a ton of anger."

"Who *didn't* notice?" Seth said. "He was brooding in the corner of the group like a black cloud. I was relieved he didn't want to say anything."

"Me too. Not sure I could have held Kit back if he opened his mouth again," Nico said, taking Kit's hand in his as he drove.

"I'll be good," she promised. "I'll just avoid him with everything I have."

"Good plan," Nico said, as they pulled up to the main house and got out of the vehicle. "Better idea would be t' disappear for the rest of the day, but that would look bad."

"That still may be called for," Kit yawned, stretching. "I'm thinking a nap may be in order by the time this is over."

"Let's just pray that after t'day this mess is over," Nico said, as they walked into the house.

*   *   *

Arriving in Cairns only a few days before Nick's funeral, Dominic, known by his ID as Michael Esposito, began his journey. Using Katie's photos from her profile of her previous trip to Australia, he drove to the places in the pictures from Cairns. Stumbling into a coffee shop one morning, he picked up a newspaper and read it while eating his breakfast. He about choked on his toast when he found Nick's obituary in the paper, along with an article about him in the local news section, and what happened to Nick and Katie in The States.

Tucking the paper under his arm when he left the coffee shop, Dominic knew what he needed to do. Going to a local clothing store, he purchased a white dress shirt, dark pants, and a tie. He had to look like he fit in at the funeral. His size, stature, and lack of Australian accent would be more than enough to make him stand out. He would have to be careful on how he did it, but he intended to see Nick buried for not protecting Katie. It would only be then, that he would know it was for real. It would be at that moment, he would have closure.

*   *   *

Standing in the middle of the crowd of eighty to a hundred people who gathered around Nick's gravesite, Dominic listened as over twenty people got up to talk about Nick. The one that got to him the most was Nick's mom. Seeing the pain in her eyes broke his heart. As much as he hated Nick, he didn't want anyone to hurt like that, and have to bury their child.

From where he stood, he had a good view of the family. It amazed him how much each of the family members resembled each other. That's when he saw her. Rubbing his eyes, he squinted to get a better view. *The wife of the new owner of the station looked a lot like Katie.* He heard someone call her Kit Sullivan. *Could she be Katie? She was supposed to be buried in Oklahoma two weeks ago.*

Using his fingers, he covered her hair from a distance in order to center on her face. Feeling the color drain from his face, as fear, excitement, and anger all churned deep within him, he would swear in a court of law that Kit Sullivan was Katie MacKenna. There would be only one way to find out.

Chapter 3

Indian Summer

Walking up the dirt drive that seemed to go on forever after the funeral, Dominic stayed as close as possible to the tree line. Not wanting to be seen, he crouched down when he got closer to the house. He would have to be sneaky in how he would talk with her, but he *had* to talk to her. He *had* to find out if she was Katie or not. As he sat there waiting for his moment, he formulated a plan.

*   *   *

"This is exhausting," Kit whispered to Nico about an hour into the time at the house.

"Y'er lookin' a little pale. Stay here," he said, leaving her on the couch, only to return with Pete a couple of minutes later.

"You okay, Kit?" Pete asked, checking her forehead. "No fever."

"No. I'm not hot. I'm tired. Just really tired."

"How's yer stomach?"

"Fine. Why?"

"No reason. Just checkin' different things. It may still be the medicine she's on. How many days does she still have of that?" Pete asked Nico.

"Today was the last day."

Pete sighed. "Right-oh. We'll keep an eye on ya, but I reckon it's just the medicine. Why don't ya go get somethin' t' eat an' drink, an' then head out t' the porch t' get some fresh air?"

After grabbing a glass of ice-cold lemonade, Kit headed out to the bench near what was left of the horse barn. Happy to know the demolition and rebuilding would start the next day, she settled in to watch the sunset that was still a couple of hours away. It was a stressful day, but she held onto the promise that each day would start fresh and new, with no mistakes.

Hearing something in the corner of one of the stalls still standing, she set her lemonade aside and walked over. Peeking into the darkness of the stall, she was stunned when a board smacked into the back of her head. Falling to the ground, the only thing she saw before passing out was the ground.

*   *   *

From where he sat in the bushes, Dominic watched Kit walk out to the bench. He furrowed his brow when she got up, heading into what looked like remnants of a barn. Jumping when he saw her fall to the ground, he waited. If he showed himself too soon, whoever just hit Kit may kill her.

He watched as a burly man, who looked like Nick, scooped her off the ground. Glancing toward where the graveyard was before turning back to Kit, his heart raced out of control. *Was that Nick's ghost?*

Realizing he saw the man at the graveyard, he concluded it had to be Nick's brother. Baffled by the resemblance, he collected himself and decided to follow him at a distance. If Kit needed immediate help, he would step in, but his goal was to see where the man took her first. If he could give the cousin information, it may help when he proclaimed his innocence once he made his appearance.

*   *   *

Following the man and Kit for what seemed like forever, Dominic was relieved when he finally stopped. Nate took Kit into an old metal storage shed on a property that didn't look like anyone had occupied in years. With the door open, Dominic could see into the tiny building. He watched as the man tied Kit to a chair, and then used duct tape to cover her mouth before pulling up a chair to wait until she regained consciousness.

This was his moment. Turning from the scene, he ran back to the station as fast as he could. By the time he returned, most of the crowd of people had left. Taking a slow, deep breath, he said aloud to the Lord, "If You're there like Katie said You were, I ask You to be with that girl, and be with me here. Please show me that You are real. If so, I promise to follow You for whatever time I have left. Just please, don't let that man hurt the girl?"

Taking a brave step forward, he walked into the living room of the main house to see Seth, Nico, Nana, Pop, Flynn, Adam, Zack, and Paige scattered about the room.

"Dominic?" Seth stood, reaching for a firearm that wasn't there.

"Who? Why?" Nico asked, stunned. "What are you –?"

"I saw someone who looked like Nick take that girl from here," Dominic quickly explained, cutting him off.

"*What*?" Nico stood in shock. "Who? What girl?"

"Your wife. At least I assume it was your wife," Dominic clarified.

Running up the stairs, Pop momentarily returned with a gun. Tucking it into the back of his pants, he ordered, "Show us."

"Y'er not supposed t' have that," Nana warned.

"Charlotte, you know it'll be needed if Nate has Kit."

"Please stay here," Nico pleaded. "You have t' stay here an' take care of the station. I can't let you go."

"You can…an' you will. This is *still my* station, an' she's a member of this family. I will protect everyone here with everything I have," he said sternly. Turning back to Dominic, he ordered, "Show us."

"Just a minute," Nico said before running up the staircase.

"You remember where she is?" Pop asked.

"Y-yes, sir," Dominic stammered.

"Fine. Pop an' I will go," Nico said, after returning from upstairs with his knife attached to his belt. As he rested his hand on the doorknob, he stopped and turned toward the others, "Everyone else secure this station. With Kit missin', we're a target for Akoonah."

"You can count on us," Seth acknowledged before Pop and Nico ran out the door with Dominic.

"Dom, explain t' me why y'er here again?" Nico asked, as they made their way through the bush. "An' be careful. This isn't a nice area when it comes to crocs."

"Got it." He nodded in understanding. "As for me? I came here to do a memorial visit for you and Katie. You *are* Nick, aren't you? An', that girl *is* Katie, isn't she?"

"I'm Nico, an' my wife, the one y'er tellin' me Nate took, is Kit. My dad, Fletcher, is Nana's brother."

"You look awful young to be his son," Dominic pointed out.

"I was a late-in-life baby. Can we concentrate on Kit, please? What did ya see?"

"I thought I saw Katie at the funeral, so to get a better look I came to your house. That's when she went out to the bench with a glass of lemonade. Are you *sure* that's not Katie? She sure walks and looks *a lot* like her."

"Shut it about Kit, an' keep talkin'!" Nico snapped. "That blokes got my wife!"

Dominic continued pushing through, deeper into the bush, as he finished his story. "He made a noise in what was left of a barn. When she went to check it out, he hit her in the head with a board."

"You have the gun, right?" Nico checked with Pop.

"Yep."

"Good, because the way this story is goin', I may have t' use it on sight."

"No worries. I won't let you," Pop said, sternly. "This isn't yer fight. It's mine an' Charlotte's. *I* will end it if I have to."

"Let's pray it doesn't go that way. What else can ya tell us?" Nico asked Dominic.

Huffing and puffing, not used to the amount of exercise he was doing, Dominic explained, "He took her to a metal storage shed and tied her to a chair. Then he sat in another one, waiting for her to wake up. That's when I ran to get you. Look, I don't want to hurt her or anything. I just want to make sure she's safe and happy. Katie or Kit, whoever she is, deserves all the happiness she can get."

"Just get us there. How much longer?"

"Shhhh," Dominic shushed Nico as they approached an abandoned house, with a storage shed out back. "Last time I saw them, he had her in there."

"Let's go get her," Pop said, pulling Nico with him around toward the back of the house.

Not wanting to be left out, Dominic slowly followed them.

"Be careful," Pop warned Nico, "the anger is extremely strong in him. He operates and feeds off it."

Nico only nodded in response. Narrowing his eyes, he was forced to keep his own anger under control when he saw exactly what Dominic described. "We have t' get her outta there."

"We will," Pop whispered. "We need somethin' t' throw him off, though, so we can take him by surprise."

"Got it," Dominic said. Before either man could object, Dominic stepped out into the clearing between the shed and the house. "Hello?" he called.

Nate jumped at first. Then he saw the slightly overweight man, who looked to be in his upper forties, and chuckled. "This should be easy," he remarked, walking out of the shed.

Seeing Nate get off his chair, Dominic gulped. *He would do this for the girl. Whether she was Kit or Katie, he would help her. He had enough blood on his hands.* "Howdy, friend," Dominic said, doing his best to act like nothing was wrong. "I'm just checking on the property for the owners. Is there a reason why you're in their shed?"

"Really?" Nate sneered, as he pushed the door partially closed with his foot before crossing his arms. "Y'er watchin' the property of a dead man?" Taking several steps forward when Dom didn't immediately respond, he asked, "Why are ya watchin' the property of a dead man?"

"It-it's for the family," Dominic stammered, watching Nico and Pop silently creep toward the shed behind Nate.

"Well, you can tell 'em that I've got it covered. They don't need t' send ya anymore. I got permission from the son t' stay here."

"We'll have to verify that. Wanna, um, come in the house with me, and we'll give him a call?" Dominic asked, doing his best to bait him away from the shed.

As he took another step forward, Nate heard the creak of the door, and spun toward the shed. "What do you think y'er doin'?" he demanded.

Nico swung the door wide open, to see Kit looking at him in wide-eyed terror. Tied to the chair with duct tape on her mouth, she screamed, trying to warn him of Nate headed his way.

Dominic jumped on Nate, who sent Dominic flying into the air, landing on the ground with a thud several feet away as if he were a sac of potatoes, instead of a two hundred and fifty pound man. Nate barely got turned around, to see Nico dive for his legs, knocking him to the ground.

While Pop watched the pair on the ground, Dominic ran into the shed. Seeing Kit's eyes get even bigger, she screamed in terror, as her two worst nightmares collided right in front of her.

"I'm not going to hurt you," Dominic said to calm her, while he searched for a knife to cut her lose. When he found it, he crouched in front of her and explained, "I'm here to help. I promise you that I won't hurt you, Kit."

Kit stopped screaming and watched as he cut her lose. Ripping off the tape once her hands were free, she bolted from the chair to see Nate over Nico, with Nico's knife in his hands. "Someone stop this!" she screamed, running toward the pair, but Dominic caught her in his arms to stop her from running toward them.

Just as Nate was about to plunge the knife into Nico's heart, a shot rang out, echoing around them. With the incessant ringing left in her ears, Kit's scream sounded hollow when Nate looked up at her, blood dripping from his mouth.

"Nico?" Kit squeaked out, pale and shaking, as she ran over to the pair and dropped to her knees near Nico and Nate.

Nico grabbed the knife before he shoved Nate off him. Passing the knife to Kit, Nico then scooped Nate up in his arms.

"Why? Why did you do that?" Nico pleaded, tears in his eyes. "As much as I don't like yer actions, y'er still my family. I love you."

"How could you?" Nate whispered. He let out a screech that sounded like a bat from the depths of a cavern before his body lost its rigidness. "It's gone," he said, relieved. "It's finally gone."

"The anger?"

"Yes."

"Nate. Do you love me?"

"Yes. I know it's you, Nick," he said, resting his hand on the side of Nico's face. "I know my brother by sight."

"I know you know who the Lord is. Do you believe Jesus died for yer sins? Do you believe He loves *you* too?"

"Not what I –" he stopped and gulped, struggling to get air. "Not what I did."

"Yes. He died for even yer sins. Please? Do you believe Jesus died for you? He only wants t' forgive you."

"Some things should not be forgiven. I only want t' ask for *yer* forgiveness."

"You have it, brother. But, Jesus wants t' forgive you too. Tell me you know this. Tell me you understand He loves you an' wants t' forgive you. He's already paid the penalty."

"No, mate. Not me. You live yer life t' its fullest," he said, and was gone.

Nico growled in frustration. Looking at Pop, Dominic, and Kit, he asked, "Why? Why wouldn't he accept Jesus' gift of forgiveness? That's all he had t' do!"

"Did ya feel the demon leave him?" Pop asked.

"Yes. Why didn't he make the choice, though? He was free!"

Placing her hand on his shoulder, Kit quietly explained, "Not everyone will accept His gift. Our job is to tell them, not make them believe. That's the gift of free will that God has given each of us. We each have to make a choice to believe and trust in Him. Nate thought he was too far-gone, but even Nate's sins were not too great that God wouldn't forgive him. Jesus already paid the penalty for *all* sins."

"Even mine?" Dominic asked, wiping the tears from his eyes. "Did Jesus pay the penalty for *my* sin? Is there enough grace in there for me too?"

Kit's heart broke at his words.

"Katie…and don't deny it, I know you're Katie. Katie, do you think this Jesus would forgive me for my sins of attacking those girls, killing Jillian and Aaron, and even kidnapping and almost killing you? Do you *really* think I have a chance? I've heard you say before that, 'sin, is sin, is sin – they're all equal.' Does that apply to me?"

Kit gulped. *Could she really forgive him for what he did? Would Jesus really forgive him? A murderer? Dominic, the man who took two young lives, and attacked several girls. The man who kidnapped Katie and even tried to kill her? Could she forgive him?*

Praying in her heart for strength and mercy, along with the massive amount of grace that was going to be needed for this, she went over to Dominic. "Dom, I don't know what to say to that," she admitted. "I do know that while Jesus was dying on the cross, He forgave a murderer who was on another cross right next to His. I know He said that man would be in paradise that very day. You're going to have to ask *Him* for forgiveness. As far as me, that will take some time. I'm sorry, but I don't trust you."

"I know your secret. I know you're still alive."

"Are you blackmailin' her?" Nico asked, stunned.

"No. What I was going to ask is if I could join you on the ranch. I want to help. I promise you that I won't hurt her. If I wanted her dead, I would have let Nate do whatever he wanted to do with her, but I didn't. All I want is for her to be happy…and as much as I hate to admit it, *you* make her happy."

"We'll talk about it when we get back t' the station. Right now we have another problem," Pop pointed out, as he gestured to Nate's body still in Nico's arms.

Nico looked down at Nate's body. Seeing all the blood covering his clothing from where the bullet penetrated his chest, he shook his head and whispered, "I don't know what to do."

"I did it, boy," Pop said, taking over the situation. "You don't have t' worry about him anymore. He's gone. There's a pond infested by crocs a short distance down that way," he said, pointing past the shed further into the woods.

"We're fixin' to feed him to the crocs?" Kit asked, stunned.

Nico nodded, solidifying his decision. "If we don't, then Pop will get arrested. I'll carry him. Dominic, you stay here with Kit. I'm trusting you," he warned, standing with Nate's body in his arms. "Don't make me feed *you* t' the crocs too."

"I won't let anything get her," Dominic assured him.

Several long minutes after Nico and Pop left for the swamp, Kit turned to Dominic and explained, "You can't tell anyone you know we're alive. If you do, Lucca and Joey Rossi will kill us. That's the reason we ran in the first place. If you truly mean what you say, you *will not* tell anyone what you saw and heard here today. Am I clear?"

"Katie, I meant it when I said I only want to see you happy. That's all I've *ever* wanted. I thought I could make you happy, but now I know it's always been Nick. *And,* now that I know you're still alive, I want to protect you and keep you safe…whatever it takes."

"It's gonna take you keeping your mouth shut. No one knows we're alive."

"I promise you that I will keep your secret. I hurt you and you're friends. For that, I'm sure there is never going to be enough time to forgive all the pain and agony I caused. I will keep your secret, though. I promise you. No one will ever get it out of me."

"Thank you."

"Katie?"

"It's Kit now," she reminded him.

"Kit, I am really sorry. Some day, I hope you will forgive me."

Kit rested her hands on her hips and sighed. "Do you know what grace stands for?"

"No."

"There's an acrostic that explains it best. It's God's Restoration At Christ's Expense. Jesus *did* pay the penalty for your sins. Despite just how much I don't like you right now, and how much pain and agony you caused, only God can forgive your soul. Now, I *am* only human, so it will take me a lot longer before I could even begin to forgive you for that, but Jesus already knows it all and is only waiting for you to ask. If you're fixin' to ask Him to forgive you and restore you using the grace and mercy He's already paid for, then that's between the two of you. I want nothing to do with it for now."

"I understand. I know it's a lot to ask."

"Not too much to ask of Jesus, though," she corrected. "That will be between the two of you. For now, I have to trust that you won't hurt me."

"I wish I could say I never would, but we both know I already did," Dominic said, somberly. "All I can say is that I hope one day down the road you can find it in your heart to forgive me."

"That's something the good Lord and I will have to work out. In the meantime, maybe we should see where they went."

"No. I promised to keep you safe. You need to stay here," Dominic said sternly. "I want to do good. I want to do what I promised."

"All right," she said, crossing her arms. After a moment of silence, Kit said, "I don't know what we're going to tell the family."

"Tell them that Nate fell into the swamp an' the crocs got him," Nico said, walking out of the brush with his grandfather. "I don't want Pop t' go t' jail for Nate's actions."

"I deserve it, though," Pop admitted. "Charlotte's gonna kill me when she finds out what *really* happened."

"Pop, this *has* t' stay between us. I have lost too much already. I don't want t' lose you too."

"The only people who know are us," Dominic pointed out, "and, I'm not saying a word."

Realizing he needed to keep his friends close and his enemies closer, Nico got an idea. "Dominic, did you really mean it when you said you wanted to find God's grace?"

"Yes."

"Then, I'm goin' t' make ya an offer."

Cocking his head to the side in curiosity, Dominic asked, "What is it?"

"Wanna work on Serenity Wells Station as the cook?"

"*Have you lost your mind?*" Kit asked, jaw dropped.

"Nope. Nana could use a break in the kitchen, an' he's a good cook. Besides, what better way t' keep an eye on him?" Nick pointed out.

"Yes," Dominic said, decisively. "I'll do it. That way you know I'm serious."

"If you even hurt one hair on Kit's head –"

"I won't!" He said, putting his hands in the air in surrender. "I promise to help protect her."

"I'll get the paperwork that'll let ya stay started in the mornin'," Nico agreed, shaking his hand.

"Nana's fixin' to have your head on a silver platter!" Kit argued. "The kitchen is *her* territory."

"An' when they sign the station over t' me an' you, *who* do ya think will be doi'g all of the cookin'?" Nico asked. "Y'er goin' t' have enough on yer plate. Besides, we already know he's a great cook, right?"

"Right," Kit said, cautiously.

"Then, give him a chance? If he screws up, he's dealin' with me," Nico warned.

"I promise to give you only my best," Dominic promised.

"Let's just hope you're as good as your word," Kit said, feeling apprehensive and frustrated by Nico's offer. While she understood what Nico was doing in hiring him to protect both secrets, she would have to see the man who killed Jillian and Aaron, and held her captive, every day for the rest of her life. *Would she be able to handle it? This would take some amazing grace to work through this one!*

Chapter 4

And the Leaves Came Tumbling Down

When the group returned to the station, the family and Seth greeted them about halfway down the drive, anxious to hear what went on. "What happened?" Nana demanded. "Was it Nate?"

"Yes," Pop sadly confirmed, knowing full well what her next question would be.

"Where is he? What happened t' the drongo?"

"He dropped into a pond infested by crocs," Nico said, bailing his grandfather out. "He's no more."

"Bloody hell!"

"Nana!" Nico snapped. "Watch yer mouth!"

"That's the cleanest I could think of," she explained, in shock. "The sins of the father will be passed down, even into the fourth generation. *Please*," Nana grabbed Nico's collar and pulled him down to her, "do *not* let this take another generation! Stop this!"

"I plan to," Nico assured her. "I've already started prayin' for the next generation. Without God, another one will fall. *He* is our only hope of breakin' this curse."

Taking a step back, Nana did her best to stop her world from spinning. Kicking herself into organization mode, she said, "Looks like we'll need t' do another funeral."

"Let's just make this a quiet one," Pop suggested. "Keep it within the family."

"Yeah," Zack agreed. "I have a feelin' it wouldn't be that well attended anyway."

"Just a simple gravestone will work," Nana said, decisively. "We'll need that pastor back here, though. He may have been a drongo, but he deserves a proper burial. He was still one a' my grandsons."

"Just have the courtesy of not puttin' him next t' Nick?" Nico asked.

"Oh no. There's a particular section for those taken by the curse," she explained. "He'll be the fourth one placed there…an' hopefully the last."

"Here's prayin'," Pop agreed.

*   *   *

While Nana and Pop went about reporting Nate's death to the authorities, as well as setting up for his funeral, Seth pulled Nico and Kit aside. "What's with Dom? Why is he still here? You *know* I need to arrest him and get him back to The States to face charges, right?"

"You can't," Nico said quietly.

Seth narrowed his eyes. "What did you do?"

"Just a sec," Nico said, and then went over to Dom. "Just have a seat on the couch, mate. Let me sort this out."

"Will do," Dom said, and anxiously sat down under the watchful eyes of Zack, Adam, and Flynn. Meanwhile, Paige headed into the kitchen to clean up, keeping herself busy.

When Nico got back to Seth, he pulled him and Kit off on their own, on the other side of the burnt barn so no one would hear them. "Here's the thing," Nico started, "we're goin' t' keep Dom here on the station."

"*Have you lost your mind?*" Seth snapped. "Are *you* okay with this?" he asked Kit.

"I'm dealing with it," she mumbled, nibbling on her fingernails. "It's for the best."

Seth crossed his arms. "Why? What happened out there?"

"Exactly what Dom an' I said happened," Nico explained.

"What am I missing? This doesn't sound like the whole story."

"Please just know it's for the best?" Nico asked. "Trust me?"

"You're serious? I'm just supposed to ignore the fact that there's a murderer on the station with you guys? Do you understand how difficult you're making this for me to leave?"

"We'll be fine. There are plenty of guys around here t' look out for us. Today was a fluke. What I may do is get the heads of each group a walkie-talkie for better communication, makin' sure Kit an' I have one too."

"That's a start. What else are you going to do? Use that FBI brain of yours. There needs to be more done."

Nico sighed, rubbing the back of his neck. "I could set up video surveillance throughout the station. That way, if somethin' happens we'll be able t' have video proof."

"What about a security crew?"

"That's a good idea. We have plenty of hands. We can use a couple of them for patrol."

"Nick…I mean, Nico," Seth corrected himself mid-sentence, as he put his hands on his hips, "From what I've seen and heard since I've been here, you are at war whether you want to admit it or not. And now you've invited a wolf into the sheep's pen by offering Dom a job?"

"Y'er right, but Dom *needs* t' stay here."

"Why?" Seth pressed.

"Because he knows who we are."

"How?"

"I can't tell you. Just know I need t' keep him here t' keep an eye on him."

"Even with Katie…I mean, Kit…I mean…grrrr!" he growled. "This is confusing at best!" Seth sighed, collecting his thoughts for a moment. "Let me try this again. Even with Kit in the house with him? Is that safe?"

"I feel this is the best decision."

"Kit, what about you? How do *you* feel about this?"

Kit crossed her arms, almost hugging herself. "I trust my husband."

"Look at her body language!" Seth shouted. "Does she even *remotely* look comfortable with this?"

In a quiet voice, Nico asked her, "Kit, *are* you okay with this?"

"I don't know. What I *do* know is that he's looking for Jesus. If my comfort is to be sacrificed for his salvation, then yes, I'm okay with this. If you're asking me if I trust you and your decisions, then, yes, I do. If you're asking if it unnerves me to have him here on the station, then once again, yes, it does, but I will trust that God will still protect me. If it's true grace he's looking for, then he'll find it here."

"That paints a pretty clear picture," Seth observed. "If those are your answers, then I'll abide by it. I'm not comfortable at all with leaving him here. If Director Shaw even *remotely* catches wind of this, we're *all* in trouble."

"Seth, if *any* of this gets out, then we don't have t' worry about Director Shaw…we're dead," Nico pointed out. "Lucca an' Joey Rossi won't hesitate t' pull the trigger."

"I get that, but feeding her to Dominic is not helping this situation."

"Guys?" Kit said, feeling the pit in her stomach. "I was just kidnapped and had two of my worst nightmares collide right in front of me."

"I know. I'm sorry," Nico said, wrapping his arms around her. "I'm really sorry. I don't know what t' do here."

Looking up at him, she said, "We've kind of been winging this."

"I know. I didn't plan on Dom showin' up though. He knows who we are, that we're alive, an' where we are. I don't want t' have t' pull you from my family too. If we leave here, we won't have anyone t' watch our backs."

"I get that."

"Then know I'm tryin' everythin' I can do t' protect you as much as possible."

"But, you can only do so much."

"I know. I'm tryin' t' control as many factors as I can. With Dom here, I can control that factor. I can't control Lucca and Joey Rossi. Now that Nate is dead, that's a factor I don't need t' worry about."

"I understand."

"Then you have t' know by now that I'll do everythin' in my power t' protect you."

"It obviously wasn't enough today."

Seth cringed. "Ouch."

"Look. I didn't say that to hurt you. I said it so you would know that I understand God is my ultimate protector," Kit explained. "As head of this household, you are responsible to God for any decisions made and for what happens to this family. *You* are the one ultimately responsible to the Lord God Almighty for me, and any future children we may have. Having said that, I'm going to trust your decisions. I know you take each decision to the Lord. I just pray you did this one as well."

"It was a snap decision, but I feel it's the lesser of the two evils," Nico admitted.

"Then let's just pray the good Lord will protect us."

"I agree."

Seth cleared his throat to get their attention.

"Anything else?" Nico asked, his hands on his hips.

"What *really* happened to Nate?"

"This is goin' t' have t' be somethin' I can't share with you."

"We don't have secrets. After the whole death thing, we made a promise of no more secrets. I really didn't think we had any before then."

"We didn't," Nico admitted. "I need t' protect the person who took him out, though."

"Was it Kit?" Seth asked, horrified.

"No. It wasn't Dom either."

"Was it *you*?"

"No!"

"No. It wasn't him," Kit said, feeling pressured. "Look. Nate attacked Nico, and was about to kill him, when Pop shot him."

"*Kit*!" Nico shouted, upset.

"He needs to know," Kit insisted, as tears poured down her cheeks and her body shook. "I'm tired of all the secrets. There is no such thing as a good secret! It *will* bite us if he doesn't know."

"Now I have to figure out how to *not* arrest Pop *and* Dom," Seth said, throwing his hands in the air. "Why are you doing this to me?"

When Nico rested his hands on Seth's shoulders, for the first time since he knew him, Seth saw panic in Nico's eyes. "You can't arrest either one," Nico pleaded. "Please. *Please* don't take Pop away from us. With everythin' that has happened t' us, can't ya just give this t' me?"

Seth let out a slow breath of air, as he tossed around the many scenarios that could happen. "If you guys stay here, you'll at least be protected. I can't take Pop from you. He was trying to save your life. At least tell me something good came out of this?"

"At this point, Nate is out of our lives, an' he's free from the demon," Nico said, hesitantly. "If Dom wasn't here, Kit may not be either. Nate had her. He was goin' t' hurt or even kill her just t' get back at me. Dom saved her life. Now he wants t' know more about Jesus."

"Likely story." Seth huffed. "Look, I get that he saved her. I get that if he wasn't here, then Kit may not be here. What I *don't* get is why he's *still* here."

"Because he knows where we are, *an'* he knows what happened t' Nate. We *need* t' keep him here. An' if he ends up findin' the Lord in the process, then good *will* come out of this."

"You'd better hope there's not anything worse still to come. Look, I don't agree with this, but I trust you. Now that I know it all, it makes more sense. I'm going to go pray. There's a lot I need to work through."

"I appreciate it."

"Your secrets are your secrets," Seth agreed. "I don't have control over what you do with them. Is there anything else I don't know?"

"No."

"Then keep a close eye on Dom. If he makes the slightest move, you contact me immediately and I will have his tail end arrested so fast it'll make his head spin. The only reason I'm even slightly okay with this is because I know you will rip him limb from limb if he steps even a toenail over the line."

"You know I will."

*   *   *

"What do you *mean* Dominic is going t' be our cook?" Nana asked in shock, as she and Nico argued in the kitchen. Everyone else was out on the porch, relaxing after the day's events. "Who is this Dominic? How do you know him?"

"I can't answer that," Nico confessed.

"Then how am I supposed t' trust him? I don't let just *anyone* in my kitchen."

"I get that. How about if I prove t' you how good he is?"

"How?"

"Go grab a drink, an' go out t' the porch. I'll give him a test."

"Okay," Nana said, giving up.

Walking out to the porch, Nico called Dominic back to the kitchen. When he got there, Nico explained, "I need you t' do somethin' for me."

"What's that?"

"How badly do you want t' stay?"

"Really bad. I know this'll be a chance for me to finally have a life again. I also want to explore this Jesus some more."

"Then I need ya t' cook the best meal you have ever cooked in yer life. I'm tryin' t' fight for ya, but I need *you* t' step up an' cook for them. You need t' impress that entire bunch out there."

"*All of them*?" Dom asked, wide-eyed.

"Nothin' big, mind you. A sample plate will work. Just do yer best. I have t' stay in here with you, but the kitchen's yers for now. Ya have t' get Nana's blessin' in order t' stay here."

"I see," he said, with his hands on his hips. Going over to the walk-ins, he looked around, wracking his brain to think of what to cook.

"Do you know any Aussie foods?"

"Yep. I studied them before I came. Let me think for a moment."

Watching Dom pull a variety of ingredients from the coolers, Nico asked, "What are ya makin'?"

"Just watch," Dom said, working feverishly. In a blender, he combined shallots, onion, garlic, jalapeno peppers, cilantro, soy and Worchester sauce, pepper, a blood orange, and limes before he then topped it off with some beer.

"Really? What *are* ya doin'?"

"Shhh," Dom said before he ran the blender. Then he took five steaks and poured most of the mixture over it, covering it with clear wrap before placing it in the cooler. Then he made garlic and cheese mashed potatoes. While the potatoes were boiling, he reduced the remaining marinade into gravy for the potatoes. Once that was finished, he put the potatoes together, and then left them on the stove with a lid to stay warm. "Please get out a small plate for each person out there," Dom asked Nico, as he continued to fly around the kitchen, completely in his element.

While Nico got the plates out, with a fork on each one, Dom ran out the back. Using the gas grill, he cooked the steaks. "That smells great!" Nico remarked, and then tasted the potatoes. "Ohhhh," he groaned. "This is amazin'!"

"Mashed potatoes are Kit's favorite," Dom remarked. "Pretty sure *she's* the one I need to impress the most, not Nana."

"How do ya figure?"

"Kit's the one I did the damage to. There's nothing I can do to change our past, but I *can* show her the risk to let me stay here is worth it."

"True. Just give her space, though," Nico warned. "You know her well enough t' know that she's on her guard."

"At the very least," Dominic said, retrieving the steaks from the grill.

Cutting the steaks into bite-sized pieces, he placed three bites on each plate before he put a spoon full of potatoes with gravy covering them. For the final touch, he added a thin slice of apple on each plate. "There! Colorful, yet tasty."

"Looks great! Let's get it out t' everyone," Nico said. "Family first."

"Got it," Dom agreed, as they each carried out the plates, four at a time.

Once the plates were out, Nico and Dom each grabbed the remaining two and headed out with everyone else. "Well?" Nico asked.

"We were waitin' for you," Nana explained.

"Pretty sure we're waitin' for *you*," Paige pointed out to Nana.

Taking the hint, Nana took the first bite. With a look of pure bliss on her face, she shook her head. "Eat up, boys," was all she got out before diving into the rest of the plate.

Remarks of how great everything was came from all over the area. Centering on Kit, Dom asked her, "Well?"

"Wonderful. As always," Kit responded, her tone cool. That was all she *could* say. The steak was amazing, and the potatoes and gravy melted in her mouth. She knew there was no way she could *ever* touch Dom's cooking.

Dom beamed with pleasure. Soaking in all the accolades, he was grateful for the new lease in life Nico and Kit offered him. No more looking over his shoulder. No more living behind the computer screen. He could enjoy the beautiful scenery and hopefully the camaraderie that came with living on the station. He didn't mind the early and late hours. He would be able to cook again, and he was happy!

Chapter 5

Shades of Autumn

Working on the barn for the over a week began to wear on the workers. Between the added work of demolishing and then rebuilding the barn, they still needed to keep up with the daily chores. Having Dominic in the kitchen, allowed Nana to be more of a presence in keeping everything organized, mainly supervising the barn build. She, Nico, Pop, and Pete took a day to do the blueprints until they were all satisfied. Nico wanted to use a prefabricated barn out of convenience, but Nana stated that everything on the station was hand-made and this would be no exception. Once the supplies arrived, Nana took over the foreman position of building the barn, allowing Nico to take charge of the rest of the station.

With the stress of everything spinning around her, Kit was thrilled the next day would be Sunday. Able to center herself at church, allowed her to take the focal point off herself, and back where it belonged…on God. Concentrating on the Lord, focusing on Him, helped her keep things in perspective.

Also on Sundays, the station normally ran on a skeleton crew. While this week was no exception in the main part of the station, the remaining men volunteered to finish the barn, where they normally would be resting. The ranch hands would alternate what Sunday they worked, so no one worked two Sundays in a row, but they agreed this week would be an exception so they could finish the build and be done with it. They all wanted the station back to normal.

The other blessing was that this would be the first day Kit would be going to church in a long time. They were supposed to go when they were in Australia the first time, but it never happened. Nico pressured Nana to go with them since they arrived, but she continued to resist. After Nick's funeral, and she met the pastor, Nana gave in. Nico and Kit, Seth, Paige and Zack, and Nana and Pop were going to go to church the following morning as a family, and Kit was excited to see what they thought about it.

*   *   *

The morning rush of getting ready and getting out the door in time was chaotic at best. Nana, Pop, Paige, and Zack got into one truck, while Nico, Kit, and Seth went for the other…only to be met by Dominic.

"What are you doin' here?" Nico asked, stunned.

"Would it be okay if I went with you to church? I'm serious about finding out more about this Jesus. In what I saw out there the other day, I know there's a lot I don't know about in this world, and part of it has to do with God."

Nico glanced at Kit for her reaction. Seeing her slight nod, Nico agreed, so they piled into the truck. As Kit and Nico sat in the front, Seth and Dom got in the back.

"Have to admit I feel very irritated with you," Seth said, halfway to church.

"I know," Dom said. "There's nothing I can do about my past, but ask for forgiveness."

"I'm *not* the one you need to ask it from."

"I realize you may think that's true," Dom said, "but it's not. I need to ask for forgiveness from anyone I can that my actions have affected. While there are very few I *can* ask, you *are* one of them. I've already talked to Nico and Kit."

"I see."

"Having said that, I'm sorry for all of the hurt I caused. There's nothing I can do to bring Jillian and Aaron back –"

"Do *not* say their names," Kit snapped.

Nico's head quickly whipped toward her before turning back to the road. "What was that?"

"He doesn't have the right to speak their names out loud."

"Obviously *she* hasn't forgiven you," Seth pointed out.

"Kit, don't let the anger get ahold of you," Nico warned.

"It won't, but he's still not allowed to say their names. He was the one who took their lives. That's a fact no one can deny. In doing so, he is not allowed to speak their names."

"So, like Nana has made sure no one speaks Jasper's name, no one can speak Jillian or Aaron's names? That didn't work so well for her. Pretty sure it won't work so well for you either."

Kit sighed, looking out the truck window. "You can be a pain in the behind sometimes."

"But…am I right?"

Narrowing her eyes at him, she said, "If you're trying to get me to forgive him, this is *not* the way to do it."

"Do you not agree with me?"

Kit growled in frustration. "Fine! Just use their names sparingly," she said to Dom. "It hurts hearing it from your mouth."

Nico looked at her, appalled. "Kit!"

"It's the truth," Dom said. "That's fine. I can work with that."

"As my mother used to say, 'It's easier to work with the truth, than sort through a lie,'" Kit reminded him. "If we're supposed to begin to work through this, he has to know how I'm feeling."

"Right, but could ya say it a little nicer?"

"Afraid not…at least at this moment."

Dom rested his hand on Nico's shoulder. "Nico, I'm okay with that. Really. She's at least being open and honest, and not quiet."

Nico chuckled. "Yeah. When she's quiet, you'd better duck."

"Excuse me, but I'm still here!" Kit growled. "Please don't talk around me."

"Y'er right. I'm sorry," Nico apologized, taking her hand into his. "If that's how ya feel, then that's how ya feel."

"I'm doing my best to work through this. Trying to find a common enough ground to restart with is not easy. Having said that, I can*not* have him speak their names."

"Fair enough," Dom agreed. "There's a lot we're going to have to work through. I'm sorry I used their names, and I won't do it again."

"That would be appreciated," Kit said, looking back out the window again as a tear slowly crawled down her cheek. Wiping it away, she added, "Go on with what you were saying. I need to get in a better frame of mind to go to church."

While Seth and Dom talked quietly in the back seat, Nico turned the radio on to praise music. Hoping the adage was true that 'music soothes the savage beast' he hoped it worked for Kit as well. With everything going on around her, he prayed life would slow down soon.

*   *   *

Walking into the church, feeling his nerves on edge, Dominic hoped this place would give him the answers he was looking for about God and Jesus. Taking a seat on the end of the row of chairs, with only Seth next to him, he sat there, his body tense.

As several people introduced themselves to the group, Dom's nerves began to thaw. *Could this be a season of change for him? Could this God really do everything he heard about Him?*

Amazed to see a band with drums, guitars, keyboard, and a base guitar, he immediately fell in love with the music. It flowed through him like he had never experienced before. Closing his eyes, he soaked in the love and grace he felt envelope him. This peace was a new feeling, and he wanted to enjoy it. Leaning over to Seth in the middle of a song, he whispered, "What does it mean by, 'Spirit, lead me where my trust is without borders'? Who is the Spirit?"

"I think Nico needs to trade places with me," Seth said. He quietly whispered to Nico before they switched places.

When he was settled, Nico leaned over and whispered, "The singer is askin' the Lord's Spirit t' guide an' direct them, leading them where they didn't even think possible. They don't want t' put boundaries on the Spirit's guidance. They're stating that they have faith Jesus will give them the strength they need t' make it through whatever this world throws at them."

"Who is this Jesus that He has so much power? Why would people place so much faith and trust in Him?"

Looking around, not wanting to ruin someone's worship time, Nico pulled Dom out into the foyer with him. "Have a seat. This may take a while."

"Who is this Jesus?" Dom asked again. "I've heard of Him. I've even heard of God. But, this Spirit thing is new."

"What do you know about Jesus?"

"That He was a carpenter from Nazarene, a long time ago. If I remember right."

"Hmm. Okay. Let me try to give you the basic gist…" Nico started. He took the next several minutes to explain that people had to leave an animal blood sacrifice back in the old times as the final atonement for their sin. Then he went on to explain that God agreed to send His only Son to be that sacrifice to the world, so no further blood shed would be needed. By sending Him into the world through a virgin, this allowed Jesus to experience what it was like to be in human form, but still have the Lord God Almighty as His Father. It allowed others to have an example to follow, knowing Jesus lived among them. He felt the pain of betrayal from His inner circle. He felt the sting of being denied by one of His best friends. Through all of that, He still had compassion for the world flowing through Him. He knew what the soldiers were going to do to Him, but it would be nothing compared to what He would experience on the cross. "They beat Him, shreddin' His skin, exposin' even the bone," Nico explained. "They mocked an' tormented Him with their words, an' then shoved a three-inch crown of thorns down on His skull. An', if that wasn't bad enough, they tried t' make Him carry His cross through the streets. He was so badly beaten, though, that they ended up pullin' someone else t' carry it the rest of the way."

"Wow," Dom said, listening intently, as the worship music continued to flow in the background.

"When they finally arrived t' the appointed place, they hammered three-inch spikes in His hands an' feet int' the cross before puttin' it int' an upright position. On that day, as the world mocked Him, people spit on Him, an' literally crucified Him, He voluntarily took the sin of the world on His body. Through all of that, He *still* had compassion for our pathetic human race. He even forgave a man on a cross next t' Him, so he could enjoy Heaven on that very day. He made sure that John would look after His mother. He loved this world so much, that He gave everythin' in Him t' save it. But, the story doesn't end there. Ya see, on that day, He *did* die on the cross. He carried the sins of the world t' the grave, but, an' this is very important, He fought back. Three days after He died, He fought the very gates of Hell an' came back t' life, so the world knows we, in fact, serve a *livin'* Savior. He is the *only* way t' God. Now, when He came back, the first thing He did was forgive His friend for denyin' Him. He then encouraged His disciples before He left. There were around five *hundred* other people saw Him as well, so people couldn't say the apostles were makin' it up. An' t' answer yer question about the Spirit, before He left He made sure t' leave a guide for those who follow Him, called the Spirit."

"What does it mean to follow Him?"

"For every scar an' beatin' He took, consider that a sin of yers is bein' paid for. He took the penalty of every sin you would commit. He *knew* you would take the life of Jillian an' Aaron. As much as He hoped you wouldn't, He knew you would, an' paid the penalty for it. Just like when Pop took Nate's life, he sacrificed the possibility of goin' t' jail in order t' save my life, Jesus went through torture an' torment t' save yers. Ya see, the gift of His salvation from yer sins is already there. You only have t' accept it. You have t' ask Jesus t' forgive you of yer sins, so you can start fresh an' anew. While Kit may still be workin' on that forgiveness aspect, once you confess yer sins t' Jesus, He'll wipe them away, givin' you a clean slate in His book…an' *His* book is the one that counts."

"I see." Glancing into the sanctuary as the pastor was doing announcements, Dom turned back to Nico and asked, "So, if I ask Jesus to forgive me of my sins, do I get this guide or Spirit you talked about?"

"Yep. He didn't leave the Spirit just for His apostles. He left the Spirit for every one of His disciples. He did it for every person who truly believes in His grace, mercy, love, an' gift of salvation. He did it for everyone who asks Jesus t' forgive them of their sins, an' asks Him t' guide their life. He will give you the gift of not only the Spirit t' guide you, but also access t' God Himself, *an'* the assurance of knowin' that when you pass from this world, that you will be with Him in Heaven on that very day. He wants you t' enjoy all eternity with Him."

"I see," Dom said, processing. Seeing everyone stand up for another song, he asked, "Can we go back in? I think I need to hear more, but before the singing is finished I want to feel what I felt earlier."

"What do ya mean?"

"When we were singing, I felt this amazing peace flow through me."

Setting his hand on Dom's shoulder, Nico explained, "That, my man, would be the Spirit. Pay attention t' Him. I'm pretty sure He's callin' ya t' listen."

"I think you may be right. Would you mind sitting next to me so I can ask you questions if I need to?"

"Sure. I'll just have Kit switch places with Seth."

"Thank you. I know I don't deserve this opportunity, but I'm grateful for it."

As they stood, Nico remarked, "None of us do, mate. None of us do."

*   *   *

All through the service, Dominic paid as close attention as he could. At one point, Kit gave him her notepad and a pen so he could take notes, and Nico would look the Bible references up, so Dominic could read directly from the Bible, with the three of them sharing.

Spirit lead, Pastor Paul spoke that day on forgiveness. He mentioned several examples in the Bible. He explained how Joseph forgave his brothers in Genesis 50 for selling him. Then he went into the story of David. Explaining that David had taken Bathsheba, conceiving a child through adultery. He had her husband killed so he could marry her. Having said all of that, because of the Lord's grace, once David repented He forgave David, and David still became known as a man after God's own heart. He then explained the story of Peter, and how he denied that he knew Jesus three times prior to Jesus' crucifixion. He reminded the people that when Jesus returned from the grave, He forgave Peter…three times…therefore canceling Peter's denial of Him. And then, there was the most important story of forgiveness. Taking the story from where Adam sinned, causing the initial rupture in the relationship between God and man, Pastor continued all the way through, explaining the sin sacrifice and what it was, even up to the crucifixion, and where Jesus' death and resurrection would allow Jesus to forgive the sins of man…if only they would turn to Him and ask. Pastor went on to explain just what grace and mercy was, and why it is important to the truth of Jesus. He clearly went through the attributes of all three parts of the trinity – the Father (God), the Son (Jesus), and the Holy Spirit – and what role they played in their lives.

By the time he was finished, Kit felt horribly guilty for yelling at Dom before church, and for holding Aaron and Jillian's deaths as strongly as she did against him. It wasn't *her* place to judge him. Now, that didn't mean she would necessarily let him just pick back up at a friend level, that trust would have to be rebuilt brick by tedious brick, but it *was* possible. Praying in her seat at that moment for harboring bitterness against Dominic, she asked Jesus to forgive her.

When she finished, she knew she would have to speak with Dom, and prayed for God to provide the right moment. Praying with ever fiber of her being for the Spirit to give her the words and strength she would need to work through not only the conversation, but also the rebuilding of a friendship obliterated, she had the confidence of knowing the Lord would help her. After all, He created an entire planet…He owns cattle on a thousand hills…He even knows how many hairs are on her head…and knows how many days were in her life.

*   *   *

After church, Nico and Kit stayed around to wait for Dominic, who insisted on speaking with the pastor, while Seth went home in the other vehicle. Seth was having issues with Dominic around, and wasn't exactly sure how Kit was doing it. He really didn't want to have to wait for him too.

It took a good half-hour before Dominic walked out with Pastor.

"G'day, sir," Nico said, shaking Pastor's hand. "Thank you for takin' time t' talk t' our friend."

"Oh, no worries, mate. Totally a pleasure. I don't mind if it's for a good cause. Have t' say it was great t' see Nana an' Pop here."

Nico chuckled. "Not surprised she made ya call them that."

"Actually, she refused t' tell me their real name until I gave my word t' call them that. They said everyone in the territory knows them as Nana an' Pop, an' hearin' their real names make her cringe."

Kit sighed. "Ain't that the truth!"

"Y'er not lookin' too good, love," Nico pointed out, putting his arm over her shoulders.

"I don't feel the best, but I have to talk to Dom," she said, grabbing Dom's arm, pulling him off to the side.

Dom cringed. "I know that look. Am I in trouble?"

"No. Actually, I am."

"What do you mean?"

"I was playing judge, when that is *not* my place. If you would forgive me for holding bitterness against you, I would appreciate it. The rest of the feelings need to be between God and me, but playing judge and jury was my fault. I shouldn't have done that. That wasn't my place."

"I killed your best friends and kidnapped you. I almost killed you too," Dominic pointed out.

As soon as he said it, Kit's stomach rolled and churned, sending her over to the side yard just in time for her to throw up in the grass. Shaking afterward, she wiped her mouth, praying against any more vomit from coming up. "I'm sorry. Please forgive me," Kit pleaded.

"Kit?" Nico called to her, but she waved him off, signaling him to stay where he was.

Dom went over to Kit and put his arm over her shoulders as he knelt beside her. Whispering so neither the pastor, nor Nico could hear, Dom said, "Katie, I'm really sorry for my actions. I'm sorry that it caused the lives of your best friends. I'm sorry I killed Jillian and Aaron. I'm sorry I attacked those women. I'm sorry I kidnapped you and held you against your will. And,

I'm sorry I choked you and almost killed you. Is there anyway you could possibly forgive me for all of that?"

Kit broke out in hot tears, streaming down her face. Body still shaking, she whispered, "Yes. I forgive you. Will you forgive me for…for holding anger and bitterness against you?"

"There's nothing to forgive, but if you're looking for it, I forgive you. I would do anything to keep you as a friend." While Kit crouched on the ground holding her stomach, with the tears streaming down her cheeks, Dom pressed forward with what all he had to tell her, "I talked to Nico and Pastor, and I asked Jesus to forgive me of my sins. I asked Him to guide my steps, words, and actions. I asked Him to strengthen my faith and trust in Him…and He did through your actions. There is nothing I can ever do to undo what I did, but through Jesus' forgiveness, and now yours, I feel pounds lighter. I cannot thank you for what all you and Nico have done for me, and it is my hope and prayer that I will live up to Jesus' expectations and plan for me – whatever they may be."

Kit only nodded as she curled up on the ground in a fetal position, holding her stomach.

"That's enough," Nico said, coming over. Brushing her hair out of her face, he was stunned at how pale she was. "What's wrong, love?"

"Sick," she moaned. "Just really sick."

Scooping her off the ground, he carried her to the truck, closely followed by Dom. After laying her in the back of the truck, Nico and Dom said goodbye to Pastor and got in the front, heading back to the station.

"Now, what *exactly* happened?" Nico asked, as they pulled out of the parking lot.

"She asked me to forgive her. She didn't need to, but she insisted. She also forgave me for everything." Grinning like a little boy on Christmas, Dom added, "Jesus did too."

"Are you serious?"

"Yep! All of it. I'm excited to see what Jesus is going to do with all of this. While it's all still new –"

Dom was cut off by Kit moaning, "Nico, I need you to pull over."

Jerking the truck to the side of the road in one swift motion, Nico threw the truck into park and got her door open just in time for her to stick her head out of the truck and throw up.

"Nice timing," Dom remarked. "Can I get anything for you?"

"There's a bathroom in that park," Nico pointed out to Kit. "Want t' go over there an' freshen up."

Nodding in response, she crawled out of the truck, stumbling to the bathroom in a blind stupor. Her head spun out of control and she felt disconnected from her body. Wracking her brain to remember what she ate, she thrust the bathroom door open and let out a blood-curdling scream!

On the mirror in the bathroom, was a spider looking right at her, about eight inches in diameter. Slowly stepping back from the bathroom, she screamed and jumped when Nico was instantly at her side.

"What is it?" he asked, concern evident.

Unable to say a word as Dom caught up to them, Kit just pointed toward the bathroom, her body trembling.

"You want to do it, or should I?" Dom asked.

"Probably me. Keep a close eye on her. She's scared t' death," Nico said, saying a prayer in his head for strength to handle whatever was on the other side of the door. Opening it wide, he gasped before getting a better look at it. Fascination raced through his body as he saw the creature staring at him, just as fascinated and scared. The spider bowed-up, making it look even bigger than it was already. While he had seen them throughout his life, he never got the chance to see one up close and personal like this. "Sorry little fella, but my wife needs t' come in here, an' she isn't goin' to if y'er here. Ya got two choices. Either you come willingly with me an' I let ya loose outside, or I smash ya. What's it gonna be?"

"Who are you talking to?" Dom called.

"A spider."

"You're talking to a spider?" he asked, poking his head into the bathroom. Eyes widened in terror, he exclaimed, "That's not a spider, that's spiderzilla!"

"Welcome t' Australia, mate." Nico smirked. "Hold open the door for me an' have Kit turn away."

"Okay. Just a sec." Disappearing for only a moment, he returned, holding the door as wide as he could.

"What's it gonna be, lil' guy?" Nico asked, slowly maneuvering himself between the spider and the door. Going to the back part of the spider, he checked with Dom, "Keep it open. I'm goin' t' throw it out the door."

"Go for it. Just make sure your aim is good, or you'll hear me scream like Kit."

Nico chuckled, partially out of being tickled by Dom's reaction to the spider, partially out of nervousness. Saying another quick prayer, he quickly snatched the back leg of the spider. Before the spider knew what was going on, it was flying through the air and out the door.

"It's clear," Nico said.

Kit ran into the bathroom and buried her face into Nico's shirt. "*What was that?*"

"A spider."

"I have *never* seen one that big!"

"Oh, that's not as big as they *can* get," Nico pointed out. "That was a young adult."

"Just let me freshen up and go to the bathroom," Kit grumbled, going over to the sink.

Leaving her in the bathroom, Nico headed out to find Dom nowhere in sight. "Dom?"

"Over here," he called from inside the truck.

"Chicken," Nico said under his breath. Hearing another blood-curdling scream, Nico bolted into the bathroom again, to find Kit plastered against the wall.

Looking up when a small stick dropped, Kit screamed again before running from the bathroom for the truck, arms flailing. Leaving Nico standing near what looked to be a spider nest, he sighed, "Oh boy. I'm gettin' outta here before mama spider returns."

*   *   *

Running outside, Nico looked around for Kit. "Over here," Dom yelled for him from inside the truck.

When Nico got over there, he found Kit in her seat, with her arms wrapped around her legs, rocking in place. "Shame, love. You look traumatized beyond words."

Breathing heavily, she looked up at him and ordered, "Get-me-home!"

"Will do."

Driving as fast as the truck would go, he would periodically hear Kit shudder or wipe her legs and arms. Feeling bad for her, knowing spiders of that size were around the station, he knew eventually she would work through it. Remembering her fear of spiders, he was actually surprised the subject hadn't come up sooner.

"Is she going to be okay?" Dom asked, concerned, as they started up the drive toward the main house.

"Do me a favor? When we pull up, run an' grab Pete t' make a tea for her. With her throwin' up an' shaking, along with what she saw, she's goin' t' need somethin'."

"Got it. Um," glancing back to Kit for a moment, he asked Nico, "What will people say about me being here?"

"They don't know who you are. You've been given a rare opportunity t' start over, fresh, with no mistakes. Don't mess it up."

"I won't. Trust me. I won't. You and Jesus both gave me a second chance. I won't mess it up. I know my word doesn't mean much at this point, but you have my word."

"Just do your absolute best, an' don't make me regret it."

"I won't."

When they pulled up to the main house, Dom ran for the barn, while Nico carried Kit into the house.

"Bloody hell! What happened?" Nana stood in shock, while everyone was sitting at the table.

"He's not –" Dom stopped himself when he saw everyone around the table. "They're all in here."

Pete got up from the table and checked Kit's forehead. "Where ya been? And what happened t' her? She doesn't have a fever, but she looks like a dog's breakkie!"

"Shock, an' she threw up multiple times on the way home," Nico explained.

"Hmmm. Take 'er upstairs an' let me talk t' Dad on this one," Pete said, heading back to the table to talk to his dad, Buri.

*   *   *

When she was settled in bed, Nico told her, "I'm goin' t' go see what they've come up with. In the meantime," he brushed her hair out of her face, "get some rest."

"I will. Thank you," she mumbled, rolling over to face the wall, grateful to be in a bed.

Closing the door behind him, Nico ran downstairs to a silent dining room. "Okayyyy," Nico said uneasy, "why is this room so quiet?"

"Because Dom told us what happened t' Kit today. We're kind of wonderin' about somethin'," Nana explained.

"What's that?"

"We worried 'bout givin' 'er tea," Buri explained, "She could be full a' paws an' claws."

"What? No. It's too soon."

"Not really." Nana shook her head. "It only takes once, an' you have been married for a good two t' three weeks."

"You don't think..." Nico's voice trailed, as the color drained from his face. "She can't be."

"Why not?" Nana probed. "Pretty sure you've consummated. So, unless you've done somethin' t' stop that, it could very well be a possibility."

"I – no," Nico said adamantly. "It's too early. There's no way."

"Do ya use anythin'?" Pete asked.

"This is *not* somethin' I want t' discuss in front of everyone."

Pete pulled Nico into the kitchen, with Buri and Nana on their heels. "Look, if she is, then she is, but we can't give her anythin' until we know," Pete explained. "Do ya use anythin'?"

"No," Nico admitted, shoving his hands into his pockets.

"Y'er married. It's fine if she is," Nana said, not sure why he was upset. "You seem bothered. Why would it be bad if she were preggers?"

"Because she's had these nightmares. One was where she got kidnapped – which proved true when Nate took her. Another one was where she dies in childbirth here on the station. The third has somethin' t' do with findin' a dead child in the north field."

"Those are just dreams."

"Her dreams have come true before." Nico sighed, shaking his head as he crossed his arms. "Look, if she's preggers, she could die."

"That's where you're going to have to trust God," Seth said, leaning on the doorway. Making his way into the kitchen, he placed his hand on Nico's shoulder. "If she's that sick, she may very well be pregnant. If she is, then pray against the outcome of the dream with everything you have."

"I can't lose her," Nico desperately pleaded with them.

"None of us want t' lose her, but if she's preggers she can't have the tea," Pete reiterated.

"No. No tea. Let me see her?" Buri asked.

Nico shook his head. "I don't know about that. What if we wait it out an' see if the nausea clears?"

"Take her some food?" Buri offered. "Then I talk t' 'er?"

"Fine," Nico huffed, knowing it would be a losing battle to even attempt to fight Buri. Nana followed his every instruction when it came to medical issues.

"I go," Buri said, grabbing a plate full of food before he headed upstairs.

When Nico went to follow him, Nana grabbed his arm. "Let 'im do 'is work."

"She would want me in there. I need –"

"T' let Buri do his job. He knows what he's talkin' about. Go get some tucker so you blokes can get t' work."

"Yes, ma'am," Nico grumbled. "I know better than t' fight with you."

"Y'er a wise one," Nana said with a smile before they all headed back into the dining room.

*   *   *

Hearing a light knock on the door, Kit called out, "Come on in." When she saw Buri was the one coming in, she slowly sat up, curiosity getting the best of her. "What are *you* doing here? I thought it was Pete."

"Pete not give you tea. Here. You eat," he said, handing her the plate. Grabbing a chair from the corner of the room, he pulled it over to her bedside. "Try t' do my best in talk."

105

"I can follow your English," Kit said, nibbling on the bread. The rest looked gross. As a matter of fact, the smell was beginning to overpower her senses. "Please put the plate in the hall?"

"No. You eat."

"No. It stinks."

"You like steak an' rice. I seen you eat it before."

"I *do* like it, but it stinks right now."

"No. Smell normal. What is wrong?" he asked, cocking his head to the side.

Buri's curly and bushy hair hung between his chin and shoulder. His skin was darker than average, due to his Aboriginal heritage and being in the blistering sun all day, but his mind was sharper than most twenty-year-olds. Standing all of five-foot-five, he seemed timid and mild, but he was anything *but* timid *or* mild. He was a force to be reckoned with in his worst day, deadly on his best.

"Sick. Please don't make me eat."

"When you start sick?"

"Woke up this morning sick."

"I see. An' did ya eat anythin' t'day?"

"No. Not besides this," she said, holding up the bread.

"Hmm." Stroking his chin in thought, he asked, "When you last period?"

"*What?*" Kit about choked on her bread. "Why would you ask that?"

"You be here for three weeks?"

"Almost."

"Maybe preggers."

"Pregnant? What? No!" Kit panicked, flashing back to her nightmare. "I can't be."

"You can."

"No. I can't."

"Yes. You can. We cannot give you tea if ya are."

"What do I do?"

"Nothin'." He chuckled. "It already done if you are."

"Ugh! What do I do now?"

"You rest, an' eat whatever you are given. It for baby an' you. You not eat, you –"

He was cut off when Kit bolted from the bed for the bathroom, barely making it before she threw up again. Groaning when she finished, she dropped her head onto her arm. "Make it stop…please?"

"You rest," he said, patting her head. "Get rest."

When he returned downstairs to a full table of concerned people, Nico was the first to speak. "Well?"

"Not sure, but think so."

Nico dropped his head in his hands and sighed. "When are ya goin' home, mate?" he asked Seth.

"Not anytime soon at the rate things are flipping around here. Whiplash seems to be common lately. Why?"

"I may need a good friend."

"Let's take a walk," he said, and the two of them left into the station.

"Okay, now that he's out of earshot, what's the verdict?" Nana pressed.

Buri sighed. "I feel she full a' paws an' claws."

Chapter 6

As Autumn Leaves Turn

Over the next two weeks, Kit did her best to keep food down, but it was to no avail. She would eat, but promptly throw it up. The family and ranch hands were worried, but there was nothing anyone could do but watch her slowly melt away with each day. When she wasn't throwing up, she was sleeping…and when she wasn't sleeping, she was throwing up.

"Enough already!" Nico yelled, as Kit made a mad dash for upstairs after trying to eat lunch. "Buri, find out what's goin' on with her!"

"I know what wrong."

"What's wrong?" Nico asked, surprised Buri never told him he figured it out.

"She preggers."

"Okay. What are we goin' t' do about it?"

"We can do nothin'."

"What do ya mean by that?"

Resting his hand on Nico's shoulder, Dom said, "God has to take care of her."

"But, if that nightmare a' hers comes true, she's as good as dead!"

"I haven't stopped praying, neither should you."

Running his hands through his hair as he sighed, Nico admitted, "I'm at a loss here. I don't know what t' do."

"Pray," Dom reiterated.

"I need t' walk," he grumbled, and left out the door for the station.

"When will she be feelin' better?" Nana asked Buri. "She's not keepin' anythin' down. At this rate, both Kit *an'* the baby will starve before it's born."

"Shouldn't she take a pregnancy test or something?" Seth asked.

"She preggers," Buri said confidently. "You get yer test, but she preggers."

"How do you know?" Seth asked, and the table burst out in laughter. "What?"

"He's been practicin' medicine before you were born," Nana explained. "If he says Kit's full a' paws an' claws, then she is."

Seth sighed. "Then God better help her, because she's not going to make it without Him."

*   *   *

About two months after their arrival to Australia, Kit finally had a day where she didn't wake throwing up. "Y'er lookin' better t'day," Nico commented, as Kit took her seat at the table.

"Thanks. I need to keep it light, though."

After Nana said grace, Seth announced, "Um, need to tell you guys something, but I wanted to wait until everyone was here."

"What is it?" Nico groaned. After not seeing much of Kit for weeks, his greatest fear was that Seth would be leaving. He was getting used to having him around. While he knew Seth had a job to do, the selfish part of him wanted Seth to stay.

"Talked to Director Shaw early this morning, and he wants me to come back."

Nico sighed, dropping his head into his hands. "When?"

"You're leaving?" Kit asked, upset.

"Afraid so. There are some things I need to get taken care of. Trust me. The last thing I want to do is leave, but I have a job to do."

"Sorry t' see ya leave," Nana said, echoing the feeling around the table. "We're kinda gettin' used t' ya 'round here."

"I'll be back. I just don't know when. I'll also keep in touch."

"Please do. Y'er welcome here anytime."

"Thank you. I'll get back here as soon as I can."

"When are you leavin'?" Nico asked, crossing his arms in front of him with a thousand thoughts running through his mind.

"Tomorrow. I leave tonight for Cairns."

"Wow. Um, okay. Wish I knew a little sooner."

"Would it really have made a difference?"

Nico sighed. "Not really."

"Look, brother, I need to get back. I've pushed it as far as I could."

"I know. And I appreciate it. I'm just gonna miss ya."

"Well, if I'm to come back when she has that little one, I need to go now."

"Good point," Nico agreed. "Just keep in touch, huh?"

"I will."

"And, be careful," Kit added. "Don't make us come back just to hunt you down because someone killed you."

"I wouldn't dare." Seth chuckled. "I wouldn't dare."

*   *   *

Saying goodbye to Seth was heartbreaking for all involved. Even the guys he worked with each day on the station had gotten used to having him around. That night, before he left, Seth pulled Nico aside to have a serious conversation. "We gotta talk."

"What is it?" Nico asked, as they headed out to walk around.

"While I have been keeping an eye on Dom, it still makes me nervous to have him so close to Kit."

"I know. Trust me, though. With all the security of the cameras, walkie-talkies, an' security patrols I have set up, we're well protected. Everyone on here will protect her with everythin' they have."

"He has *killed* people! Her friends at that! He kidnapped *her and* left her for dead! And here, you just leave her dangling in front of him?"

"Seth, this is a decision I've prayed about an' feel comfortable with. God has given me peace. I've kept a close eye on him, an' have seen the changes in him. He's hungry for the Lord."

"That doesn't discount what he's done."

"No. It doesn't, but I'm goin' t' let him an' God sort that out. I've given him a gift of a fresh start. Havin' said that, while Kit has forgiven him, I've not stopped watchin' him. He's continuously on my radar."

"Why? Why are you doing this?"

"I know he hasn't spent any time in jail, but he *has* lived in solitude for years. He's lived on edge, continuously lookin' over his shoulder t' see if his past would catch up t' him. In givin' him a fresh start, he has not only found the Lord, but it has also allowed Kit the grace t' find forgiveness for him. It's as much for Dom, as it is for Kit."

"Fine!" Seth huffed. "Just keep a close eye on him. I *do not* want to have to go to another funeral for the two of you in the near future because of him. Am I making myself clear?"

"Yes. I'll protect her with everythin' I have. I'm also prayin' for God t' protect her as well…an' He's stronger than anythin' this world can dish out."

"I know. I'm a Christian too. I'm just having trouble with this forgiveness thing in regards to a cold-blooded murderer."

"Seth," Nico rested his hands on his shoulders, "that, with all due respect brother, is between you an' God, not me, Kit, an' Dom."

Crossing his arms, he admitted, "I know. I just don't understand how I'm supposed to forgive him for that one."

"Pray, brother. And in the meantime, I'll pray for you as well."

"Thanks. I have a feeling I'm going to need it."

"Don't we all."

*   *   *

Returning to work for Seth was not easy. Leaving Nico and Kit was harder than he thought it would be. With going to their 'funerals' only days before finding them alive, it took him time to recover. Then, getting used to them in their new environment, and getting used to working on a station itself, the idea of heading back to a crowded city and dealing with the daily stresses that came with being an agent really didn't sound appealing to him. He knew what his responsibility was, and he would do it, but his heart wasn't in it anymore. Not sure how much longer he would be able to go into work each day with his heart elsewhere, he headed into the office the morning after he landed back in Cleveland.

"Hey! He lives!" Dakota commented when he walked in.

"Yeah. Not sure if I really want to be here, but I'm here," he mumbled.

114

Looking up from the paperwork he was working on, Chad said, "Ya look like crap, my friend."

"Thanks. I love you too."

"Seriously, dude. You just got back from vacation. Shouldn't you be more relaxed?" Todd asked.

"I came back from burying my best friend, and spending weeks consoling his family, getting them to a stable mental state," Seth corrected.

"Right. Know we all feel for you and understand, as we have had *two* vacant desks during your hiatus," Eugene pointed out.

Looking at each of his teammates, Seth sighed. "I know you guys need me to be in tip-top shape, but I just don't know if my heart's in it anymore," he admitted. When the tapping of her keyboard came to a sudden halt by his admittance, Seth looked at Claire in concern. "What?"

"Um, what if we take a break for coffee? You look like you need to talk."

"I *need* to catch up."

"You *need* to get re-centered," Emma countered.

Grunting in frustration, Seth dropped his head in his hands. "I *need* to do my job!"

"Go for coffee with Claire, and then try it again. There's nothing here that can't wait for an hour or so," Emma pointed out. "If not Claire, then grab someone else. You need to get focused again."

"Fine. Let's go," Seth said, grabbing Claire on the way out. When they were clear of the building, he commented, "That was subtle."

"What was?"

"We're supposed to be secret."

"We are." She shrugged. "I'm playing the concerned friend."

"When in reality, you're the concerned girlfriend."

Sighing, she shoved her hands in her pockets, and then added, "Who you haven't been in much contact with over the last several weeks."

"I've had a lot on my mind. Besides, I've also been on a working station. They work you to the point of exhaustion, stuff you full of food, and then send you to bed to start it all over again early the next morning."

"If it was so rough, why did you stay?"

"Because in between, we had a funeral for my best friend, and I spent my spare time consoling his family."

"Is that all?"

"What do you mean?"

"I *mean* you seem different."

"You got that in all of ten sentences?"

"No, I got that from a feeling I've had since you got on that plane."

"What do you mean?"

Sighing again, she admitted. "I don't know if I can explain it."

"Try."

"It's kind of the same feeling I had when Nick found…you haven't found God, have you?" she asked, her face pale at the thought of losing another one.

"Yes," he admitted. "Is that a problem?"

"Does that mean our relationship has to change?"

"Wow. I come back from probably the worst possible trip of my life, and you're concerned whether or not we can have intimacy in our relationship? Are you serious?"

"I just don't want to lose another one."

"Another what?"

"Another guy to this God thing."

"It's not a *God thing*. It's a relationship with the living God. And, if that's all you're concerned with, then maybe it's for the better that we *don't* continue our relationship," he snapped. "That's the most self-centered thing I've heard from you. And trust me, I've heard some doozies from you!"

Stopping in the middle of the sidewalk, Claire crossed her arms in a huff. "That's rude!"

"Like you're *not* being rude? Look, Claire," he said, putting his hands on her arms, "I love you. We've been together for two years. If you don't understand just how much I love you, then you're missing the element that truly makes a relationship. As much as we fight and fuss, at the end of the day our love needs to stay strong."

"I know. I feel that too. I just don't understand why a relationship with this God requires *our* relationship to change. The same thing happened with Nick."

"Quit comparing me to Nick!" Seth growled, crossing his arms. "I'm getting tired of whenever we have an argument his name comes up. I am *not* Nick. I will *never* be Nick. If you want to be with *me*, then let me know. If you want to be with Nick, you're out of luck."

"Wow! That was harsh!"

"That's reality!"

"I love you!"

"Then quit comparing me to Nick! He's gone! He hasn't been yours for *years*! He and Katie were together, and you *never* cut her a break either because you were jealous she was with Nick. Well, how does it feel to know that in the end they were together?"

Tears stung Claire's eyes as her bottom lip trembled. "Why would you say that?"

"Because I am tired of dealing with your past. It's killing our future. Do you love me?"

"Not at the moment."

"Nooooo, you may not like what I'm saying, but do you love me?"

"Yes." She sighed. "Not sure why, but I do."

"Tell my why you love *me* and do it *without* comparing me to Nick."

"I –" she stopped short. "I'm sorry. You're right. I haven't been fair to you."

"Finally!" Seth threw his hands in the air. "You finally admit that you're wrong!"

"Yes. I was wrong. I'm sorry."

"Okay then. Do you want to start over?"

"What do you mean?"

"I feel that you need to get to know *me* for who I am…without comparing me to Nick."

"I don't –" Claire wiped the tears from her eyes. "You're right. Will you forgive me?"

Wrapping his arms around her, he kissed her head. "You, nutcase. I love you with all my heart. I only want you to love me the same."

"I do."

"Don't go back there again."

"Okay. I get it." Looking up at him, she asked, "Can we try this again?"

"If we do, you're right…things are going to have to change. We can't be anywhere near as intimate as we have been. I would also like it if you went to church with me."

"No way!"

"Just try it with an open mind? I'm not forcing God on you. I only want you to go with me with an open mind. It may not be as bad as you think."

"So, you're saying since we're turning over a new leaf in our relationship, I may have to consider doing the same in my own heart?"

"I'm praying it's a new start all the way around. It's my hope that you would at least *consider* God."

"I'm not making any promises."

"I don't want you to, but I *do* expect you to respect me in regards to my decision to follow Jesus. That's going to require some changes. Since you're getting to know me without comparing me to Nick, this may be a good time for you to get an understanding of the new me as well. I've had a lot going on inside of me over the last several weeks. There've been many struggles and I've discovered quite a bit about myself – a lot of which I didn't like, so I've changed it."

"I see," she said, taking a step back.

"That doesn't change how I feel about you. I love you beyond words. I *need* you to understand who *I* am and what makes me tick. In the meantime, I'll do what I can to show you that while we may not have those intimate times until we're married, there are many aspects of our relationship that we haven't been using."

"Such as?"

"Such as taking you out. We've gotten stuck in a rut. Once intimacy entered into our relationship, that seems to be all it is. I want to take you places and show you my interests. I also want you to take me places that spark *your* interests. Of course I'll pay, but I want you to plan them."

She thought about it for a moment before she agreed. "That sounds refreshing."

Resting his arm over her shoulder, he escorted her the rest of the way to the café around the corner from the office for coffee. "Now, let's go get to know each other. I know this cute little café you may enjoy."

"Of course I'll enjoy it. *I* was the one who introduced *you* to it," she said, playfully elbowing him.

"Starting over, sweetheart. Starting over."

"Right. Fresh, new, with no mistakes or past."

* * *

After a long conversation with his sister Sandy, Seth forgave her for lying, but asked her to trust him in the future. It was a relief to him to know he at least had Sandy to talk to about Nick and Katie still being alive, but felt bad for keeping the secret from Claire. Knowing her and Katie's past, he wasn't secure enough in their relationship yet to trust her with something so big. He justified it by keeping in mind that if it only affected him, he would have told her right away. However, this would affect Nick, Katie, and the new little one Katie was carrying if this secret got out, and he agreed with Nick – the fewer who knew their secret, the better off they would be.

Over the next few weeks, Seth and Claire went out quite a bit. After a couple of Sundays, Claire admitted that she didn't mind going to church. She even started asking questions, that Seth had to refer her to the pastor to answer.

One Sunday, about four weeks after he got back from Australia, Seth and Claire were talking as they sat in MacGreggor's Sports Bar. "I'm really not sure what I'm going to do."

"With what?" Claire asked.

Seth took a deep breath, knowing this conversation would be tough. "I have to tell you something that we need to keep between us."

"Of course."

"I don't think my heart's in this job anymore."

"What do you mean?"

"In working at the station, I found it peaceful. While it was hard work, I wasn't dodging bullets or hunting down criminals. I wasn't looking over my shoulder, wondering if my team would all be coming back at the end of the day." He sighed. "I don't like knowing if we go on a raid, that I may not see *you* again. You have to listen on the other end of the radio, probably praying with every bone in your body that I'll come back. I hate the idea of you having to listen to or watch my death in a camera."

"This is true," she admitted. "But I know it's for a noble cause. We don't do it for glory. We do it to keep this country safe. We do it to keep our neighbors and families safe."

"I realize that. I'm struggling with the fact that I'm not getting any younger. Don't you want to settle down? Have you ever thought of having children?"

"To be honest, not really."

"You don't want children?"

"Haven't really thought about it. I'm just hoping to make it day-to-day."

"That's sad."

"That's my life. I've been on my own since I was seventeen. Hacking is what allowed me to have money. Granted, it was an illegal way to get it, but it *was* a way to get it."

"I guess I never thought much about your past. I'm sorry about that. Now that you've had some stability, what do you think?"

"Like I said, I've never thought about it."

"And, now that I've brought it up? Would you want children?"

"Aren't they a pain?"

"A pain? No! It's in how you raise them. Granted, while genetics does play a part in it, it's mostly in how you raise them. There are five kids in our family, and each of us has found ourselves in a good place, working with the integrity our parents instilled in us."

"Can't imagine that's the norm."

"Unfortunately, it's not. People tend to let society raise their child instead of doing the work in raising them themselves."

"I agree, but what can we do differently?"

"We can raise them how the Bible tells us to raise them."

"You mean spanking?" Claire asked, appalled.

"Spare the rod, spoil the child. I don't want a spoiled child. Now, depending on the child's temperament, we may not have to spank them often."

"If it's *us* we're talking about, let's be realistic. You're the poster boy for a type 'A' personality, and I've got a stubborn streak a mile long. Our children won't stand a chance!"

"They will…if we do it right."

"And, where do you plan on getting this expert advice?"

"My parents are a good resource."

"Okay, so, how many are you thinking?"

"Two, maybe three. What about you?"

"Guess that'll depend on just how much pain we're talking about here."

Seth chuckled. "Well, there *are* pain meds you can take."

"I'm sure, but I'm also sure there'll be recovery, etcetera. I'll have to answer that question after the first one."

"You really want to possibly stop at one? They'll need a playmate."

"What if pregnancy turns me into a fat pig?"

"You'll never be a fat pig. I know you. You take very good care of your body."

"Sometimes it does stuff to your body, especially when you postpone having them."

"When would you want to get married?"

"Where are these questions coming from?"

"Honestly?"

"I *thought* we covered that when we started over," Claire said, raising an eyebrow at him.

"I'm thinking of leaving the FBI."

"*What*? You can't!"

"Yes, I can. And yes, I'm seriously thinking about doing just that."

"What are you going to do instead?"

"I'm going back to Australia to work on the station."

"You're going to *what*? Where is this coming from? How can you seriously think about going to another country to live? What's wrong with the U.S.?"

"Well, I know we haven't talked much about it, but I got close to his cousin while I was there."

Narrowing her eyes, Claire hissed, "I *knew* it!"

"You're really an absolute nutcase!" Seth laughed loudly.

"You're laughing at me?"

"Claire," he said, taking her hand into his, "I love you, but you have absolutely *nothing* to be jealous of. Nick's cousin is a male. Nana was training him to take over the station. We got to know each other, and he's really cool. You'd like his wife, too. She's due in about six months."

"Is that where all these questions are coming from?"

"Claire, we're not getting any younger."

Propping her chin on her hand, she sighed. "I know. We covered that."

"What do you want from us?"

"We've been dating for over two years. I know we've started over," she said, "but the main thing about you that's different is how you process things, otherwise you're the same."

"What do you mean?"

"Instead of processing things through just your experience, you added the element of God to your processor."

"Interesting."

"Otherwise, you're still the man I love."

"What about you? Has your processor begun to change at all?"

"Oh, it has," she admitted. "I'm a bit tougher to get through, though. I have a difficult time adapting to change."

"Oh, I disagree. You adapt quite well, and quickly when you have to."

"Just how *quickly* do I need to adjust?" she asked, suddenly catching on to what he was telling her.

"That depends on how quickly you want *us* to go forward."

Claire gulped, as her face went pale. "What *exactly* are you telling me?"

"That I am thinking of moving there in a couple of weeks."

Gasping, Claire slapped her hand over her mouth in shock.

"Before you ask, yes, I'm serious."

"You can't be!"

"I can. And I am. I'm tired of this. What if we get that call tomorrow, go out for a raid, and I never come back? I don't want to have any regrets. I'm going tomorrow to talk to Director Shaw and tell him my recommendation for my replacement."

"Who are you going to recommend?"

"Dakota did a great job while I was gone. I'm thinking he deserves the position permanently."

"Wow."

"So, what do you think?"

"Have you talked to Nick's grandmother about how long she needs to get you over there?"

"Already done. I was waiting to talk to you until she was ready."

"So you're…wow. You're *really* going to do it? Plan already in place and everything?"

"If I didn't have a plan in place, I wouldn't potentially upset you. I wanted to make sure Nico and Kit were open to it."

"Nico and Kit?" Claire asked, suspiciously. "Their names are *Nico* and *Kit*?"

"Yes. Nico and Kit Sullivan. They're the ones who have taken over the station from Nana."

"And, how *exactly* are they related to Nana?" Claire asked, studying him as she crossed her arms.

"I know what you're thinking, but Nico is Nana's brother Fletcher's son. It seems Fletcher was a playboy, and he got caught. Nico's mom died when he was younger in a car accident, and Fletcher stopped running around at that point to raise him."

"I see. And Kit?"

"Her father and two brothers still live in Texas."

"Okay, and where is Nico from?"

"He's from Perth."

"I find the coincidences eerily similar to Nick and Katie."

"They met when Kit made a college trip to Mt. Uluru with some friends. Nico was living on a station in Alice Springs about the same time, and took a day off to go to the Mt. Uluru on the day Kit and her friends happen to be there. He followed her back to The States afterward, and they continued their relationship down in Texas, where he worked on her dad's ranch. They got married about a year ago. When Nick got killed, Nana wanted to keep the station in the family, so she asked Fletcher if he thought Nico and Kit wanted it. They did, so they moved out there, and she's been training him since."

"So, Nick and Katie are *not* Nico and Kit?"

"Nick has brown hair and Kit's is auburn. Also, since you knew Katie, did she *ever* cut her hair?"

"No."

"Kit's is shoulder length."

"I see. She wouldn't cut her hair off. If she were in another country, there would be no need," Claire said, sorting it out in her mind. "So, when are you leaving?"

"Well, I'd like it if you came with me. With her due in about six months, she's going to need all the help she can get around the house, and potentially with the new little one."

"Like a nanny?"

"Yeah."

"What about internet? Will I be able to access the internet?" she asked, the panic in her voice evident.

"It'll be limited, but you won't really need it out there. Everything is old school. As a matter of fact, maybe you can get them updated into this century by helping with a computer system."

"Do you really think I would fit there?"

"Have to tell you that if you go, we're not coming back."

"Well, I don't have a family except the FBI, but you do. What's your family going to say?"

"They know. They also understand. There are many ways this day and age to stay connected, but knowing Nana and Nico, and how hard they work people, I highly doubt we'll have a lot of spare time."

"Sounds like it'll be difficult."

"It will, but it'll be worth it. Look, I'll be leaving in two weeks. It's up to you if you want to come with me. If you do, then I ask that we get married before we go."

"You're serious? I have two weeks to make a decision that will effect the rest of my life?"

"Not necessarily. If you want to stay here, you can, but I'm going."

"Without taking my feelings into consideration?"

"Would you really want me to do something where not paying attention could get me killed?"

"Would you really want me to do something that is not in me?"

"Nope," Seth said adamantly. "That's why I'm giving you a choice. We're not married. There may very well still be someone here that you could fall for."

"But, I love *you*."

"And, *I'm* going to Australia. Do you want to come?"

*   *   *

"I can't believe you're leaving," Dakota said, sitting in Director Shaw's office, stunned. "You just got back."

"My heart's not in it anymore. I don't want to not be paying attention some day and get myself, or worse yet, someone else, killed," Seth explained. "Look, I know it seems sudden, but you've already been doing the job. I feel you would make an excellent agent-in-charge."

"*We* feel you would make an excellent agent-in-charge," Director Shaw corrected.

Dakota sighed, running his fingers through his hair. "I understand. If something happened to Todd, I would potentially be thrown for a loop as well. If it happened to Todd *and* Emma or Claire, I definitely would. Our unit is close, so you have to understand my anxiety in you leaving."

"I do, but we have confidence in you," Seth reiterated. "You're good. I *know* you won't let them down."

"There's one more thing," Director Shaw added.

Dakota looked from one man to the other, on edge. "I don't know if I *want* to know."

"Claire's going with him."

Chapter 7

A Harvest of Memories

"You sure about this?" Seth asked, as they stood next to security before going in. The rest of the unit was there as well.

"We're already married. If you were going to ask me if I was sure, the alter would have been a more appropriate time," Claire pointed out.

"I did."

"And what was my response?"

"Well, Mrs. Simmons, I do believe it was *yes*," he said, grabbing her hand.

"You guys are seriously going to leave…for good?" Todd asked, upset.

"Now is not the time to get upset, Todd," Emma said, "You should have done that two weeks ago."

"I did."

"I know you guys may not understand this, but know it's what's best for us," Seth explained. "We love you guys and hope you understand and support us."

"We wouldn't be here if we didn't," Emma clarified. "Look, I'll probably be retiring here in a about five years. Who knows where I'll end up? I actually think it's smart to be thinking of your future. Besides, raising kids on a ranch? I have to admit I'm kind of envious."

"Thank you," Seth said, as he and Claire hugged everyone. "Well, we need to go."

Wiping her face, Claire said, "Be safe, and take care, huh?"

"Lasso a cow or two for me, eh?" Chad smirked.

"Riding horses will be interesting." Claire rolled her eyes. "Talk about culture shock."

"It could be interesting, that's for sure." Todd smiled at the thought. "Almost wish I was going with you just to see that one."

"You guys just keep an eye out for each other," Seth said, giving everyone another hug. After Claire did as well, they headed through security. "Nervous?" Seth asked when they were on the other side.

As they walked down the terminal, hand-in-hand, Claire said, "As Todd said, this could be interesting."

*   *   *

Walking down the terminal in Cairns, Seth was nervous as to what Claire's reaction would be when she found out the reality of the situation at the station. Deciding his best bet would be the surprise approach, he kept his mouth shut for the time being. There was no internet on the station, and he knew they would have to calm Claire down once she found everything out, so he held his breath and prepared for the worst.

Pulling their suitcases from the conveyor, Seth spotted their escorts by the doors. "There's Nana and Pete. Nana was Nick's grandmother, and Pete was his best friend growing up."

"Interesting," Claire said, taking everything in. Truth be told, her brain was on overload. Even in just the airport she was hearing the difference in speech. This would be a challenge for her, but she loved Seth so she was determined to make it work.

"Seth! Hey, mate! Glad t' see ya!" Pete greeted them, throwing his arms around Seth. "Missed ya!"

"Glad to be back," Seth said, returning the hug before he hugged Nana as well. "Missed you, you feisty young thing."

"Missed yer silver Yankee tongue," Nana countered, "But, glad t' have ya back. Nico's missed ya too."

"Can't wait to see him. Nana, Pete, this is my wife, Claire," he introduced her.

"Glad ya gave me the head's up about yer trouble an' strife," Nana said, giving Claire a welcome hug. "Paperwork shouldn't be a problem. We can finish when you've gotten some rest."

At first Claire froze before she hugged Nana back. "Thank you," Claire said, uncomfortable, yet liked the hug. "I know I seem out of sorts, but we've been on a plane for what feels like days, and I feel a bit out of place in hearing the language."

Pete furrowed his brow. "It's English."

"Right, but it's not American English. It'll take some getting used to."

"No worries." Nana waved her off. "It'll come in time. C'mon, the others are waitin'."

"Right. Just so ya know, she doesn't know a thing," Seth mentioned.

"About what?" Claire asked, heart racing. "What did I just walk into?"

"Do you trust me?" Seth asked.

"I do."

"Then, trust me," he said, draping his arm over her shoulder on the way toward the truck.

*   *   *

As they pulled into the drive of the station, Claire continued to look in every direction possible, not wanting to miss anything. The terrain was nothing like she had ever seen before. The animals fascinated her. At one point, she saw a group of kangaroo racing across the open weary wasteland.

"You can breathe, love," Nana mentioned. "You haven't since ya got off the plane."

"It's beautiful, just different. You have to understand that I've never been out of the city."

"You didn't go out in the country for Katie's funeral?"

"I didn't go to Katie's funeral," Claire admitted. "She and I didn't get along very well."

"Not Katie's doing," Seth explained. "Claire had a problem with Katie that had absolutely nothing to do with her."

"Oh really? What was the issue?"

"Katie was with Nick," Claire said. When Pete and Nana looked at each other in shock, Claire asked, "What?"

"Nothing," Nana said quickly. "Park it over there," she said, pointing toward the barn.

Putting the truck into park, Pete got out of the truck and out of earshot of Claire before he said to Seth, "Go ahead an' get her inside. You two will be in the guest room with the queen bed. I'll grab a couple a' blokes t' get yer stuff upstairs."

"Thanks, man. She may be needing to go to bed sooner than later."

"Need some tea?"

"Might not be a bad idea," Seth agreed, getting out of the truck, closing the door behind him. "Shock may be the word of the day."

"That's puttin' it mildly. Should be interestin' t' say the least."

"Good news is she can't go anywhere."

"But the bad news is, she can't go anywhere," Pete countered before Seth headed to the other side of the truck to get Claire out. "They're in the kitchen."

*   *   *

Walking into the house, Claire got an uneasy feeling. "Why do I feel like the hair on the back of my neck is standing on end?" she whispered to Seth.

"Could be what's in the kitchen," he said, directing her toward the kitchen. Shocking her all at once would either be a good thing or a bad thing. Time would tell.

"What the…?" Claire asked, eyes wide, as she looked into the eyes of Kit, Nico, and Dom. Rubbing her eyes before she looked again to make sure it wasn't due to exhaustion, Claire asked, "Nick? Katie?" Then Nick grabbed her as she went to jump at Dom. "You! What are *you* doing here?"

"Calm down, Claire," Nico ordered, doing his best to keep his arms around Claire so she wouldn't hurt anyone, while Kit stood between Claire and Dom. "Seth! Do somethin' with yer wife!" he growled. "Preferably before she hurts Kit or Dom."

Claire turned, stunned. "You're worried about me hurting *Dom*? Really? Are you insane? He *killed* people! He almost killed Katie," she reminded him.

"He's not the same person you knew before, an' none a' these blokes know about his past. I would prefer it stay that way," Nico said sternly.

"Nick! You can't be serious!"

"It's Nico now, an' yes I am. You guys comin' here will upset the natural order enough without you spoilin' everythin'. You'll put *a lot* of people in danger…mainly my wife an' baby."

"Baby…*what*?" Claire glared at Kit. "You're pregnant?"

"I told you Kit was pregnant," Seth reminded her.

"You didn't tell me *Katie* was pregnant!" she growled. "What *else* haven't you told me?"

"This is it. I didn't tell you, in order to protect them. Katie is Kit, and Nick is Nico. You have to call them by those names."

"And what about Dominic? Is his name changed too…in order to protect the guilty? Because he *certainly* isn't innocent," Claire said snidely, standing on her own as Nico let her go. "I cannot *believe* what I'm seeing."

"You better quiet her down. You can hear her all the way outside," Pete warned, coming into the kitchen. Pouring some cooled tea into a cup, he handed it to Claire, "This'll help ease any travel sickness, as well as help ya with yer jetlag."

"Fine!" Claire huffed before she chugged the cup. Thrusting it toward Pete, she narrowed her eyes at Seth. "What did you think would happen when I saw this?"

"Look, we have a lot we need to explain to you, but first let's get you to lay –" Stopping when Claire dropped to her knees, Seth protectively draped his arm over her. "We need to get you to bed."

"What did you do?" Claire mumbled, dropping her head on his shoulder. "Are Katie and Nick really alive?"

"Yes."

"Katie's pregnant with Nick's baby?"

"Yes. They're married too."

"And Dominic's here? For real?"

"Yes. Let that sink in while you sleep."

"While I….*what*?" she asked. Shaking her head to clear it, her body suddenly gave out.

Catching her before she hit the floor, Seth scooped her off the ground. "She's gonna kill me when she wakes up."

"Probably, but she'll forgive you eventually," Nico pointed out as Seth went upstairs. "She always does."

After tucking her in, Seth headed back down to the group in the living room. "What did you mean she always does?" Seth asked Nico.

"Over the last couple of years, you were able t' get away with sayin' stuff that the average person would have gotten their head ripped off for."

"How long did you know?"

"To be honest, I didn't know right away. I figured it out the spring after Kit an' I got together. That was one of the reasons I was prayin' Claire had nothin' t' do with Joey Rossi's torture of Kit."

"Speaking of which," Kit said, taking her seat on the couch beside Nico, "Do you think Lucca and Joey Rossi believe the story that we died?"

"According to Dakota," Seth said, "Joey did some digging after your funerals. He got the information to Lucca, confirming your deaths through the autopsy reports Sandy filed."

"How did he get those?" Nico asked, stunned. When Seth just gave him a look, Nico shook his head. "Yeah. I get it. As long as they believe it, I don't care *how* they got it. As long as they're no longer our problem, I'm happy."

"Claire also intercepted multiple emails, that when decoded, indicated they do believe the story. I think it helps that no one has seen you in The States since your so-called deaths. You're not in any papers. Your pictures are nowhere on the internet either. Just stay off-line and you guys should be fine."

"That's our intention. We may be mentioned in birth announcements, but it won't have any photos."

"You won't be mentioned as Katie MacKenna or Nick Locke either. You'll be Nico and Kit Sullivan. Just don't do photos. The more you guys stay out of the spotlight, the better off you'll be."

"That's the plan."

*   *   *

Since Nico needed Seth out in the station, Kit went in to sit in a chair by Claire's bed while she slept. Drawing a sunrise picture of the station to pass the time, Kit periodically reflected on her and Claire's journey together, finding it ironic that they ended up together in the end after all.

Struggling a few moments to wake up, Claire's eyes slowly fluttered open. When she realized she didn't recognize the room, she gasped as she sat up straight in bed.

"Morning, sunshine," Kit said, setting her sketchpad to the side.

"Katie?"

"It's actually Kit now," she corrected her. "You can't call me Katie, and you have to call Nick, Nico."

"Are you really here…and alive?"

"Yes, ma'am."

"Your hair?" she asked, as Kit moved over to the side of her bed. Touching it, she asked, "You cut your beautiful hair. Did you color it too?"

Before Kit could answer, Claire scrambled out of the covers, bolting for the bathroom. Kit stayed in the room until she returned, fearing she would join Claire in her condition, as Claire violently threw up several times.

When Claire returned, she curled up on the end of the bed. Resting her head on her arm, while she held her stomach with the other, weak was a mild term for how she felt. "What was that?"

"Unfortunately, that's a side effect of the tea. Here," Kit said, getting her a small garbage can. "Just in case you decide to toss your cookies again."

"Thanks." Looking up at her, Claire asked, "Why did you cut your hair off? Why would you change it to red?"

"It was the best way to disguise me. Blond was *not* an option for me. It wouldn't match my coloring, so I chose auburn to add warmth. Nico colored his hair as well. With the little adjustment in our looks and name, it allows us, and others around us, to feel more comfortable safety wise. The new guys don't know any better."

"And, you're pregnant?" she asked, resting her hand on Kit's stomach.

"Three and a half months. Seems it didn't take Nico long to get one past the goalie."

"When did you two get married?" Looking at the ring on Kit's finger, Claire gushed, "Oh my word! That's stunning!"

"It's Nana's. It's an heirloom from her family. It goes with the owner of the station. When we got married upon our arrival here, Nana insisted that we take the ring since the station was going to us anyway."

"So much has changed," she remarked. Suddenly it registered in her mind what she saw downstairs, and asked, "Was that really Dom in the kitchen?"

"Yes. Please let me explain that before you go downstairs and kill our cook."

"You're letting him cook your food? Are you not concerned that he'll poison you?"

Chuckling, Kit shook her head. "No. He wouldn't dare. There are too many guys on this station who would kill him with their bare hands, and he knows it."

"How did this happen?"

"It's been an amazing journey. Sit back and relax while I explain," she said, using a calm tone in order to keep Claire as relaxed as possible. As Kit went through the events that led up to Dom being on the station, making sure to leave out the part where Pop was the one who killed Nate, she continued until Claire was caught up to their current status.

Two hours later, Claire sat there, dumbfounded. "Seriously? Are you *sure* this transformation is genuine?"

"I can say with all honesty and confidence, yes. Wanna hear the really cool part?"

"What?"

"He has a love interest. Her name is Charlene. She's such a sweetheart!"

"What? Does she know?"

"No. And she'll never know his past either, unless *he* tells her. That's not our secret to tell. Just like there are people protecting us, we're protecting him."

"But, how *can* you? He *killed* Jillian and Aaron. He tried to kill you and he attacked all those girls. How *can* you protect him? I don't understand."

"Seth didn't either. I'm still not completely sure he does. What I *do* know is that I have a peace about it. I also have a feeling Nico did it for me, as well as for him."

"What does *that* mean? You never asked for that!"

"No, but I realized just how much anger I was holding against him when I saw him again. I was judging him. It wasn't my place to do that. God is the only Judge. He's the one who Dom has to answer to…and personally? I wouldn't want to be him when he gets to Heaven. That's going to be one heavy conversation."

"He still needs to face a human judge and jury for what he did. Technically, you're harboring a fugitive."

"Technically, yes. We choose to look at it as giving him a second chance at life. Jesus did that for us. We're doing it for him."

"I just don't understand."

"You don't have to."

"But, I don't get it."

"That's okay. Look, we're all starting fresh and new here…even you."

"What do you mean?"

"How rough of a past do we have?"

"Well, it hasn't been the best," Claire admitted.

"Right, but you and Kit don't have one, so we get to start over."

"How can you do that?"

"Like this," she said, sticking her hand out, "Hi! My name's Kit Sullivan. What's yours?"

Claire smiled as she shook Kit's hand in understanding. "Claire Bren…I mean, Claire Simmons."

"See, we both have new names. With that in mind, we're starting fresh, with no mistakes. Also, Claire Simmons doesn't know Dominic Cook, so you guys can start fresh and new as well."

"I don't know about that," Claire said, hesitantly.

"You can do this. You never really got to know him. You only knew what he was accused of and what he did, not who he is."

Contemplating for a long few moments, Claire finally nodded. "While you're right, I still don't agree about not turning him in."

"You don't have to. The only thing we ask is that you respect those on this station, and they are to respect you as well. That includes Dom."

"I understand."

"Good. Now that we have an understanding, you just sit here and rest while I go get you something to eat. You must be starving."

"Now that you mention it, I am."

"Be right back. Just relax," Kit said, and disappeared.

While she was gone, Claire looked up toward Heaven. "Okay, if You're real, You and I have *a lot* to talk about. Is this really okay for Dom to be here? Is it really okay for us to be here too?"

"Of course it is," Seth said, walking into the room with a plate of food he got from Dom, who was bringing it up because he heard Claire awake.

"What did you hear?"

"All of it. I'm glad you're opening the door to at least talking to Him. Here, Dom put together a plate for you," he said, giving her the plate with a glass of lemonade.

After several bites, Claire shook her head. "I don't know about this whole Dom on the station thing, but I *do* know he's an excellent cook. And this lemonade? It's amazing!"

"I know. Concentrate on that portion of him."

"How are *you* okay with this?"

"I'm not, but it's not my call. It's Nico's."

"How are you okay with calling him Nico, and Katie, Kit?"

"Got used to it when I was here before. I struggled for a bit, but eventually got through it. It's for their safety."

"I understand that. It's just a lot to take in."

Lightly knocking on the door, Pete poked his head in, "Kit told me Claire was awake. Has she forgiven me yet?" he asked with a grin.

Claire couldn't help the laughter that escaped her. His white teeth stood out among his dark skin and curly hair. "I forgive you. It was probably for the best."

"Good. How are ya feelin'?"

"Better."

"Head hurt?"

"Actually, it does."

"Probably because y'er dehydrated. Drink that lemonade, along with at least three more glasses before dinner."

"I will."

"Good. Glad t' have ya here. Get some rest an' see ya at dinner," he said, and disappeared down the stairs.

"He's funny."

"You have no idea. They're all characters. It may take a bit for you to get used to them, but once you're accepted, you're golden."

"It's a fresh start, right?"

"Right."

"Good. Then no one knows I'm a turkey."

"That's putting it mildly," he said with a grin. Then he added, "I'm only kidding. Look, no one knows your past with Kit. As far as they know, you're my wife. That's it. That's all anyone knows of you. Even Dom doesn't know you. It's up to you what type of person you want to be."

"I get it."

"So, who are you going to be?"

After a moment of reflection, she responded, "I'm Claire Simmons – computer expert, and, it seems, soon to be nanny."

"And, who knows? Maybe we'll have one of our own soon as well."

"That'll be up to that God of yours."

"He can be yours too."

"I know. Just let me take this in a little at a time. Things in my life have done a complete one-eighty. There are a lot of memories and stories I have to filter through."

"Just breathe and take it one day at a time."

"Now *that* sounds like a plan."

Chapter 8

Autumn Blessings

Over the next several months, Claire worked hard on her reputation, along with her attitude with Dom and those around the station. She even went to church after a couple of weeks. This allowed her to see Dom in a new element. She watched him every chance she could, checking to see if she saw any of the man she read about in the file.

Also, along that time, Kit and Nico got some unique news. It seems when Kit went for her ultrasound, they discovered she was carrying twin boys. One night while everyone was on the porch, when Kit still had a little under a month left of her pregnancy, there was a debate among the people on the station as to what to name the boys.

"You could name them Cain and Able," Seth suggested.

Kit vetoed that idea. "No, because the one named Cain will think he's evil."

"What about Jonathon and David?" Dom suggested. "They were best friends in the Bible, right?"

"Right," Nico acknowledged. "That's a possibility."

"What about Jacob an' Esau?" Flynn asked. "If you want t' go Biblical, that's another possibility."

"True," Nico agreed.

"You could also go with rhyming names, such as Taylor and Tyler?" Claire suggested.

"Or, Barwon an' Jarrah are good choices, hey brother?" Barwon said, wrapping his arm around Jarrah's neck before rubbing his head.

"Daniel an' David are good Biblical names too," Adam suggested.

"Or John an' James," Nana pointed out, "they're in the Bible."

"Or Peter an' Paul," Pop suggested. "Aren't they apostles?"

"These are all good suggestions," Kit said, excitement running through her.

"Really?" Jarrah asked, thrilled that she liked his suggestion.

Nico chuckled. "Sorry, Barwon an' Jarrah, have t' veto those."

"Aww, man!" Jarrah said, throwing a rock at a spider crawling on the ground near him. Flynn jumped up and killed it before Kit saw it.

"Some other rhymin' names could be Jayden an' Jordan," Kalti suggested.

"Or, Landon an' Logan," Steve offered. "Also, Gabriel an' Michael are Biblical."

"Archangels. Not bad," Nico nodded in agreement.

"There are so many choices," Kit said, feeling overwhelmed. "I don't know what we're going to do."

"We'll make the decision by the time they come," Nico said, confidently.

"Hate t' tell ya, but y'er runnin' outta time," Nana pointed out. "She's over eight months along. Kinda surprised she's still carryin' 'em."

"Shush! I really don't want her t' have 'em yet. They're not ready."

"You mean *you're* not ready," Seth hinted.

"What do ya mean?" Pete asked.

"He's afraid something's going to happen to her in childbirth," Seth said, reminding them of Kit's nightmare.

Standing, Pete stared out down the road, jaw dropped. "Who is…?"

Nana squinted, hoping to get a better view. "Who's that?"

"I think it's Charlie," Pete said, heart racing.

"*Our* Charlie?" Buri asked, stunned. "Why he here?"

"I'm goin' t' find out," Pete said, jogging over to him. As they talked, the others nervously watched.

"Okay, who's Charlie?" Claire asked. "Haven't heard of him yet."

"He's Pete's wife's brother," Nico explained.

When they walked up to the group, Pete introduced him, "This is Charlie, my brother-in-law."

"Why you here?" Buri asked, curious.

"I was sent," Charlie explained, "by Danny Hawk."

"Hawk sent ya?" Nana perked up at hearing his name. "Has anyone heard from Shawn O'Brien?"

"Afraid so." Charlie nodded, with a solemn look on his face. "He not here no more."

"What do ya mean?"

"He gone."

"Gone where?"

Charlie sighed, placing his hands on his hips. "Shawn with God."

"Oh," Nana said, sitting back in her chair, upset.

"What happened t' him?" Pop pressed.

"Him ran into a baaaaaad woman. Evil. She an' her people took him an' his love, Victoria, out," he explained. "Hawk tell me t' come an' pray over dat," he said, pointing to the north field. "Him say she close, an' don't want anythin' t' happen t' her," he pointed to Kit.

"Where's Hawk?" Nana asked.

"He an' others go t' big battle elsewhere. Him tell me t' come here, so I come here. I do what he tell me."

"Are you a follower a' Jesus?" Nico asked.

"Yes."

"Right-oh. Have at it. Any help is appreciated."

"I go?" Charlie asked, pointing toward the field.

"You eat yet?" Dom asked.

"No."

"How about I go get you a plate of food, and then you can go?" he offered.

"No. I need t' pray first. In the mornin', I eat."

"Sounds good."

"I go? Very important. Hawk tell me *very* important mission," Charlie explained.

"Yes. Thank you," Nico said, relieved to get help. "We appreciate it."

As he walked toward the field, Barwon asked, "What's he doin'?"

"He's goin' t' pray over the field," Nico explained.

"Why?"

"There's a reason I haven't let any cattle there. There's a problem between the fields."

"Uh, Nico?" Kit asked, holding her breath as a contraction suddenly tightened her mid-section. When it did, she felt a 'pop' before pain spiked up, making it so painful that she couldn't talk.

"Her water broke," Nana said, seeing the liquid on the porch below her. "Nico, when her contraction slows, get her up t' yer room. Claire, go call an ambulance. Buri?"

"I know what t' do. Pete, go get ready," Buri said before disappearing into the woods to gather herbs for pain in case the ambulance couldn't make it in time.

Once the contraction went down, Kit begged, "Make it stop. It's too early!"

Following Nico up the stairs while Nico carried Kit to their room, Pete said, "Can't."

"They might not make it. It's too early!"

"Yer water's broke, Kit. Ya can't stop a runnin' freight train. Those boys are comin'."

*   *   *

"Kit?" Andi said, coming into the room several minutes after they got upstairs. "Claire called to tell me that y'er…oh boy!" she said, when another contraction took over Kit's body. Looking to Pete, she asked, "How far apart?"

"They're close," Pete said, doing his best to make her comfortable. "Her water also broke."

"Hate t' tell ya, but we're deliverin' these little guys here. One a' the Thompson's boys broke his leg. The ambulance is already on its way t' the hospital. There's no stoppin' it. That's why Claire called me."

"Y'er serious?" Pete asked, stunned. "Which one?"

"Benji."

"Again? That boy's broken just about every bone in his body already an' he's only eight! Can ya imagine what he's gonna be when he grows up…*if* he grows up?"

"A stuntman," Kit said, breathing heavily as the contraction slowed. "Will you people shut up when I'm in the middle of a contraction? It hurts and I'm just trying to get through this. Where's the pain medicine?"

Walking into the room with a cup in his hand, Buri announced, "No ambulance. Babies comin' here. Drink," he said shoving the cup at Kit.

"Fine!" she huffed before chugging the cup. Shoving it at him, she said, "I love you, but I'm fixin' to hurt someone here if this pain docsn't stop!"

"Kit, you need t' calm down, love," Nico coaxed. "Just relax."

"Relax?" Kit narrowed her eyes at him. "This is *not* easy!"

"I know. I'm sorry. Is there anythin' I can do?"

"No. Just shhhhhhheeeeeeeeoooowwwwww!" Kit howled in pain before she started breathing heavily. "Oh God! Please! It's severe pain! Ahhhhheeeee!" she said, and couldn't talk anymore.

Pete spun on his heels toward her. "Kit?"

Breathing heavily, Kit just glared at him as she did her best to get through the immense pain levels.

Over the next hour, Kit's pain was intense. Just when she didn't think she could take anymore, the first little one made his way into the world, screaming at the top of his lungs. As the second baby made his appearance, the ambulance pulled up to the main house.

After the paramedics loaded Kit and the babies up into the ambulance, Nico, Seth, and Claire jumped into the truck and followed them to the hospital. By the time they arrived, Kit was beyond exhausted. Her excitement mixed with fear, as she knew the babies were way too early.

*   *   *

"Right-oh," their doctor, Doctor Anderson, came into the room reading the chart. "Here's the thing. Yer ankle biters are a bit too early."

"I was afraid of that," Kit said, beside herself.

"Unfortunately, some things are not in our control. They're up in our neonatal intensive care unit, getting the best possible care. They'll be screamin' an' yellin' at ya in no time."

"Here's prayin'," Nico said, sitting down beside Kit, grabbing her hand.

"I'm gonna be honest with ya, here. They're both havin' trouble with keepin' their body temperature, so they're in the incubator. They're also not quite ready t' drink yet, so we have them on an IV. We'll start feedin' them on a dropper, an' then move t' a bottle. Once they're fluent in their use with the bottle, we'll wean them off the IV. Now, durin' this, we're goin' t' continue t' monitor their heart rates an' breathin'."

"Is that a heavy concern?" Nico asked.

"Yes, it is. I'll keep you posted on their progress, of course. Right now, though, they are bein' called baby boy 'A' Sullivan, an' baby boy 'B' Sullivan. That's gettin' t' be a mouthful. Do you have any idea of how we can shorten that yet?"

"Are ya askin' for names?"

"In a round about way, yes. Here's the paperwork you have t' fill out," he said, plopping a small stack of papers, along with a pen, onto the side table. "Would ya like t' give me an idea?"

"Well," Nico started, glancing at Kit, who nodded before he continued, "The first will be Joshua Nicholas, an' baby 'B', as you call him, is Caleb James."

"Strong biblical names," the doctor nodded in approval. "I'll inform the nursing staff t' add Joshua t' the first baby's ID band, an' Caleb to the second baby's band."

"That would be appreciated. Now, what about Kit?"

"Well, young lady, you have done amazingly well through all of this. You'll be released probably in three days. Make sure you eat foods high in iron an' protein. We're also goin' t' keep an IV goin' for a couple a' days as well. Once released, I'll want a follow-up appointment with you in couple weeks t' make sure y'er continuin' t' do well."

"Um, how long will the boys be in here?" Kit asked, anxiously.

"If things go well, they'll be in the NICU for about two weeks, an' the regular nursery for about a week before we release them."

"Are you telling me that we're going to have to leave them here?" Kit asked, feeling sick to her stomach about the idea.

"You're welcome t' come back as often as you wish. We completely understand yer concern an' apprehension in leavin' them here. Call as frequently as you feel ya need to. We don't mind bein' harassed. These are yer babies an' we understand that."

"I appreciate that, but –" Kit looked over to Nico, terror written all over her face.

"If you want, I'll get you a hotel room in the hotel next t' the hospital. I can't be gone from the station that long, but I understand that you will," Nico offered.

"If you want," Claire spoke up, "I'll stay with you. Since I'm supposed to be the nanny anyway, I would think it would be a good thing for me to know what's going on from the nurses."

Wiping the tear from her cheek, Kit only nodded in response.

"Done. I'll set that up for, what, three days from now?" Nico asked the doctor.

"Yep," he confirmed. "Baring anythin' unforeseen, that is."

"Good. Seth, are you okay with this?"

"Yep. We'll come into town often right?" he asked.

"Yeah. I'll get us here as often as possible. I don't want t' be apart from her either."

"And, you won't," Nana said, coming in with Pop. "I ran that station for years. Pretty sure I can cover a few weeks."

Nico shook his head. "Nana, you don't need t' do that."

"Yes, I do. You have a family now. You two need t' stay united. Charlie's got the north field, an' those boys know what they need t' do. We got this."

"Good then," the doctor stood, "it's settled. I'm gonna go check on the boys. Y'er welcome t' go see them as soon as you'd like. There can only be two in at a time. The nurses'll make sure you follow that rule as well. They're very strict up there."

"Thanks for the head's up," Nico said, appreciatively.

After the doctor left the room, Nana asked, "So, what are the little bugger's names?"

"Joshua Nicholas, spelled like my original first name, an' Caleb James," Nico told them.

"Joshua an' Caleb? I know they were in the Bible. I've heard Pastor mention them, but who were they?"

"Joshua and Caleb were selected, along with ten other men, to scout out the Promised Land for the Israelites," Kit explained. "While the other ten were afraid by what they found, Caleb and Joshua stood up for the Lord, and said they should go in and take the land He provided. As a matter of fact, Joshua took over Moses' position after he died, and led the Israelites into the Promised Land. Their story teaches us that regardless of what others say, we need to stand up for the Lord."

"Well, if anyone can break this curse, they sound like the pair t' do it," Nana said, confidently.

"With the Lord on our side, we can't lose," Nico agreed.

*　*　*

Going into the NICU, Kit and Nico were both nervous as to what to expect. Once in there, they scrubbed their hands before finding the boys, and sat near them. Since Kit was in a wheelchair, Nico pulled a chair next to her.

"So, it's my understandin' that one is named Joshua, an' the other is Caleb?" a nurse asked, coming into their area.

Kit just nodded, looking at all of the little ones in the NICU. The shape some of them were in broke her heart. Their ages in weeks were on the cards next to their incubators. There was a twenty-seven-week-old boy under a bilirubin light to help with jaundice. Others in there had multiple tubing, and monitors attached to them. Shaking her head as tears slowly crawled down her cheek, Kit asked, "Are the boys okay to come out?"

"Only for a half-hour at a time. Then we have t' get them back in t' get their temperatures regulated again."

"What about their monitors?" Nico asked. "Doc said they were bein' monitored."

"Well, Joshua's a bit stronger than Caleb in some areas, an' Caleb's got him beat in others. Joshua's been doin' what he's supposed t' be doin' in regards t' his heart rate an' breathin', while Caleb's set off some alarms. Meanwhile, Caleb's doin' better with eatin'."

"Can we hold them?" Kit asked.

"Which one do you want first?"

"Let Nico hold Joshua, while I'll take Caleb. Then we can switch," Kit said, half to the nurse, half to Nico.

"Sounds good," Nico agreed. "This first time is for us. The others out there will have t' wait an' only get to see them in their cradles for this round."

"Agreed," the nurse said. "Since Joshua's holdin' his temp a little more, I'll pull him out first."

As she got him out of his cradle, Kit's heart rate picked up. Their birth, to her, was a blur. She barely remembered what they looked like. As a matter of fact, the entire day felt like a blur.

Seeing the tiny body of their son in Nico's big hands almost made Kit's heart burst. "That's so sweet!" she gushed.

"Yer turn, love," the nurse said, handing Caleb to her.

Both boys were identical in looks. They had jet-black hair, like Kit's used to be, and at that moment, they had blue eyes. Knowing Nico's eyes were blue, and hers were hazel, she was curious to see which color the boys would have.

"I'm feelin' a lot at one time," Nico admitted. "I can't believe these little buggers are from us."

"I know. Right?" Kit smiled as she looked down at Caleb. Picking up his tiny hand, she wiggled her finger in between his so he was grasping her finger. "Look at these tiny fingers and nails. Quick, count," she said, counting his fingers and toes. "Good. Ten fingers and ten toes."

"Same with Joshua," Nico pointed out. "Look at these little feet an' nails."

"And all that hair," Kit remarked at their hair, that was an inch and a half long all over their little heads.

"Marryin' you was the happiest day of my life, an' I didn't think anythin' else could make me any happier. But this? Havin' little ones that God created from me an' you? This is out of this world. I never want t' forget this feelin'."

"Your heart amazes me," Kit said, as a tear dropped onto Caleb's blanket while he slept peacefully in her arms. "I can't believe they're here. They're amazing."

"How are *you* feelin'?"

"I'm in pain down there, but I'm not leaving them until I have to."

"I don't blame you."

After about ten minutes, they switched the babies, having the nurse put them back in their cribs after being out for a total of twenty minutes. They didn't want to take any chances.

"Nico, can they come in with you here and let me go back to my room?" Kit asked when their time was up. "I'm exhausted."

"Here, take these with you," the nurse said, handing Kit digital printouts of the boys so she would have them with her at all times. "Do ya need me t' send someone t' take ya back t' yer room?"

"No. Seth and Claire can take me back while Nana and Pop trade out," Kit said.

Nico kissed Kit before she left. "See you in a bit, love."

On the way back to the room, Claire doted over the photos. "I can't wait to see them! They're so cute!"

"Thank you. We're excited. I never want to forget what they looked like in Nico's arms. I'm grateful the nurse took these photos of them in our arms for the first time," Kit said, accepting the photos, holding them close to her for the rest of the ride back to the room. Grateful the boys looked stable, and that she was doing so well, Kit snuggled under the covers, relieved to be safe and sound and in the place she was in life. Knowing the Lord was looking over them and keeping them safe, it allowed her to fall into a deep, peaceful sleep.

Chapter 9

Harvest Delights

The next couple of weeks were tough for Kit and Nico. Joshua was released about a week earlier than Caleb, so they kept him in the hotel with them until they could bring them home together. While he was with them, Kit had to feed him every two hours. This made for a rough schedule, but to her every minute with her boys held precious value.

When they weren't in the hotel, they were in the NICU with Caleb, or sleeping. Every time Kit went into the NICU, it broke her heart. She would see baby after baby in rough shape, and couldn't imagine working there every day. As a matter of fact, the only bright spot Kit saw was when the twenty-seven-week-old made it through, but there were others who didn't and she felt for those families, praying with every bone in her body that neither Joshua, nor Caleb, would be next.

* * *

The day Caleb was released was a joyous time for the entire station. Knowing they were coming in, the family planned a welcome home party. Through the weeks, Nico and Seth would pop in and out at the station, but otherwise, they were with their wives in town.

Pulling up to the main house, Kit immediately started crying. Seeing the welcome home sign and the two 'It's a Boy!' signs made her heart burst with joy. While they unloaded the boys, cheering and hollering could be heard throughout the station, which was upsetting the animals, but no one cared.

Charlie met the group at the truck, while the others waited on the porch. "Bless?" he asked.

"You wanna bless the boys?" Nico checked, making sure he understood him.

Grinning, Charlie only nodded in response. When they agreed, Charlie said a beautiful prayer in his own language before he continued in English, "We want t' thank You, Father, for dese beautiful babies. We ask You t' make dem strong young men for You. We ask You t' protect dem an' keep 'em safe. We ask You t' give Kit an' Nico strength in upcomin' days t' care for da lil' ones. We ask You t' bring dem t' You at an early age, an' allow dem t' continue t' grow stronger in You each day," he prayed before finishing in his own language once again.

Charlie never ceased to amaze Kit. Standing all of five-foot-seven, his kinky-curly black hair hung to about his shoulders. His dark brown eyes matched the darkness of his skin, making his snow-white teeth stand out when he smiled…which was constantly. His mellow disposition allowed a calmness to surround him wherever he went.

"Thank you," Kit said, feeling the weight of the last few weeks.

"It okay, boss lady. You need t' rest with da babies. God will bless all a' ya. Jus' keep Him first in yer life. I need t' get back t' the field t' walk an' pray."

"Gotta ask," Seth said, rubbing the back of his neck as he tried to figure out how to politely ask what he wanted to know.

Charlie stopped in his tracks. "What?"

"What are you doing up there? And why?"

"Oh," he said, relieved that was all he wanted to know. "Dat field has bad spirit connected t' it 'cuz a' da other station. I walk around da field an' pray for a shield a' protection. Maybe in time you use, but not now."

"I see. And, how does prayer stop the influence of whatever is coming from the other station?"

"Prayer is verrry powerful. People not give prayer credit it deserves. Dis is as much for da station, as is for da babies," Charlie said, nodding toward the twins. "Break curse, yeah?"

"That would be nice," Nico agreed. "We've been prayin' for that for a long time."

"I pray over babies. You pray over babies. Babies be okay. Blood a' Jesus will keep dem pure an' safe."

"Right-oh," Nico sighed, picking up the twins while Kit had the bags. "In the meantime, the others are waitin'."

"Dey wait for me t' pray," Charlie explained. "Nana not want da anger on da station. She know possibly come in dru dem." Gesturing toward the boys, he went on, "But, I pray first. I pray every day until Hawk tell me otherwise. Boys will grow strong in Jesus. Dat's yer duty too, though."

"We're aware, an' we take that seriously," Nico agreed.

"Den go in faith dat da babies are being prayed for. I go back t' da north field. Somedin' up dere *real* bad. It tryin' t' break through, but I keep prayin', an' God an' His angels keepin' 'em back."

"Then, go do yer thing," Nico said, as they separated from Charlie, heading toward the house.

"Funny little man," Kit commented.

"But, strong in faith."

"We need that."

"I agree. We need t' keep everyone safe."

"And, covered in the blood of Jesus."

*   *   *

Joshua and Caleb were born on June twenty-eighth. Kit would have loved to have them born on July third, her birthday, but either way she was happy to have them, and that they were healthy.

Over the next several years, stress was the order of the day. Kit felt as if she wasn't feeding a baby, she was cleaning one. If she wasn't cleaning one, she was feeding one. Feeling like she was running on autopilot, she was grateful when they began to do more on their own. By the time they were two, they were potty-trained, eating on their own, and picking out their own clothes. She knew not every set of twins was that easy, but she was blessed and happy to have them at all. With all of the events surrounding their lives, the two years of stress of raising twins seemed like a breeze!

"Kit," Pete said, coming into the kitchen as she was cleaning their highchairs from lunch and Dom was starting dinner and lunch preparations. The boys were outside with a very pregnant Claire – who was due in about two weeks. "We need t' talk."

"Sure. What's up?"

"Nico wanted me t' talk t' you, because he's kind of nervous t' mention it."

"Mention what?"

"Y'er preggers again."

"*What*? No!" She said, color draining from her face. "I can't be! Nico even got fixed about a month ago so I wouldn't get pregnant again."

"Did you," he cleared his throat in nervousness, "Did you, um, use anythin' the first few times afterward?"

"Well, no. He was fixed."

Pete shook his head, while he rested his hands on his hips. Dom just about dropped his bowl of potatoes, when Pete explained, "Ya have t' use somethin' for the first six or so weeks. Kit, Dad told me about a week ago that he thought you were pregnant, an' I've been watchin'. Y'er preggers."

"No. I'm not," she said adamantly. "I can't be. I haven't had a whole lot of energy because of the boys."

With his face red in embarrassment, Pete sighed. Looking up at the ceiling in hopes of organizing his thoughts, Pete groaned, "Ohhhhh, Nico owes me *big time*!"

"You can't be serious?" Kit's eyes popped wide-open when she realized he *was* serious. "I'm…I'm pregnant again?" Sitting down on the stool in the kitchen, stunned, she asked, "Am I really pregnant again?"

"Afraid so. We'll test ya if ya want, but you know how accurate Dad is."

"But, I beat the dream last time. I didn't die in childbirth with the twins. Do you think it's possible to have two sets of twins?"

"Not likely. While twins *do* run in the Sullivan side of the family, it's traditionally only one set. Pretty sure yer dream on that one was inaccurate."

"The kidnapping dream came true."

"What about the north field one?" Pete challenged.

"Give it time. Charlie's still up there."

"For now."

"I'm fixin' to get irritated at you!" Kit snapped, narrowing her eyes as she crossed her arms. "You're not being very encouraging here."

"Kit!" Nico flew in through the front door. "Kit! Call Anna at Koala Pass!"

She stood, stunned. "What? Why?"

"A cop just came an' arrested Alec. He said somethin' about child molestation an' rape charges. Anna's only seventeen."

"Oh no," Kit groaned, dropping her head. "You don't think they did anything, do you?"

"Well, I don't think they would risk our stations havin' an issue over a simple datin' thing. Call her."

Dialing the number, Kit prayed that this was some mistake. When Aaron (Anna's brother) answered the phone, Kit asked, "Aaron? This is Kit. Is either Anna or your mom available?"

"Umm, may not want t' talk t' either right now."

"What's going on?"

"Between you, me, an' the fencepost?"

"I'll have t' tell Nico."

"I understand. Thing is, Anna's preggers…an' it's Alec's."

"How do you know?"

"Anna told us. She pulled some dreamy story about 'meetin' under the stars' bullocks. Mum an' Dad are furious."

"I'll bet. We'll be over in a few."

"Be prepared for anger."

"I'll leave the boys here."

"Probably a good idea."

"Be there shortly," she said, and hung up. "Um, Anna's pregnant, and it's Alec's."

"*Our* Alec? How did this happen?" Nico demanded, face red in anger.

"Before you lose yer temper, keep in mind that the anger's still roamin'," Pete pointed out.

"How far along is she?"

"Don't know," Kit explained. "Aaron said everyone's angry over there, but we have to go."

"I agree. Pete, make sure Charlie knows, an' have him prayin'. I have a feelin' we're goin' t' need all the back-up we can get."

"Will do."

As Nico and Kit jumped in the truck, Kit mentioned, "You're a chicken."

"Who? Me?" he asked, chuckling.

"You sent Pete in to tell me I'm pregnant."

"Because I had my hands full with a cow givin' birth when he came t' me. Between fightin' with a cow t' give birth, or tellin' you y'er pregnant, sorry babe, I chose the cow."

"Chicken," she said again.

"I'm really sorry. I thought gettin' done what I did would have cured that."

"We'll just get me done when the little one's born. Obviously it was meant to be here or I wouldn't be pregnant."

"Good way t' look at it."

"Nico," Kit said, taking his hand into hers, "God is blessing us once again. I'm not fixin' to look a gift horse in the mouth. If He wants to bless us once again, then I'll take it."

"Good. Keep those positive thoughts in mind," he said, pulling up to Koala Pass's main house. As they got out, Nico grabbed Kit's hand, and whispered, "Pray."

"Have been since you mentioned Alec being arrested. This is all going to be up to the Lord."

"Isn't it always?"

"Kit!" Anna ran off the porch in tears, throwing her arms around her. Near her ear, Anna whispered, "They want me t' have an abortion."

"*What*?" Kit shouted, horrified. Pulling her away, she looked into Anna's eyes to see that Anna was telling the truth. Pale, Kit quietly said to Nico, "Her parents want her to have an abortion."

"We gotta talk," Nico said, pulling the two girls with him to the porch. As they walked, Nico could sense every eye on them who was on the station. He could feel the anger churning around them, trying to penetrate their spirit. "G'day, Tommy, Andi," Nico greeted them with a hug.

"Have a seat," Tommy nodded toward two empty seats. Andi and Tommy's boys, Alex, Adam, Andrew, and Aaron, along with Tommy and Andi, occupied the other chairs, leaving three. "Figured you would be here shortly."

"Can we talk?"

"Kinda thought we were."

As Kit and Nico got settled in their seats, Nico started, "Got a visit t'day from the police. Seems there's been some contact between Alec an' Anna?"

"*More than contact*!" Andrew roared. "She's full a' paws an' claws!"

"An' y'er sure it's Alec's?"

"Yes," Anna answered. "I'm even willin' t' do a paternity test when it's born."

"It's not goin' t' *be* born!" Adam growled. He swore as he sat back in his chair, crossing his arms in a huff.

"Is this final?" Nico asked, cautiously. "Is there room for discussion in this?"

"We're *not* gonna let her ruin her life because some drongo decided he wanted her," Andi insisted.

"Right, but there *are* alternatives," Nico pointed out. "She could adopt it out, *or* you two could raise it as yer own."

"Have you lost yer mind?" Tommy snapped.

"No. Bear with me a minute."

"By all means," Tommy waved his arm in the air, "please enlighten us."

"If ya make her have an abortion, she'll always remember that she killed her child, but –"

Adam scoffed. "It's *not* a child yet!"

"Yes. From the point of conception, it's a child," Nico explained, "By eighteen days, the baby has a heartbeat. By forty-two, brain waves can be detected. At fifty-two days, the baby yawns, an' can hiccup. By eight *weeks* all organs are functional. Look, even by nine weeks, it has fingerprints. At ten weeks it can feel pain. An', at twelve, it can smile. Now, I dunno about you, but t' me, that spells life."

"Wow," Andi said, mulling over his words. "I didn't realize that."

"Y'all became Christians only about four years ago. You weren't able to raise your kids in the Lord since birth. Y'all can look at it as a second chance if you raise it," Kit explained. "You will also give Anna the gift of watching her little one grow and see what the Lord will do for it. *Or* if you don't want to do that, there are many loving couples who can't have children of their own. You can give *them* the gift of a little one. We'll even take it. We would much rather raise it than see it die. Whatever you decide, but please, *please* don't make her have an abortion. Y'all have weeks to decide if you two want to raise it or if she'll have to put it up for adoption, but don't take the life of that little one. It's not the baby's fault how it was conceived."

"Yeah. Worst case scenario, she graduates a year later than she expected," Nico suggested. "If yer only concern is for her education, there are other options than killin' yer grandchild."

"Killin' our *what*?" Andi asked, appalled. "We would never!"

"That baby is part Alec, but it's also part Anna, which makes it part you by blood. No matter what you do, you can never change that. Do you really want t' kill yer grandchild?"

"No, I –" Andi stopped, mid-sentence. "I never thought of it that way."

"As Christians, we value life," Kit pointed out. "We all know that God doesn't make mistakes. Take time to pray as to which of the two options you want to go with, but *please* don't make her kill her baby?"

Tommy sighed, deep in thought. "Ya bring up some valid points."

"We only want t' protect her reputation," Alex explained.

"You already had Alec arrested," Nico pointed out.

"He has t' pay for what he did!" Tommy shouted.

"I get that," Nico agreed, "but her reputation has already been blown by you arrestin' him. You wanna continue t' deal blows by makin' her kill her baby too?"

"What would *you* do if it were *your* daughter?" Andi asked.

Nico shrugged. "Already told you. We would raise her as our own. As far as the other option, we would give her the choice of adoption. Either way, we wouldn't let her kill her baby. We're not God. It's not our place t' decide who lives or dies."

"You put up a valid argument," Andi said, mulling his words around in her mind. "I guess we'll have t' give her the option. Anna? It's yer life. What do *you* want t' do?"

"Really?" Anna smiled, hopeful.

"Really."

"I would love to be able t' see the little one grow. If you're willin', I would like it if you raised it. If not, then I would much rather adopt it out or give it t' Kit an' Nico."

"If we raise it, you can*not* have any say in what we do," Tommy warned. "If it's cryin', you can't go pick it up. If you don't agree with our discipline, you can't jump in t' try t' stop it."

"I understand."

"You say this now, but do you *really* understand? It won't be easy."

"But my child will be alive an' in yer good hands. You raised five of us. Pretty sure y'er competent t' raise another."

"Fair enough. We'll start the paperwork tomorrow."

"What about Alec?" Nico asked.

"What *about* Alec?" Tommy asked, irritated.

"Well, he's the dad," Kit pointed out. "Legally, while she can sign her rights away, you still have to worry about Alec fighting for it. If you cut a deal with him where you drop the charges in exchange for him signing over custody, pretty sure he would do it."

"But if we do, he gets off scot-free!" Andi objected.

"You don't think he's learned his lesson in the cooler?" Kit asked. "I'll be willing to bet that if you offer that deal, he'll take it. His arrest is already on record. If he signs the paperwork, at least he gets out of the charges."

"We'll have a strong discussion with him as well," Nico added.

"Think it'll work?" Andi asked.

"If he doesn't sign, then he goes t' jail an' ends up losin' custody a' the baby anyway," Nico pointed out. "It's in his best interest t' sign the papers."

"Are ya willin' t' do this?" Tommy asked Anna.

"Yes. Please!" Anna pleaded. "Please don't make me kill it!"

"Right-oh. Reckon that's the plan," Tommy said, declaring his final decision.

"Are you bloody serious?" Aaron snapped.

"That ocker got her pregnant!" Adam added.

"What's gonna stop her from seein' him again?" Alex demanded.

"Andrew?" Tommy asked. "What's yer opinion?"

Andrew shrugged. "I don't have one. If I see him near her again, I'll kill him with my bare hands."

"Enough said," Tommy agreed. "Do you understand what will happen if you even consider seein' him again?"

Anna sighed. "Yes, sir."

"We mean it," Andrew warned. "Don't push us."

"Don't even consider it," Aaron threatened. "We *will* take him out."

"Yes. I understand," Anna agreed. "I won't see him again."

"Settled?" Nico asked.

"Yes," Tommy agreed. "We'll go t' the lawyer in the mornin'."

"May I walk them t' the car?" Anna asked her parents.

"Yes, but afterward, you need t' come back here so we can lay down some rules an' guidelines."

As they walked to the truck, Anna glanced over her shoulder to make sure they were out of earshot before she said, "I don't know how ya did that, but thank you."

Kit hugged Anna, and whispered, "Don't you *ever* do that again. Do you understand?"

"Yes, ma'am."

"Yer brothers *will not* hesitate t' do some major damage t' him," Nico warned, giving her a hug before they left. As they were driving down the road, Nico mentioned, "Well, that was fun."

"We really need to bathe all the babies in prayer. When Andi asked what we would do, I agree with your answer, but I gotta ask myself if they're raised right, would they do the same thing? Will they fall into that trap?"

"If they do, then I'll do what I said we would do. We'll keep it an' raise it."

Resting her hand on her stomach, Kit said, "I feel that this one is a girl. If she is, then we need to take good care of her."

"We will, just as much as we will the twins."

"*Will* we be able to protect them?"

"That's not our job," Nico reminded her. "Ours is t' pray. The Lord's is t' protect. We have t' trust His will."

* * *

Over the next several months, things around the station once again did a one-eighty. Claire and Seth had a baby boy, who they named Scott Allen Simmons. In the meantime, Anna had a baby girl, who Andi and Tommy adopted, and named her Willow Ann. Alec agreed to sign the papers, and then he returned to his parent's home in Brisbane. He wasn't wanted on the station anymore. Kit and Nico weren't willing to risk relations between the two stations.

The good news was that Kit's pregnancy was going well. On her five-month ultrasound, they found out that once again, they were having twins. The technician was unsure of the sex of the babies, though, so that would be a mystery until the day of their delivery. They were just happy the babies and Kit were healthy.

* * *

"You don't think I'm going to die in this birth, do you?" Kit asked one night while they were cuddling before bed.

"I think God is in control of things. You haven't had that dream for a while, though."

"Not since the birth of the boys."

"Then we'll leave it up t' God, love."

"Speaking of that," Kit said, then doubled over in pain.

Nico sat up in alarm. "Are you serious?"

"We need to get to the hospital," Kit groaned.

*   *   *

To Nico and Kit's delight, Kit carried the twins to full term. She delivered healthy baby girls within five hours of arriving to the hospital. Unfortunately, the babies experienced distress during the delivery to the point that a caesarean section was needed to get them out quickly.

"Since she's in a happy place," Nana said, walking into the room with Pop, Paige, Zack, Adam, Flynn, Claire, and Seth, "what are the names of the newest Sullivan babies?"

Sitting at Kit's bedside, Nico didn't bother looking up. His concern was for Kit. It was a rough delivery for her, and she also had surgery to tie her tubes while she was under. To Nico, Kit looked pale at best. "They're Rachel Elizabeth an' Leah Grace."

"Pretty names," Claire remarked.

"Yeah."

"Are you okay, brother?" Seth asked, resting his hand on Nico's shoulder.

"No. She looks horrible. This is the worst I've *ever* seen her."

"What about the babies?"

"They're doin' pretty good. They said they'll keep them in the NICU for twenty-four hours, but chances are they'll probably get moved t' regular nursery in the next day or so.

They said the babies would probably be ready t' go before she is."

"What all did they do to her?"

"C-section and tied her tubes. She hasn't been awake for long. She hasn't eaten yet either."

"Did they say when she should be awake?" Paige asked, walking over to Kit's other side, picking up her hand. "Her skin is chilly."

"They said she could wake at any time."

"Your voice sounds so hollow," Nana observed.

"She looks horrible!"

"Have you seen the babies yet?"

"Yes. I followed them up t' the NICU. They called me back down after she woke a couple of hours ago, an' I haven't been back yet."

"Mind if we go see them?"

"You can. I'm not goin' anywhere until I see her eat somethin'."

"That would require her to wake up first," Claire pointed out.

"Then I'll sit here until then."

"Have *you* eaten yet?" Seth asked.

"No."

"What if we go get you something to eat while Claire, Nana, and Paige go upstairs to see the babies?"

"You can't go in without one of us with you," Nico explained. "If you want t' go get some food, that's fine."

"What do you want?"

"Anythin'."

"Are these the babies?" Nana asked, picking up the pictures.

"Yes. Nana, nothin' personal, but I'm really not wantin' t' talk at the moment."

"I understand. We'll leave you for now an' get ya some food."

"Thank you."

Several minutes after they left, Kit woke up. Hope filled Nico to see her hazel eyes, but the twinkle was lost in them and that concerned him deeply. He knew it would take her quite a while to recover from this one, but he knew she would. Raising two sets of twins would take pretty much everything in them. He had faith that God would carry them through.

Chapter 10

Cutest Little Pumpkins in the Patch

Over the next several years, life around the station often resembled a zoo. With the two sets of twins, Claire and Seth's three children (Scott Allen, Caitlyn Leigh, and Samuel Alexander), the ranch hands, and the animals, Nico said it was often a fine balance between complete chaos and somewhat organized.

Due to crowded quarters in the main house, they built a house for Seth and Claire on the property, as well as a guesthouse for Pete and his wife, Victoria, and their five children. Since Charlie was Victoria's brother, he slept in the house when he wasn't praying over the field. For the time being, with the amount of children Pete and Victoria had, Victoria's sister, Grace, was staying with them to help as well.

Since Andi and Tommy adopted and were raising Anna's baby, Willow hung out quite a bit with the kids of Serenity Wells to give Andi a break. Kit and Claire tag-teamed the young group until they were in school.

Once the kids entered school, Kit and Nico started working with the youth group at church. They felt a burden for teens, but with two sets of twins, there wasn't a lot of time left, so when the kids got into school, it allowed them the time to join the ministry. During that time, Nico started a home-based ministry of devotions on the porch on Monday nights. This opened the station to the Lord. At first, Scott, Claire, Andi, Tommy, Pop, Nana, Dom, and a couple other ranch hands attended the study session. After several weeks, several more ranch hands ventured toward the porch. Then after a few months, they even joined in the discussion, much to Nico's delight.

One afternoon, when the boys were around ten years old, Pastor Paul stopped by the station to see Nico and Kit.

"What can we do for ya?" Nico asked, as they all three took a seat on the porch.

"Well, there's somethin' I wanted t' talk t' you both about. There are a few youngsters you know very well who go t' the church that need a little extra attention."

Kit shook her head, confused. "I don't understand."

"Well, their parents approached me with a proposal I wanted t' talk to ya about."

Kit snickered. "That sounds scary."

"We wanted t' talk t' you about a camp a' sorts."

"What *kind* of camp?" Nico asked, suspiciously.

Pastor nervously cleared his throat before he explained, "They're a bit troubled. The parents thought maybe if they had some exposure t' hard work, that when it came time for them t' take over what they were supposed to, they may actually appreciate the hard work it would take t' normally get the position. They're also hopin' the boys would appreciate the gift their parents were providin' in those positions."

"Who *exactly* are we talkin' about?"

"Well, the first one is t' take over as CEO in his father's company when he graduates college. He's a leader, but it's normally not in a good way. Quinton Walker is – "

"*Quinton*? You want *Quinton* to come *here*?" Sitting back in her chair, Kit crossed her arms as she said, "You done lost your mind!"

Nico chuckled before he asked, "You want Quinton t' come here? For how long?"

"Well, let me finish the list first. I want you t' get a full picture a' the young men we're talkin' about here."

"Um, okay," Nico said, uneasy.

"I started with the roughest of the characters on purpose," Pastor admitted. "That way maybe you would consider the proposition."

Sitting back in his chair, Nico waved for Pastor to go on.

"Liam Thompson is the next one. He's in line to be a partner in his father's law firm when he graduates. His dad wants him t' understand all of the hard work it took for him –"

"We get it. They want their sons t' understand the value of a hard day's work. Please finish the list so we can get a better understandin' as t' who y'er talkin' about here?" Nico pressed.

"Okay. It's Quinton Walker, Liam Thompson, Wesley Martin, Dawson Lee, Rhys Robinson, Preston White, Felix Abbot, Cedric Barnes, Winston Beckett, an' Evan Buchannan."

The color slowly drained from Kit's face as each name was said. When he finished, she asked, "Did you just go through and pick the most troubled kids in the youth group, or what?"

"Well, actually the parents got together an' they approached *me*," Pastor admitted.

"Why aren't *they* here?" Nico asked.

"Because they wanted me t' represent them, an' maybe soften the blow, so t' speak."

"How long are we talkin' here?"

"Two weeks."

"What are the guidelines?"

"None."

Silence hung in the air for several moments before Nico asked, "Y'er sayin' that we keep them for two weeks t' do whatever we want with them?"

"Their parents trust you."

"That means no cell phones."

"Understood."

"If they call their parents, the parents are t' back us up an' support whatever we're doing?"

"Yes."

"So, for two whole weeks –"

"You will have ten slaves, yes," Pastor finished.

Rubbing his chin in thought, Nico weighed the proposition.

"You're seriously considering this?" Kit asked, stunned. "You *do* know who he's asking us to keep for fourteen days. As in, they *cannot* be taken back to their parents for those two weeks. You get that, right? There's no calling the parents to bail us out either."

"If they're here, there *is no* bailing out. If they're here, they're mine."

"You *have* lost your mind!"

"Kit, if God can do an amazin' thing in the hearts of these boys, it'll be worth two weeks of our lives. These boys are goin' t' be in influential positions when they graduate. God can an' *will* use them. I, for one, would love t' see what He has in mind for them."

Kit scoffed. "You *have* lost your mind."

"It's possible, but what do ya think?"

"I *think* you've lost your mind!"

"I need you t' help me in this."

"Fine. If we do this, the best way would be to pair them up with another ranch hand."

"They're not goin' t' like that."

"Quinton is yours," Kit insisted. "No one else will forgive you if you pair them with him."

Pastor and Nico burst out in laughter for several moments before Pastor said, "Quinton's goin' t' be yer toughest one. I gave them in the order of toughness."

Kit sighed, lifting her hands in surrender. "Fine. We'll do it."

"Bonzer!" Nico grinned. "I knew you were a good one!"

"Just make sure they know that I speak softly, but carry a big stick."

"What does that mean?" Pastor asked.

"That means I don't yell, but I make my point beyond a shadow of a doubt."

"You raised two sets of twins," Pastor pointed out. "If you did that without yellin', pretty sure you can handle this bunch."

"Oh, I have no doubt. My concern was for my husband's sanity afterward," Kit added.

While Pastor thought that was funny, Nico wasn't amused. "I can handle them," Nico said confidently. "They'll have a rough go of it, though. That's why I need the parent's backing."

"They're nervous, but at this point y'er their last hope," Pastor explained. "They've tried everythin'."

"Okay. No electronics at all. No phones, computers, iPods, iPads, ebook readers, nothin' even remotely electronic is t' be brought t' the station. They are t' bring only jeans, t-shirts, an' sunscreen. Preferably boots if they have them, if not, runners will work. They may want a light jacket an' some lightweight shirts t' wear over their t-shirt."

"Done."

"They'll have t' do their own laundry, be up with the others, sleep in the bunkhouse, etc."

"Got it," Pastor agreed.

"Most importantly, they are t' bring their Bibles, along with a journal an' pen."

"Sounds reasonable."

"When do we get 'em?"

Pastor stood and shook Nico and Kit's hands. "They'll be here on Monday."

"Good. That'll give us the weekend to warn the crew," Kit said. "They'll need it."

*   *   *

"Mumsy!" eight-year-old Rachel ran into the room on Monday morning while Kit was making the bed, with Leah close behind. They plunged into the covers, giggling while they twirled in the king size sheets.

"Hey, little ones," Kit said when the two blond-haired, blue-eyed twins each popped their heads out of the blankets. "What are you two up to today?"

"Waitin' for those blokes t' get here," Rachel, the more outspoken of the twins, said. "The station hands say it's gonna be interestin'."

Sitting down on the bed, Kit brushed the blond hair out of both of their faces, while she asked, "What *else* have you heard?"

"That Quinton couldn't go two rounds with a revolvin' door," Leah spoke up.

Both girls giggled, as Rachel continued, "They said all a' the blokes comin' had a few roos loose in their top paddock."

"That they couldn't drive a knife through butter," Leah said, as she and Rachel alternated the sayings they heard through the station.

"Couldn't fight their way outta a wet paper bag."

"That they were about as useful as a screen door on a submarine."

"An' as useful as a one-legged man in a –" Rachel stopped mid-sentence and corrected herself, "bum-kickin' contest."

Leah giggled as she said, "They couldn't organize a fart in a chili eatin' contest."

As all three laughed aloud, Rachel continued, "They're all shine an' no shoes."

"If their brain were electricity, there would be a blackout."

"Actually," Kit halted them, "those young men are academically smart, just –"

"Have no common sense?" ten-year-old Joshua offered, as he and Caleb came into the room. Both boys had jet-black hair, and Nico's sky-blue eyes. With the boy's stocky build, Kit could tell they were going to have Nico's build, while the girls had Kit's slender build.

"That's not nice, Josh," Kit reprimanded them.

"But true, no?" he said with a sparkle in his eyes.

"True. Y'all need to be nice to them, okay?"

"Only if they're nice t' us." Caleb crossed his arms, upset. "They've been mean t' Rachel an' Leah before, an' we won't have it."

"I understand," Kit agreed. "If you hear anything you even *remotely* think we need to hear, I expect you to tell me."

"Of course," Caleb said, as the boys joined in on the pile of blankets. "We know better than t' cross ya."

"Yeah, she can be meaner than a lioness," Rachel pointed out. When Kit reached over and started tickling her, Leah, Caleb, and Joshua took the moment to jump in, and a tickle fight ensued.

"What's this?" Nico asked, leaning on the doorway, watching the scene before him in delight.

Everyone froze.

"Don't stop on my account. Of course, that *is* my wife, so I reckon I'll have t' defend her," Nico said before jumping into the middle of the bed. As he landed, the kids bounced into the air by a foot before landing back in the middle of the bed. When they landed, they jumped on their dad, and the tickle fight continued as the room filled with giggles and laughter.

* * *

Kit was in the barn with Pete when Pastor arrived with the young men that morning. They walked into the barn, each carrying a duffle bag. "G'day, Kit," Pastor greeted her.

"Morning," she said, shaking his hand. Then she took inventory of the crew of boys before her. "Pete? Wanna go get Nico?"

"Will do," Pete said, and disappeared out of the barn.

"What do ya think?" Pastor asked.

"Do they know the guidelines?"

"Yes."

"What about the list of things they can't say?"

"There's a list of things we can't say?" Quinton clicked his tongue as he crossed his arms. "That's codswallop!"

"*That* would be on the list," Kit reprimanded him. "I do *not* want my children exposed to the more colorful language known to fly around stations. Around here, the guys don't even talk like that in front of them. They do their best not to do it at all. There are seven kids living in the immediate area, and five more on the other side of the station, totaling twelve. Little ears could be anywhere."

"You lot are a fertile bunch," Winston commented, tongue in cheek.

Pastor looked at him wide-eyed. "Winston!"

"Ya know, I know *exactly* who you'll be partnered with," Kit said, her tone icy.

"I've heard that tone before," Winston said nervously. "Who are you partnerin' me with?"

"Pete, so you can shovel horse pucky for the next two weeks."

As his eyes popped wide-open, his jaw dropped. "Are you bloody serious?"

"If she said it, that's who y'er with," Nico said, walking in with Pete beside him. "What did you do t' tick her off already?"

"Made a comment about how fertile we are around here," Kit explained. "I would have given Quinton to Pete for the same reason, but that would be punishment for Pete. I think *he* should be partnered with *you*."

"I get t' be his nibs for two weeks," Quinton said, chest puffed out.

Nico chuckled as he leaned on one of the stall walls. "Y'er thinkin' I just stand around tellin' people what t' do, huh?"

"Course! That's what the boss man does."

Nico went from chuckling, to full burst out in laughter. As a matter of fact, Pete, Kit, and Pastor joined him in that one, knowing full well what Nico did all day. "You friend, have *a lot* t' learn about bein' a boss," Nico pointed out.

"My dad is the boss, an' all he does is sit in a cushy office all day."

"Oh wow!" Nico bent in half, he was laughing so hard. "I wish he coulda heard you just now." Getting his composure back after a moment, he asked Pastor, "Sorry but that was priceless. So, they know they can't call anyone, an' there are no cell phones, computers, or whatever other electronic device?"

"Correct," Pastor said with a nod. "Their bags were searched at the church. They're yers t' do with as you please for the next two weeks."

"Wait! What?" Felix asked, stunned. "Who said he could do whatever he wanted with us? We were told we were goin' t' spend our vacation on a station. You know, horseback ridin', hikin', etcetera."

"Oh no way! You're fixin' t' work harder than you've ever worked before," Kit explained. "Each of you will be paired with a guy here on the station for two weeks. You'd better be good t' them, or y'er dealin' with *me*."

"What are *you* gonna do?" Cedric demanded, crossing his arms. Then under his breath, he added, "Bloody seppo!"

Patience already running thin, Nico grabbed Kit when she went to jump at him. "They're boys, Kit," Nico reminded her. When she settled, he said, "That statement will get ya bloodied."

Cedric raised an eyebrow. "Dinkum? She goes off like Chinese New Year fireworks, an' *we* get in trouble."

"You just insulted her in a very derogatory way. Y'er lucky y'er as young as you are, or *I* would let ya know just how I feel about it."

"She couldn't go two rounds with a revolvin' door," Evan huffed. "Why did ya hold her back? What's she gonna do?"

Nico laughed, while Kit narrowed her eyes at him. "Easy on," Nico cautioned, with a chuckle, "she could beat ya within an inch a' yer life, an' hide the body so no one would know."

"How do you figure?"

"Because *I* know who trained her, mate."

"Who?"

"Me."

"Oh!" Evan looked at her, surprised.

"As a matter of fact, in a mud wrestlin' contest for the entire station, she was only beat by four other guys. The rest, she either had a hand in takin' out herself, or they dropped out on their own. She's a force t' be reckoned with."

"Not t' mention the fact that she has raised two sets of twins," Pastor reminded them. "She handles these ranch hands with ease."

"I see," Evan squeaked out.

"Now that we've cleared that up. Here's the list of terms not allowed on the station," Nico said, handing out a three-page list to each boy that Pete brought to him.

"Crikey!" Dawson exclaimed. "There's *a lot* here!"

Pastor chuckled, tickled by the reaction of the boys, as he reminded them, "They're words ya shouldn't be sayin' anyway."

"True, but…" Liam glanced at the list before he remarked, "Can't say that either. Never mind."

"It's probably a good idea t' not say anythin' right now," Cedric said, crossing his arms. "All it does is get ya in trouble."

"Good. There's yer first lesson." Nico grinned. "Winston, Pete's goin' t' be yer partner while y'er here. He's yer boss. Whatever he says t' do, you do it without question or y'er dealin' with me. Am I clear?"

"Crystal."

"Good. The rest of you can follow me. We'll drop yer bags off at the bunkhouse –"

"The bunkhouse?" Quinton's jaw dropped. "We have t' sleep with the Neanderthals?"

"Wow!" Kit said, amazed by their audacity. "Better not let them hear you say that. Your time here is already going to be tough. If you insult them, then they'll make it even worse."

"This is codswallop!" Quinton snapped. "I want t' call my father."

"Go ahead. Just keep in mind that they'll only back us up."

"Yer parents are the ones who sent you here," Pastor reminded them. "They are fully aware of what's goin' on. As a matter of fact, all of this was *their* idea. An', that particular phrase is on the list. I don't want t' hear that from yer mouth ever again."

Kicking the dirt, Quinton mumbled, "Yes, sir."

Tired of the fighting already, and warning them multiple times, Nico reached into his pocket and pulled out a hot chili pepper. Handing it to Quinton, he said, "Eat this."

"Why?"

"Because yer tongue is offendin' me, so yer tongue is what is goin' t' be punished."

"I *like* hot chili peppers, though," Quinton said, taking the chili pepper. With a smirk, he shoved the whole chili in his mouth.

What he didn't know was that Nico made sure he found an extremely hot chili pepper to use as an example in case it was needed. As Quinton's face got redder with each second, Nico asked Pete, "Pete, wanna get 'im some water?"

"Sure thing," Pete said, disappearing into the equipment room. Returning slowly, he delighted in seeing Quinton hopping around, with tears pouring down his cheeks, as he begged for water.

While Quinton downed the water, the other boys were a mix of laughter and concern. If Nico pulled the big guns on Quinton right off the bat, what would he do to them if they stepped out of line?

"Gonna say another word on that list?" Nico asked Quinton.

"No, sir," he breathed out, as Pete handed him another bottle of water.

"Good," Nico said, satisfied. "Now, before I was interrupted, I was explainin' that y'er goin' t' drop off yer bags at the bunkhouse, an' then I'll take you t' yer partner for the next couple a' weeks."

After the guys left, Pastor turned to Kit and asked, "Are they going t' make it out of this okay?"

"The ranch hands, yes. The boys, well, that'll be up to them."

"All I need is for them t' be alive when I return them. At this point, you folks can't do any worse than they already are."

"Too true. Just keep us all in prayer."

"Only every day."

*   *   *

Kit walked around the station, amused by the way the boys were responding to their counterparts. Looking forward to dinner, she headed toward the house. Halfway there, she heard Dom ring the bell, signaling dinner was ready.

As people filed into the house, they washed their hands prior to taking their seat. Silence surrounded the table as everyone settled, all keeping an eye on the boys, who were scattered with their partners.

When Quinton went to grab the rolls, Nana smacked his hand. "Nico, would you like to say grace?" she asked, narrowing her eyes at Quinton.

"That hurt!" Quinton snapped.

"No one touches the food before Nana," Nico explained. "An' Nana doesn't touch anythin' until a prayer of thanks has been said for what is before us."

"No one told me."

"You *should* be sayin' grace at yer own table."

"We don't sit at the table. The cook makes the food, tells me it's ready, an' I go in an' eat…that is, if *I'm* even home."

Feeling bad for him, Kit commented, "Shame. So, you don't eat around the table with your families?" To her amazement, each boy shook his head 'no' in response. "So, how much time *do* you spend with your parents?"

"We're supposed t' spend time with them?" Liam asked, tongue-in-cheek. "Last time I spent any decent amount of time with my parents was when I was ten. I know this, because that was my last birthday party."

"Wow," Rachel said, shaking her head. "That's sad."

Narrowing his eyes, Quinton growled, "I don't need yer pity!"

"Ease off!" Josh stood. "She's not pityin' you. She feels bad for you."

Quinton huffed. "Sit down, little man. Don't stand until y'er tall enough t' fight yer own battles."

Nico turned Quinton by his chin toward him. When Quinton went to turn away, Nico held it there. "*Those are my children. You *will* show them respect. By rights, they have the right t' boss you around. They have more seniority on this station than you. If you dare disrespect them again, you an' I are gonna have a long walk t' one a' the cow pastures, where you will scoop *all* the manure in the field into a pile until it's clean. An' I mean *all* of it." When he finished, he looked each boy in the eyes as he warned, "That goes for each of you. If you dare disrespect a single person on this station, that will be the punishment."

Rhys shuddered. "That's nasty!"

"Oh, we can handle 'em," Owen said, giving Rhys a headlock before he ruffled his hair. "This one already learned his lesson, eh Rhys?"

"Oh yeah," Rhys agreed, getting free from Owen. "Lesson learned. I'm good."

"What did they do t' you?" Quinton asked. "You folded already?"

Rhys chuckled, shaking his head. "You don't wanna know, man."

"Pathetic."

"Tell ya what," Rhys challenged him, "When you've learned yer lesson, you let me know exactly how."

"What do ya mean?"

"I already got my lesson too," Winston admitted. "I learned not t' cross Kit."

As the table burst out in laughter, Nico leaned over to Quinton and said, "If you really want me t' teach ya that lesson, jus' say the word. But know this, it will be one a' the last things you will ever want t' do. It's in yer best interest t' learn it on yer own."

Quinton rolled his eyes. "Whatever."

"Nico, I believe you should say grace an' invite the Lord into this dinin' room before somethin' else takes over," Nana hinted.

"I agree," Nico nodded, and said grace before Nana started passing the meal around the table.

"Wow! My compliments t' the cook! Y'er better than my cook at home!" Preston remarked before shoveling another bite of food into his mouth.

Dom smiled, pleased. "Thank you."

"I agree. This is great!" Rhys exclaimed.

"Can I have the recipe for this?" Wesley asked Dom. "I've never tasted anythin' like this. An' I'm pretty sure my cook can cook it with the recipe."

"Stuff this for a game of soldiers!" Quinton slammed his fork down. "What's wrong with you blokes? This is a crock! Y'er here for less than four hours, an' y'er already singin' his praises. What's wrong with you? This is a punishment, not a vacation."

Filling her spoon full of mashed potatoes, Nana took aim and shot it at Quinton, nailing him in the side of his head.

"What the –?"

"You'd better stop right there," Nico warned. "She's worse than Kit."

Narrowing his eyes at Nana, Quinton demanded, "What do you think y'er doin'?"

"Shuttin' you up," Nana simply said. "I have shot men for less, so don't even think about it."

"What are ya gonna do, ol' lady?"

Everyone froze, with the exception of Barwon, who got out of his seat and walked behind Quinton, silently standing there with his arms crossed. Barwon towered over Quinton at six-four. Wide as Nico, he was also as dark as Pete. He intimated the strongest on any other station, and anyone who knew him, respected him, and he protected the families of Serenity Wells often.

Cedric snickered. "Y'er in for it now."

"A rooster one day, a feather duster the next," Adoni warned.

"He's all shine an' no shoes," Evan said, tearing a piece of his bread before he put it in his mouth.

"Shut it!" Quinton snarled, his face getting redder by the second.

"Can I?" Barwon asked Nico.

Nico shook his head. "Not yet."

"Can you *what*?" Quinton asked.

"Keep it up an' you'll find out. If I were you I'd back down," Nico cautioned, continuing to eat his dinner.

"What can *you* do t' me?"

Setting his fork down, Nico reminded him, "Yer parents said I can do whatever I want."

Quinton sighed, shaking his head. "I can't believe we have t' put up with these drongos."

"Nico?" Barwon asked again, a little more forcefully.

Nico shook his head. "Not yet. Gonna give him a few moments t' recover."

"Don't bother. There's nothin' this Neanderthal can do t' me. I'll sue his behind. Better yet, my ol' man will."

"Go ahead," Nico told Barwon.

Barwon snatched him out of his seat and threw him over his shoulder so fast, Kit wasn't sure what was happening. The table cleared and everyone followed them out the door. Watching from the safety of the porch, they saw Quinton shouting obscenities, while Barwon carried him over to the manure pile and slammed him into it.

"You say one more word on that list, an' I'll shove yer mouth full of that," Barwon warned, satisfied he made his point, while Quinton sat there coated in manure. Walking back toward the house, over his shoulder Barwon mentioned, "Clean yerself before ya come back t' the table. Ya stink. Yer mouth does too." When he walked by Nico, he simply said, "Thank you," and then walked back into the house to commence eating his dinner.

As Quinton climbed out of the pile, he looked toward everyone on the porch. "Do *not* come back in until you've taken a shower," Nico ordered. Hearing Quinton swearing and yelling all the way to the bunkhouse, Nico said to Kit, "Get everyone else in t' eat an' save us both a plate. I think Quinton an' I need t' have a chat."

"Please, and thank you," Kit said, appreciatively. "I don't want to see that again or I'll kick his bum all the way off the station, and he'll have to walk all the way home. I don't mind following him on a horse to do it either."

Surprised by her assertiveness, Nico said, "I know y'er angry, but I've never heard you say that about a teen."

"I've never heard that level of disrespect and language come out of a teen's mouth either. In defense of every person in that house," she said sternly, pointing toward the house as everyone at the table listened, "I don't want to *ever* hear that on this station again. You want to get rid of the anger? You'd better tame that young man real fast!" she said, and spun on her heels into the house. Stopping short at feeling all eyes on her, with tears in her eyes, Kit said, "I *will not* let *anyone* disrespect *any* person on this station! *Ever!*" Running upstairs afterward, she dropped on her bed, upset and crying.

A few moments later, all four kids came up to her room and climbed on the bed. When she looked up at them, Josh explained, "Nana said she was about t' clear up any more possible issues, an' asked that we come up here, an' that Pete an' Victoria, an' Uncle Scott an' Aunt Claire take their kids outside. T' be honest, I think she's about t' rip 'em a new one."

"Besides the fact that we wanted t' be with you an' give you a hug," Rachel said, leaning over and hugging Kit, which made her cry even more.

With all four kids hugging her, Kit got her emotions under control. "I'm sorry," she apologized. "Everyone on this station is my family, an' when I hear things said to them like I heard tonight, it infuriates me beyond words."

"We know," Leah said, giving her a kiss on her cheek.

"We love you too, Mum," Josh hugged her from behind, arms around her neck.

"We appreciate you steppin' up for all of us," Caleb said, restin' his chin on her knees. "Knowin' that you have our back in whatever we do means a lot."

"Don't you *dare* be like any of those boys down there," Kit warned.

"No way!" Josh shook his head. "The guys on this station would set us straight in a heartbeat."

"Besides, we don't wanna make you an' Dad mad," Caleb said. "Disappointin' you would break all our hearts."

Josh nodded. "I agree."

"Same here," Rachel said, holding Kit's hand.

Leah shook her head. "I'm not gonna do anythin' like that."

"Thanks lil' ones." Kit smiled. "All y'all make my heart happy."

"Kit!" Nana called. "You all can come down an' eat."

"Coming!" Kit called back. Then she added, "Nana's already had a rough night. Let's see what we can do to make it easier."

"Yes, ma'am!" the kids said in unison before they all headed downstairs.

*   *   *

A few days after the arrival of the boys for their camp, things began to settle. Just after breakfast, as everyone was sent out for their chores, Charlie came to Kit and Nico, "I have t' go."

"What? Why?" Nico asked. "I mean, thank you for prayin' over the field, but why do ya have t' go?"

"Needed for mission. Hawk sent for me," he said, gesturing toward Ethan, who was standing in the doorway.

"Is someone else prayin' over the field?" Nico asked Ethan.

"Y'er goin' t' have t' cover it for a bit," Ethan explained. "We have an issue in the Black Mountain."

"Oh!" Nico said, wide-eyed. Many knew of the Black Rock legend in Queensland.

"He's needed," Ethan said sternly. "Please make sure t' continue t' pray over that field, though. The evil is just itchin' t' climb over that fence."

"We will. Thank you for allowin' him t' be here as long as he has," Nico said, appreciatively.

With that, Ethan and Charlie left. A couple of hours later, Josh ran into the house, "Mum? Have ya seen Rachel?"

"No. Isn't she with y'all outside?"

"No."

"Did she tell you where she was going?"

"No."

Kit's head snapped up from the paperwork she was working on at the table, as her heart raced. Picking up the walkie-talkie, she said into it, "Hey, has anyone seen Rachel?"

"No, love. She's not with the others?" Nico's voice came over the radio.

"Haven't seen her since lunch," Adam responded.

"Only mine are here," Claire called back.

With each response, Kit's heart rate picked up. Turning to Josh, she asked, "Are Leah and Caleb still on the play set?"

"Yes. I told Caleb not t' let Leah outta his sight."

"Nico?" Kit called.

"Go ahead."

"I hate t' ask this, because it's been a couple years since my last nightmare, but does anyone have eyes on the north field?"

"North field?" Nico's voice squeaked. Clearing his throat, he asked again, "Um, north field?"

"In my nightmare, a little girl died in the north field. Does anyone have eyes on it? If not, Nico, please go check?"

"On my way," Nico responded.

The radio stayed silent for the next few minutes before Flynn's voice came over the radio, "Kit, it's Flynn on Nico's radio. Call an ambulance. It's Rachel."

*   *   *

Kit sat alone in Rachel's room in emergency when Nico, Seth, and Nana walked in. "Where is she?" Nico asked, pulling a chair up next to Kit's.

"She's in x-ray."

"What's the doc say?" Nana asked.

"She broke her right leg and she has a concussion," Kit said, doing her best to keep herself together.

"When will we know more?" Seth asked.

"Don't know."

"Kit, y'er shakin'," Nico pointed out.

"This is the second nightmare I've had come true."

"But, you didn't die, an' neither did Rachel. Maybe the Lord gave it t' you as a warnin'."

"Then, what does the childbirth one mean?"

"Well, you *did* have the boys in the house, like you did in the dream. When you have these dreams, from now on please tell me exactly what's in them so I know what t' keep an eye out for. Maybe yer dreams are given t' you as a worst-case scenario so we know what t' prepare for, so they *don't* end that way."

"True," Kit said, wiping the tears from her eyes. "They're just so precious, I don't want anything to happen to them."

"That's where we have t' trust that God will take care of 'em. After all, they're really His. We just get 'em on loan. Look, He's provided us with a great support staff. While Charlie's no longer with us, he was here long enough for God t' bring up some other guys in order for them t' step up an' continue prayin' over the field."

"I know. I also know that while Charlie was with us for years, Hawk needed him, and he's doing other things for the Lord. I already miss the strength of the Lord that was in Him. We're strong Christians, but he had something about him I don't think I have."

"Maybe that's somethin' you should talk t' Pastor about?" Nico suggested.

"I will, when I have time to breathe."

"He's on his way," Seth pointed out. "We called him on the way here. He's supposed to be coming here shortly."

"I need to be here for Rachel."

"We're here for her. You rode in with her. If y'er in the hospital talkin' with him, I don't think she'll be offended," Nico said, resting his hand on her shoulder. "Take some time t' take care of yerself, huh?"

"When he gets here, I'll –"

"Afternoon, folks," Pastor said, walking into the room, cutting Kit off.

Nico stood and gave him a hug. "We were just talkin' about you."

Pastor smirked. "Good or bad?"

Nico chuckled. "Always good regardin' you, mate."

"First off, how's Rachel?"

"Concussion an' broken leg. She's in x-ray right now, but we have a different job for you if y'er up for it."

"Oh really? Okay, I'm intrigued."

"Well, Kit had a realization that she may not be as strong a Christian as she would like, an' wanted t' talk t' you."

"Well, the Lord works in mysterious ways. Wanna take a walk, Kit?"

"I…sure." Getting up, she followed him out to the courtyard without a word. Taking a seat at a picnic table under the shade of a tree, she finally started, "I've had a lot go on in my life. I've seen many things as well. I have to say that I've never felt the strength of the Lord as much as I did when I met Danny Hawk, Ethan Carson, Shawn O'Brien, and Charlie. There's something about them that I have never felt before. I mean, I've felt the Lord's presence tons of times, but lately I feel like I'm just surviving."

Pastor nervously cleared his throat as he said a prayer for clarity of mind and guidance. "Do you want my honest opinion?"

"I wouldn't ask for it if I didn't want it. You should know that by now."

"I do, but I wanted t' make sure. You see, in life there are a myriad of battles that happen around us that we may be blind to. You were trained t' see the incomin' fight, but what about the subtle battles."

"What do you mean?"

"Have you ever used a compass?"

"No," Kit said, chuckling. "I'm not allowed to use it, due to my, shall we say, directional inabilities."

Pastor couldn't help the laughter that escaped him. Knowing Nico, he had a feeling Nico was the navigator of the two. "Okay. Well, when you *do* use it, you basically look t' see the highest point that you want t' go to an' line it up with the compass. Periodically, as you walk, you need t' make sure t' line it up again. If you are even a degree off, while it might not affect you in the short-term, it may affect yer long-term."

"I can see that."

"While you were centered in the beginnin', things may have been knocked a degree off or so through the years that have taken yer sights off the Lord. Now, this doesn't discredit your Christianity at all. Sometimes we all need a course correction or two." Tears filled Kit's eyes, as he continued, "The devil doesn't always make direct hits. He doesn't need to. Sometimes that little shove or nudge here or there is all he needs. Then, while he does it, he fills yer schedule t' the point that you *can't* look back t' yer original focal point…Jesus."

"How do I get back on target?"

"Being a Christian takes a lot of work. We need t' keep focused on Jesus."

"Right."

"When was the last time you focused yerself solely on Him?"

Kit let out a slow breath of air as she wracked her brain. "Definitely been a *long* time. I haven't even drawn for quite a while. Last time I remember was when Claire and Seth got here. I've been too busy with helping run a station, youth group leader, and raising two sets of twins."

"They are the cutest lil' pumpkins in the patch, so I get it. An' while I understand children are a blessin' from the Lord, an' we are t' be focused on them while we have them, if we're off course what do ya think that will do in our parenting?"

"It'll be off course."

"Precisely. So, you need t' get back on course."

"Which brings me to the question I asked before. I don't want to leave my children to be put back on course."

"Who said you had to?"

"Then, how do I do it?"

"How did you do it before?"

"I went off by myself."

"For days?"

"No."

"Then why would you think you need t' do that now?"

"Because I feel so shut down. I kind of feel numb."

"Did life stop before when you had t' get refocused?"

"No, but I had time to myself."

"You mean you had time for yerself an' God," he corrected.

"Right."

"I'll be willin' t' bet if you ask Nico, he'll make it so you have at least an hour or so a day for you an' God time."

"I'm sure he would, but can I?"

"Kit!" Nico ran out of the hospital, pale and shaken.

Standing in shock by his appearance, she nervously asked, "What is it?"

"The ambulance is goin' t' the station. Flynn called. Pop had a heart attack."

"Stay on course," Pastor said, firmly. "I know this all seems overwhelmin', but focus. Take things one at a time, an' stay on course."

* * *

After the funeral three days later, everyone trudged back to the house, somber and morose. As some went to work off their feelings on the station, others sat around the porch telling stories of Pop with those who returned back to the house with the family.

As Rachel hobbled onto the porch with her crutches, Leah ran in to get her a drink.

"Okay, hop-a-long," Kit said with a smile as she nudged Rachel, "just sit there an' we'll bring you your meal. You've been standing for the last couple of hours, I need you to put your foot up." Resting Rachel's leg on another chair opposite her chair, Kit then dashed into the kitchen to see if Dominic needed any help in getting the food out. "Hey, Dom, do ya need a hand?"

"Nope. I'm good. Leah's already been in here. Didn't you pass her on the way in? I asked her to tell you to just to rest. I got this."

"What? No," Kit said as her eyes drifted toward the staircase. Groaning, she walked up the stairs. "Leah? Are you up here?" she called. Panic filled her when she didn't answer. Concern strangled her with each empty room she checked. Unable to contain the anxiety, she fumbled with the radio as she took it off her belt. "Nico?" she asked, her voices shaking.

"Go ahead, love," he responded.

"Please tell me you or someone else has seen Leah?"

"No. Quinton an' I are in the barn. Sheila's givin' birth, an' she's breech. I'm up t' my elbows in cow. Quinton's even holdin' the radio for me. Everyone check with those around you. Has anyone seen Leah?"

"I saw her headed toward the north field," Kendall Adams responded. "I told her to head back home before Preston an' I got to the south field t' check on the cattle."

"Thanks, Kendall," Nico said.

Hearing the nervousness in Nico's voice, Kit said, "I'm on my way out to the north field. Anyone able t' meet me up there?"

"Wesley an' I will," Barwon responded.

Running off the porch, Kit sprinted toward the field. As her nightmares did their best to dominate her thoughts, Kit turned to God, praying in her mind the entire way there.

When she finally reached the north field, Barwon and Wesley arrived at the same time to the empty field. "We didn't see her on the way up," Wesley explained. "An', no one else we've talked to has seen 'er either."

Looking toward Akoonah station, Kit saw the tiny body of her eight-year-old daughter, facedown in the dirt. "Leah!" Kit shrieked, climbing the fence into the other station.

"She's breathin'," Barwon announced, being the first to get to her.

"Thank you, Lord!" Kit said, relieved, as she got on her knees next to her baby girl. When she turned Leah's tiny body over, Leah's eyes popped open and she screamed bloody murder.

Wild-eyed, Leah sat up. "Where is he?"

"Who?" Kit asked, looking around.

"He said his name was Haskell," Leah explained, as her body shook. To Kit, she looked shell-shocked.

"What did he do to you?" Barwon asked, anger evident in his body at the thought that someone hurt one of the children he had grown to love.

"He-he said I had to come with him."

"You're not allowed to come to the north field," Kit explained in a soothing tone, hoping to calm her daughter while inside was an dangerous infusion of terror, panic, and thrill at seeing her alive. "Why would you leave the house? *How* did you get out of the house without anyone seeing you?"

"He said t' follow him, or he would hurt Rachel. He said Rachel was his, but I could take her place," Leah tearfully explained.

"How did you get out of the house without anyone seeing you?"

Leah sobbed. "We walked right by you an' you didn't see me. He-he made me hold his hand an' we walked right by you."

"Oh, sweetheart." Kit grabbed her as she stroked her hair. "Please don't ever do that again. I love you both."

"I know, but I didn't want him t' hurt her again."

"Did she tell you he made her go?"

Leah only nodded in response.

Looking at Barwon, Kit asked, "Please take Leah to the house and don't let her out of your sight. Make sure all four children are looked after."

Stunned, Barwon asked, "Where are you goin'?"

"I need to find Danny Hawk. Enough is enough!"

*   *   *

Jumping on a horse, Kit road out of the station at a high rate of speed without a word to anyone. She knew what she had to do. Praying for direction, Kit road out into the thick brush.

*   *   *

"What do you *mean* Kit rode out of here without tellin' anyone where she was goin'?" Nico demanded, as he was up to his elbows inside a cow delivering a set of twins.

"Look, I was told t' not let Leah outta my site," Barwon explained, holding Leah's hand. "Kendall an' Preston are watchin' Caleb, while Owen an Rhys are watchin' Josh.

Meanwhile, Rachel's surrounded by several family members on the porch."

"Here, Quinton," Nico said, pulling his arms out. Shoving Quinton's arms inside the cow, amongst his howling objections, Nico yelled, "Grab those an' maneuver it out."

"Are you bloody serious?" Quinton growled.

"You need t' help this cow give birth or she'll lose her calves…or worse yet, her life."

Looking at him in wide-eyed horror, Quinton realized Nico was not backing down. "You *are* serious!"

"Very much so," Nico said, positioning himself to help Quinton, with Quinton actually doing the work. "Pull out an' down. There ya go," Nico encouraged.

Quinton shuddered. "This is gross!"

As Barwon and Wesley laughed, Nico couldn't help the chuckle that escaped him as well. Encouraging him, Nico calmly said, "Just relax an' ease it out. There ya go."

"I'll have yer guts for garters for this!" Quinton snapped. When the cow moaned, Quinton sighed. "Fine. Just push the little bugger out so we can move on t' number two."

"Y'er talkin' t' a cow." Wesley wrapped his arms around his stomach in howls of laughter. "I wish I had a camera or my phone right now. You should see yerself."

"Sorry, mate, gonna have t' commit this one t' memory," Barwon said, resting his elbow on Wesley's shoulder. "Just wait. It gets better."

"Better than this?"

"Oh yeah."

Pulling the calf out, the baby finally plopped onto the ground. "Okay," Nico started, "Stick yer fingers into the baby's nose t' clean –"

"You want *what*?" Quinton's jaw dropped, as his arms were coated in goo.

"C'mon, mate, we don't have time t' play. Either stick yer hands in there for the second one, or clean this little guy out so he can breathe!"

"Fine!" Quinton growled. When he stuck his fingers in to clean out the fluid, his stomach wretched at the sound of the slime that coated the calf.

"Tickle his nose with this." Nico handed him a piece of hay, while he put water in the baby's ears. When the baby sneezed and shook his head, a smile formed on Quinton's face. "We're not done yet," Nico pointed out, as he gestured toward the hooves of the other calf. "This momma needs yer help. Get the other one out for yerself."

"Please tell me y'er jokin'?"

"No. I have t' find my wife. Do what ya did with the other one. If you have trouble, I'm right here," Nico explained. When Quinton proceeded to wrap the chains around the calf's legs that were sticking out, Nico turned to Barwon, "Thank you for makin' sure all the little ones are looked after, but how am I supposed t' find Kit?"

Leaning on the doorway with her arms crossed as she watched the scene unfold before her, Nana commented, "Pretty sure that'll be up t' that God of yers t' protect her."

"This is the bloody Outback!" Nico shouted.

"Watch yer mouth," Nana said, coming off the doorway, stepping closer to Nico with each phrase. "If this God of yers is so powerful, then He shouldn't have any trouble keepin' an eye on one young lady. She's a mother a' four an' one a' His. I *highly* doubt He'll let her fall prey t' some bushranger."

"I pray y'er right, but as her husband she is *my* responsibility. I am responsible t' the Lord for her an' this family. I *will not* stay here an' just *hope* she comes back!"

"Aren't we supposed t' trust the Lord, though?" Wesley asked.

"I can't just sit here an' do nothin'!"

"You don't have to," Pete pointed out, as he kept a close eye on Quinton, knowing Nico was now distracted. "If you pray, y'er not doin' 'nothin'.' Y'er askin' the Lord t' protect her."

Nico mulled this around in his mind for several long moments before he agreed. Joining hands with Nana, Pete, Wesley, Barwon, and Leah, the tiny group prayed for protection and success for Kit. "We ask this in Jesus' most precious name I pray…Amen," Nico finished. "There, it's all up t' the Lord."

"Calf's here," Quinton announced as the calf was delivered.

Leah smiled. Seeing the second calf enter the world, she confirmed, "An' we can trust He will."

*   *   *

Riding through the woods, branches ripped into her skin, but Kit pushed forward. Suddenly Star bucked, but Kit gripped the reins with every bit of strength she had. Getting the horse under control, she stared at the form in front of her in awe. "Who…or *what* are you?" Kit demanded.

"I have been sent to take you to my A.N.G.E.L.s," he responded. The man looked to be about seven foot tall, toned, wore tan pants and a white shirt. His blond hair, fair skin, and rosy cheeks allowed his royal blue eyes to stand out as he was sitting on a white horse.

"*Who* are you?"

"Does it matter?"

With a furrowed brow, Kit asked, "How can I trust you?"

"Because your husband, Nick, and others are currently in your home, are praying for your safety. The Lord God Almighty has sent me to protect you. Now, you are wasting time. Let us go find my A.N.G.E.L.s."

"Who is Nick? My husband is Nico Sullivan."

"No, Katie. You're husband is Nick Locke. You had to change your identity several years back."

"How do you know this?"

"I know this because I am one of the Lord's and He sent me to care for you. Can we leave now?"

"Okay." Kit gave up. "Let's go."

"We will go at a slower pace or the horses won't make it. Follow me," he said, and they headed deeper into the Outback.

Not sure where he was leading her, Kit felt a peace about going with him. Knowing her children were being looked after, she pushed on, deeper into the Outback.

*   *   *

Through the heat of the day, the sun climbed higher into the sky, pouring out an unrelenting heat that Kit never thought she would ever be able to escape. Her mouth felt like sandpaper, and she was sure once she found water that she would never be able to drink enough to combat the dehydration consuming her body. Pushing further into the Outback than she had ever gone, the two riders continued through into the night.

"Um, nothing personal, but the horses need water and I need t' rest," Kit pointed out around eleven that night.

"I understand, but we must push forward. We will be there by morning."

"You know I have no idea of where we are."

"I do. I know where we are going. Do not fear."

Kit sighed. "I won't. Can we talk while we ride?"

"I thought you said you needed to rest?"

"I do, but I have a feeling this happened for a reason. After all these years, I've learned that things don't happen by coincidence."

"This is true."

"Will Hawk be able to help us?"

"Yes."

"What happened to Shawn and his partner?"

"Shawn and his love, Victoria, were providing cover fire. They did not make it out alive."

"Why didn't they? I mean, why weren't they protected?"

"Those reasons are known only to the Lord," he said, guiding them south.

"I see. Can I ask if my children will all make it to adulthood?"

"They will."

"Do they have a job to do for the Lord?"

"All of God's children have a job to do."

"You're very cryptic."

He smiled. "I have been told this."

"I'm going to make it my goal to make you laugh."

Chuckling, he said, "You often make me laugh."

"Are you my guardian angel?"

"I am one of those who look out for you."

"Good grief! I need more than one!" Kit asked, stunned.

He couldn't help the burst of laughter that escaped him at how wide her eyes got. "Do not worry. We are many. You are well protected."

Kit quietly said under her breath, "Told you I could make you laugh."

"You are a joy. We must continue, though, if we are to reach our destination."

"Are we safe out here?"

"Perfectly."

"Even with the creatures out here?"

"We are safe."

"I'll trust you."

"Trust the Lord."

"Always."

"I know," he said with a smile, as they continued to ride.

*   *   *

Early in the morning, as the sun peaked through the clouds floating in the air, Kit watched the beautiful hues of gold, orange, pink, purple, and blue that colored the sky. Wishing she could enjoy it more, the lack of sleep, water, food, and rest wore her out. Eyes burning, feeling her skin fried as well, Kit knew whatever was going on at Akoonah Station would put her children's lives in jeopardy, so she would push through it to get help.

*   *   *

Around nine that morning, as the sun began to heat up the earth once again, Kit saw tents in the distance. "Is that a mirage or do I see a camp in an area with trees?"

"It is Hawk's camp."

"Really? We're here?"

"Yes."

Riding into the camp, the pair were met by several men and a couple women. Kit instantly recognized four of them. Danny Hawk, Ethan Carson, Kat Parker, and Charlie were among them.

"Welcome. We weren't expectin' you," Hawk said.

"I was," Charlie explained. "Had dream day or so ago."

"Why didn't you tell me? I told you t' let me know about yer dreams."

"Because it not seem right. Kit? Out here?"

"It's different seein' *you* out here," Kat said to the man with Kit. "An', yer clothes are different."

"I did not want to scare anyone if we ran into them," the man explained.

"Who *are* you?" Kit asked, realizing she didn't even know his name.

"Kit, why don't ya come down from there? Kat, get 'er some water. Charlie, get the horses some water as well," Hawk ordered. As Kit and the man got down, Hawk explained, "Kit, he's an angel…as in a *real* angel. We are his A.N.G.E.L.s. He's the one we report to."

"I see," Kit said, reaching the ground. As soon as her feet hit the ground, she collapsed to her hands and knees. "Sorry, I –" Shaking her head to clear it, Kit apologized, "Sorry, I haven't had anything to eat or drink since yesterday morning."

"Want me to get her an IV?" another guy asked.

"Yes. Kit, this is Rob Harper. Go with him, an' he'll get you squared away," Hawk said. As she left with Harper, she heard Hawk say to the angel, "We need t' talk, I think."

"Yes. We have much to discuss. Akoonah is a problem again."

"What did he mean by that?" Kit asked, as Harper had an arm around her, ushering her to the tent. Once inside, he had her lay on a cot before he started an IV. "What did he mean when he said, 'Akoonah is a problem again'?"

"Well," he said, pulling up a chair to take her vitals, "the woman who used t' run that station was Jacki Monroe. She died about a year after Shawn passed."

"Did they know each other?"

"She was the reason he died."

"Um, what *exactly* do you mean by that? Quit the cryptic stuff. Spell it out for me."

"Well, she was a queen bee, so t' speak, of a hive of demons."

"A *what?*" Kit sat up, stunned. She sat up too quickly, though, and the darkness that had been threatening to take over, consumed her as she dropped back down to the cot, unconscious.

*   *   *

"I don't know if she can handle this stuff, sir," Harper said quietly, as he, Hawk, and the angel stood by the door. "I mentioned demons, an' she sat up so quickly she passed out. What's she gonna do when we explain it *all* t' her?"

"She will be fine. She was dehydrated and hungry when we came in. You have cared well for her. I will leave her to you," the angel explained.

Before anyone else could say a word, Kit saw him disappear into the sky like a streak of light. Shaking her head, Kit said, "Ohhh no way!"

"Kit?" Ethan looked over to her. "Are you okay?"

"*What* was *that?*"

Hawk shrugged. "The angel. Are you okay?" he asked, coming in, sitting in the chair Harper used earlier.

"I don't understand what's going on here," she admitted. "I'm more confused than when I started."

"I know y'er familiar with Ephesians 6:12, that says, 'For our struggle is not against flesh an' blood, but against the rulers, against the authorities, against the powers of this dark world an' against the spiritual forces of evil in the heavenly realms.' Right?"

"Yes," she said, cautiously, as she sat up, wrapping her arms around her legs, taking long, deep breaths to slow the panic that wanted to take over her body.

"We live in a day an' age where the spiritual an' physical realms are collidin' more an' more each day. People don't understand what we're truly battlin'. It's my understandin' that Pastor Paul talked t' you about yer spiritual trek a few days ago before Pop passed."

"How do you know about that?"

Chuckling, he explained, "There's a lot we know, but that's beside the point. The point is t' open yer eyes a bit t' what's around you. I understand Harper shared a little with you about Jacki?"

"Yes. She's gone, right?"

"Right, but there are a lot a' them in this world. Right now, though, we need t' get t' yer station an' figure out what we're dealin' with at Akoonah."

"Do you not know?"

"Oh, I do. We need for *you* t' understand. We also need t' explain things t' Nico. This is vital."

"Why?"

"Because two a' yers are goin' t' join us eventually."

"Join you…*what*?"

"There are two of yer little ones destined t' be a part of our unit."

"What do y'all do?"

"We answer the call."

"If you're saying that two of our children are going to be joining your unit, you'd better be *a lot* clearer in your explanations!" Kit snapped.

Those standing around looked over at the pair, speechless. No one talked to Hawk that way and got away with it.

Hawk cleared his throat to break the tension before he explained, "With all due respect, you have t' understand that we need t' explain things a little slowly in order not t' overwhelm people."

"Okay. Go ahead."

"Here's some tucker," Kat said, bringing stew, bread, and water into the tent for Kit.

Accepting the food with a 'thank you,' Kit settled into her seat for the long explanation that Hawk dove into. Starting with the origin of the boxes, he went on to explain what was in them, and what significance the boxes held to the A.N.G.E.L.s around the world. He also explained the battles over the ages that have occurred in order to secure the boxes. Afterward, he explained exactly what it is the A.N.G.E.L.s did and why.

"So, ya see," Hawk finished a couple hours after he started, "we play a vital role in the Kingdom. In order t' do so, we need t' keep the next generation in circulation. I'm aware there are others trainin' up the next generation, so we need t' do the same. Unfortunately, we've learned the hard way that we're not immortal."

"I understand." Looking down for a moment to ponder his words, she then looked at him. With tears in her eyes, she explained her heart, "I understand what you're saying. I also see the immense value in the position that all y'all hold. All I ask is if you truly know they are to join your unit, that you will fully train them for both the physical *and* spiritual battles that will ensue around them prior to sending them out."

"Of course, but know as far as the spiritual, that's part yer responsibility. They're entrusted t' you by the Lord for a reason. *You* are t' be preparin' them for the world. There are lessons you an' Nico are t' teach them. That's why they were given t' you."

"I know. We've done some, but I don't know if it's enough to battle *this* type of stuff. Can you tell me which ones are going to join you guys?"

"Absolutely not. Regardless of what their job is t' be, *you an' Nico* are t' prepare them for the world. There's a reason they're given t' you for eighteen years."

"I know. Proverbs 22:6 takes on a new meaning now, though."

"Not really. It says, 'Train up a child in the way he should go, an' when he is old, he will not depart from it.' It doesn't say t' train them for a specific job, an' then disregard trainin' them in other areas. You are t' train them t' face the world...period. No matter what they end up doin', they need t' be grounded in the Lord."

"I see your point."

"Look, we need t' get ya back t' the station before Nico

comes lookin' for ya. When we get there, let *us* take care of the Akoonah Station issue."

"Who's running the station now?"

"Haskell Stephens."

"Is Haskell Stephens *really just* Haskell Stephens?"

"I give ya credit, ya learn quickly," he said with a sly smile, as he got up from his chair. "Get some rest. We leave in the mornin'."

"Thank you."

"Thank *you*. Not a lot a' people can handle what I just told you with the amount a' grace in which you handled it."

Sighing, she explained, "With everything I've seen in my life, I'm just adding it to the list."

"Keep that flexible attitude. Y'er gonna need it."

"Cryptic again?"

"No, that's being honest."

Letting out a slow breath of air, Kit shook her head. "Wonderful."

*   *   *

When Kit woke up the next day, she was still a little rough, so they gave her one more day. This allowed her the time to ask more questions and gather more information. They also shared stories with her that blew her mind. The missions this unit went on changed lives. While some of them were not so life altering, they were a blessing nonetheless. Then there were others that were life threatening, which saved the lives of those they were sent in to help. Nervous and scared didn't cover the emotions she felt when she thought of her children joining this group. She couldn't imagine what Nico was going to say.

*   *   *

"You serious?" Nico asked, stunned, as they all sat in the living room. Kit had been home for three hours. After they ate, the A.N.G.E.L.s sat Nico down and explained what was going on around them.

"Very," Hawk said, unwavering in his stance.

Rubbing his chin in thought, Nico weighed Hawk's words. "Y'er tellin' me that some demon possessed woman ran Akoonah?"

"Bloody hell!" Nana exclaimed from the porch.

"Nana, you might as well come on in. I'd imagine you've been listening this whole time," Nico said.

Blushing, Nana walked into the living room. "Sorry, bad habit," she admitted. "Not the whole time, jus' the last fifteen minutes or so."

"But it's served you well in the past," Hawk added.

"That is has. So, are ya tellin' me that a demon was runnin' Akoonah?"

Sitting back in his seat, Hawk crossed his arms in front of him. "What do you think the anger curse was?"

"What do ya mean?"

"It was a demon. That was the reason it seemed t' leave Nate right before he died. Nico, didn't he seem different at the very end?"

As Nico looked helplessly at Kit for an answer, Nana scoffed, "What are ya playin' at? Nate fell into the swamp."

Knowing what really happened to Nate, Hawk chose to not explain it to Nana at that moment. Instead, he centered more on the curse, "Before Nate died, he was released from the curse. That was the demon leavin' his body. That particular demon feeds on anger. It slowly grows as it feeds, takin' over the body of its host."

"So, yer sayin' Nate was possessed?" Nico asked.

"Are you sayin' you didn't see it?" Hawk challenged.

"I did."

"What are you two talkin' about?" Nana snapped. "Y'er talkin' circles around me! Stop!"

"Nana, please just trust us." Nico sighed. "There's a lot of information Hawk's given us. There's too much t' explain right now. At this moment, I want t' know what y'er gonna do about it?" he asked Hawk.

"We're goin' t' take care a' that right now," he said, looking toward several of his unit, who got up and left the house for Akoonah Station.

"What's this goin' t' do for future owners?"

"The station will have t' be cleansed."

"What do ya mean by *that*?" Nana demanded.

"We'll take care a' what's on the station, then afterward we'll burn it t' the ground t' cleanse it."

"You serious?" she asked, horrified.

"Very."

"This will stop the battles at the north field?"

"Afraid not, but it'll cleanse it for a bit."

"That's all we can ask," Nico said. "Just do yer best."

"We will," Hawk agreed. As he stood, he looked at Kit, conveying the unspoken words that were shared prior to their arrival. They decided it would be best not to share that two of Nico and Kit's children would be joining the A.N.G.E.L.s until the time was right. Not wanting to get between them, he was leaving it up to her and God in the timing. In the meantime, Kit was to continue to bathe the entire issue in prayer.

Taking the cue, Kit ran upstairs and pulled the guns, along with four full magazines for each gun from the safe before she grabbed Nico's knife and her set of throwing knives. When she returned back downstairs, Hawk asked. "Are you ready?"

"For what?" Nana asked, panic written all over her. "Y'er not seriously goin' over there with them, are you? What about the children?"

"Nana," Nico put his hands on her arms, "we were given the trainin' we were given for a reason. You, Claire, an' Seth will raise the children if somethin' happens t' us, but with God on our side we can't lose. The security of the station an' territory are on the line here."

"You *are* serious?"

"Here," Kit said, handing Nico a gun, magazines, and his knife before she attached hers to her belt. "Been a while, but I think I still got it."

"The others are scoutin' the situation," Hawk hinted. "They're waitin' for us."

Grabbing Nico's and Hawk's hands, Kit said, "Pretty sure we need to go in with back-up."

After praying for ten minutes, Nico closed with, "Thank You, Lord for all of these brave men an' women fightin' for You daily. Please send Yer angels of protection t' help fight with us an' keep us protected as we fight for Yer Kingdom. We ask that the blood of Jesus cover this situation an' keep everyone involved alert an' guarded. All for Yer glory, in Jesus name we pray, Amen."

"Well said, brother. Let's go t' the others," Hawk said pulling Kit with him.

When Nana grabbed Nico's arm, the trio stopped and turned to her. "You *have* t' come back. Do ya hear me, boy?" she said, with tears in her eyes. "I've lost too much. I know y'er fightin' for this family, but you'd *better* come back!"

"Yes, ma'am," Nico agreed.

"An' keep a close eye on Kit."

"I will."

"That God of yers had better be listenin' or I'm goin' t' be furious. That curse will look mild compared t' what I dish out if anythin' happens t' you two."

"I get it. We have t' go, Nana. Get the children in here, an' keep guard on this house," Nico ordered before they ran out of the house for Akoonah Station.

Ducking into the cover of the brush, Hawk easily found his team, along with their arsenal already out and ready. "Sit rep?"

"Haskell's in the main house, along with several followers. Two are guardin' each entrance, one in the front, an' one in the back," Kat explained.

"There are five in the barn," Shawn Marshall added. "As soon as we make the first move, pretty sure they'll be comin' outta the woodwork."

"What's the plan?" Patrick Grant asked.

"Kat, you an' Ethan fire a R.P.G. into the main house an' the barn simultaneously," Hawk said. "Wait until I give you the signal."

"Yes, sir," she said, as they silently crept to the rocket launchers.

Hearing the brush behind them rustle, the angel Kit was with in the Outback suddenly appeared. "Oh, thank You, Lord!" Kit said, relieved.

"Who are you?" Nico asked, on edge.

"Nico, he's the one who led me to Hawk in the Outback," Kit explained.

"And I am not alone," the angel announced. As they gathered around him, he explained, "This is not going to be like Mexico, we will all have to fight. Know the Lord stands with us and sent you His best."

"Will we lose anyone?" Kit asked.

"That is known only to the Lord."

Taking a deep breath, Hawk nodded in understanding. "Nico an' Kit, you two are with me for the main house. Shawn, take Sandra with you for the barn. Charlie an' Ethan, y'er t' stay here with Kat. Martin, Patrick, an' Rob, head toward the fields."

"When do we leave?" Kit asked.

Looking toward the sky, there were streaks that suddenly appeared as if a meteor shower hit during the daytime. "Now," the angel said, and everyone ran toward his or her assigned areas.

Kat and Ethan both counted to twenty before firing a missile at the house and the barn. "Let's get in there."

"No. We stay. If any try t' run, we stop," Charlie said sternly. "The others have this one."

"Trust them," Ethan ordered. "Hawk told us t' stay here for a reason."

"Fine!" Kat huffed, crouching down, keeping an alert eye, while praying for the Spirit's guidance for those on the grounds.

*　　*　　*

When the house blew, Nico grabbed Kit, covering her with his body. Feeling the wind knocked out of them, she was relieved to see others who resembled the angel from earlier, only dressed more for battle in their armor, fighting with those who survived the initial blast. That's when she saw it!

Walking from the fires that erupted from the main house was Haskell Stephens. Fully clothed, he walked from the demolished home, unharmed. "Whoa," Kit said, shocked and amazed. "What are we supposed to do with that?"

"*That* is *our* assignment," Hawk said, getting off the ground. "C'mon!"

The trio ran toward the house, shooting those who dared to come near them with the guns they brought. As Kit dropped her empty magazine onto the ground, she shoved a new one in just in time to take out a bat like creature that lunged for her. Hearing movement to her right, she swung around and fired again.

When she missed, Nico threw his knife, hitting the creature square between the eyes. After the creature dropped, Nico pulled the knife and wiped the yellow-ish green blood off his knife onto the grass. "Let's move, people!" he yelled over the screeches and howls of the creatures getting slaughtered around the station by the other A.N.G.E.L.s and their angel counterparts.

Surrounding Haskell, Kit remembered what Leah looked like facedown in the dirt.

"That'sssssss it!" Haskell hissed, with an evil smile. Inhaling a deep breath of air, he said, "I can feel the anger within you. It builds me stronger with each moment."

"No!" Kit shouted, as a light rain began to fall on the area, and the sun started its descent. "You have taken more than enough from this family! This ends today!"

A hideous cackle began in his throat, quickly escalating to a vigorous roar of laughter. "You are pathetic! You think you can take me out? I've been feeding off that family for years."

A shock of anger shot through her body. To her horror, he literally grew bigger right in front of her. Eyes shifting to black, she momentarily saw the demon within. "Why? Why this family?"

"You are more valuable than you know," the demon hissed, taking a step toward her while keeping an eye on both Hawk and Nico. "From when you were a child, we have watched and prepared. We did what we could to kill you before you had your spawn, but you're more resilient than even *he* gave you credit for."

"Who?"

"*Him.* He wanted you to feel hopeless, abandoned, and worthless. When that didn't work, he tried taking direct hits, but you were protected. So it called for another strategy."

"Little nudges," Kit said in understanding, as events lined up in her mind.

A female human scream suddenly pierced the air from the other end of the station. Kit's head spun in the direction of the barn, fearing the worst for either Sandra or Kat. When she turned back around, she was met face-to-face with the demon.

"Not another step!" Nico shouted, aiming for his head. "I will drop you where you stand!"

"Not before I drop this preciousss angel," he said, reaching up, stroking the side of Kit's face.

To Kit, his hands didn't feel like flesh. They felt like scales of a snake. Shuddering, she let out a slow breath of air with her eyes closed before she looked up at him. Eyes flashing momentarily green, she said, "You may take me out, but our children will live on to fight your legions. And guess what?" she asked, a twinkle in her eyes.

"What?" he asked, amused.

Slowly moving her hand to her belt, she slid out one of her throwing knives. "In the end, *we* win!" She shouted as she thrust one knife into his heart before whipping another knife off her belt. Hearing him screech in agony, she pulled up on the knife in his chest, and thrust the other into his neck.

Hearing several shots ring out around her, she felt his body crumble, taking her to the ground with him. Hawk and Nico pulled Haskell's lifeless body off her. Kit couldn't believe her eyes when she saw the body literally implode on itself until all that was left was a pile of ash.

Looking up at Hawk and Nico, her body shaking beyond belief, she asked, "Is it over?"

"Almost," Hawk said, turning to see what direction to run toward. That's when they heard a male human voice cry out.

Feeling like she was moving in slow motion, Kit looked toward the barn, and saw Kat, Ethan, and Charlie make a mad dash for what was left of it. Nico pulled Kit to her feet as the barn suddenly exploded again. Kat, Ethan, and Charlie were thrown back into the air, landing twenty yards from the barn.

"Now it's over," Hawk solemnly declared, knowing he had lost two good people. Hawk knew when Sandra Peters left the earth, and just then, when Shawn Marshall joined her in paradise.

"Who?" Kit asked, tears slowly crawling down her cheeks.

"Sandra an' Shawn," Hawk admitted. He felt them leave when they were taken.

The angel walked up to the trio. Placing his blazing sword into its sheath, he said, "It is now finished." Several angels around the station set fire to the remnants of what was left of the buildings, as others threw the bodies of the demons into fires. "I am sorry for your loss," the angel said. "The Kingdom has gained two warriors among their ranks today. Know that you are never alone. The Lord *will* protect you and keep you close to Him. Bring up your little ones for Him, and He will keep His promise to you that they will carry the divine legacy."

"Thank you," Kit said, her clothes covered in mashed concoction of soot, ash, and yellow-green blood, along with some of her own blood.

"Please return to your station and tend to your injuries while we finish here," he said, and walked toward the main house with others.

Turning her toward him, Nico saw the claw mark on her arm. "Y'er hurt."

"I didn't feel it. All I saw was the look in his eyes," Kit admitted as a shudder ran down her spine. "They went from delight, to shock, to pure terror.”

“That’s because he saw what was awaiting him,” Hawk pointed out. “I’m leavin’ Ethan Carson with you t’ tend t’ those wounds, an’ t’ help train yer children.”

“Wait! What? T’ do *what*?” Nico objected.

Sensing God’s leading, Kit explained, “Our children have a bigger purpose than the average person. He has big plans for them that were revealed to me while I was gone. We need Ethan here to train them physically and spiritually. It’s also our job to ground them in the spiritual and physical realms as well. We’ll be working together.”

“We *have* been teachin’ them, though.”

“We need to do even more. Our children will be facing things worse than even we have through our lives. They’re going to be facing things that we’ve seen here today. They’ll be a blessing to many as they do His work out there.”

“Are you serious?”

While the fires burned, creating a glow around them, Kit briefly explained some of the stories she learned over the previous forty-eight hours. When finished, Kit, Nico, and Hawk joined hands in prayer for their station, their children, their workers, their family, the A.N.G.E.L.s, and those Christians throughout the world who were facing ‘fires’ of their own. They prayed for perseverance, strength, courage, and faith to face the upcoming days.

When they finished, the sunlight said its goodbye to Australia, leaving only the darkness created by the rising smoke of the smoldering fires. As the remaining A.N.G.E.L.s walked over to the trio, they saw the Heavenly Angels return to the Heavens in the same streaks of light they used to descend to the earth, leaving only the human A.N.G.E.L.s behind.

Once they joined the trio, the group slowly made their way back to Serenity Wells. As they crossed the road, the flashing lights of the fire department and police vehicles were seen in the distance.

"Do you think they'll know what happened?" Nico asked. "They're goin' t' ask questions."

"It was shielded from the real world until the angels left," Hawk explained. "As far as they know, the fire just occurred about twenty minutes ago."

"How?"

"There are some things in this world that cannot be explained. You'll have t' trust us on this."

"Our children are gonna be a part a' this?" Nico asked, unsure.

"Two of them are," Hawk confirmed. "The good Lord is the only One who knows which two they are."

"Until then, we will continue to pray for you and the other A.N.G.E.L.s in the world, along with our children," Kit promised.

"We have brothers an' sisters all over this world who are *not* A.N.G.E.Ls that need prayer as well. They're gettin' tortured, persecuted, an' even killed for being a follower of Jesus. Those are the ones who need prayer the most."

"Can that really make a difference?" Nico asked.

"Prayer holds more power than you think," Hawk explained. "When the saints are on their knees in prayer, it gives strength t' the Lord's Angels. It helps t' carry them in times of hopelessness, an' brings comfort in the face of death. Prayer is the one way we can all be joined together, even if we are hundreds or thousands of miles apart."

Chapter 11

Harvest Moon

Losing Pop, along with the events surrounding Kit and the children immediately after the funeral, and the battle at Akoonah, threw the station for a major loop. It took everyone several long weeks before there was even a remote semblance of normalcy. Kit felt like she was on overdrive as she did her best to keep everyone's spirits up, and made sure everyone ate and stayed focused while running the station…especially Nana. Being with Pop for so long, and losing him so quickly, left Nana in a bad place. Since she wasn't even home at the time to say goodbye to him, she often mentioned that it was her biggest regret in life.

About two months after his passing, Kit and Nana were taking a walk on the station. Grabbing Kit's hand, Nana said, "Kit, I know life for you has been rough, but I want ya t' know that I'm grateful you an' Nico came here."

"So are we."

"I need t' talk t' you about somethin' Zack told me about quite some time ago, an' I wanted t' do it without Nico."

"You know we don't have secrets."

"I do, but I needed t' talk t' you first."

"Um, okay," she said, tucking her hair behind her ear.

"I know Hawk hinted toward it when he was here a couple months ago, but I already knew. Zack told me what *really* happened t' Nate quite some time ago."

Kit's eyes popped open as her heart raced. "What do you mean?"

"He told me he couldn't keep from me that he was the one who shot Nate, an' that the two of them threw his body t' the crocs. The relief t' me was that he also told me Nate was released of the anger before he passed."

"How did you react?"

"At first, the emotions were all over the place, but I understood in the long run that Nate was only gonna get worse." Nana sighed in reflection. "I understand. An' all of you have been safer for it. At this point, I haven't noticed any sign of the anger comin' against yer little ones either."

"It's our prayer it stays that way."

"I guess what I wanted t' ask was yer thoughts on the situation?"

"To be honest, it horrified me, but I've witnessed through the years that I don't have control over any of what goes on. I only have control over how I handle it. I've also learned that life has a way of balancing out. God has shown me His mercy and grace through the years, especially when I let Him do His thing. I also have learned that I need t' stay focused on Him, especially if I can't see past my own hand."

"That's how I feel right now," Nana admitted.

"Nana, you seem lost to me lately, but I want to encourage you. While you don't have Pop around, you have seven little ones who look up to you as a grandma, not to mention Pete and Victoria's little ones as well."

"Yeah, Seth an' Claire's little ones are a good bunch too. I'm glad they came here, an' that we have Ethan hangin' around workin' with the younger ones. I'm also aware he still prays over the north field."

"While what Ethan is doing with the little ones is good, you have a lot of life experience *you* need to pour into them. They need you and *your* life experience shared with them."

Nana sighed. "I know. I also know I can pour into the teens y'er bringin' into here if you continue t' do those camps."

"Yeah. This last bunch was a difficult crew. I'm glad they learned a lot, but I fear they didn't learn enough."

"Time will tell." Climbing the fence, taking a seat on the top rail, Nana continued, "I wanted t' take a walk with you in particular, because I wanted t' talk t' *you*."

"About what?" Kit asked, leaning on the railing Nana was sitting on.

"About this God of yers. Ya see, we've been goin' t' yer church for years. An' while we never took that step, Pop an' I had long talks. With his passin', an' that battle at Akoonah, it opened my eyes t' things around me. I'm concerned."

"About?"

"A couple things, actually. Number one is, if I ask Jesus t' be my Savior will I ever see Pop again?"

"Has he ever taken that step?"

"Not that I know of, but I don't know for sure. Pretty sure the rest of my family didn't either."

"Then, if that's the case I would have to say no."

"I see." Looking down, she watched a tiny lizard scurry across the sand under a rock to escape the Australian heat. "So if I accept this Jesus I won't see them?"

"If what you feel is true, then no. Having said that, you need to make the decision for you and not anyone else – this decision can *only* be made by you. I can't get you into Heaven. Neither can Nico. None of the grandkids can either. It's a decision between you, God, Jesus, and the Spirit, because it's a relationship that'll be between y'all."

"So, if I *do* ask Jesus t' be my Savior, while I *won't* see my other family, I *will* see you, Nico, an' the kids?"

"Yes, ma'am. All four kids have accepted Jesus as their Savior. I know this, because Nico and I both prayed with each of them. Seth, Claire, an' their kids are Christians as well."

"Is that all I have t' do? Just pray?"

Kit chuckled. "Yes, as far as actual salvation is concerned. As far as your relationship with the Lord is concerned, you'll need to do a bit more than that. He would prefer to be more than just fire insurance, so to speak."

"Fire insurance?"

"You know, just to keep you out of Hell."

Nana smirked as she commented, "Been there already."

"Not really. Life here on earth can be tough, but it will be *nothing* compared to Hell. Death never comes when you're in eternal torment."

"Yikes!"

"Exactly. That's what I'm saying."

She gulped. "Are you saying Pop is currently in eternal torment?"

"Unfortunately that would be accurate if what you say about him not being saved is true."

"Wow."

"You can stop yourself from having to endure that, but you can't help anyone else."

"I see."

"Jesus died for you. He's already done it. All you have to do is accept His gift of salvation, and ask for forgiveness of your sins."

"Can I do that now?"

"If you want. I can help you."

"I want."

*   *   *

Over the next following weeks, Kit was pleased to see a change in Nana. There was a renewed vigor in her eyes that Kit realized was missing since Pop passed.

Sitting around the dinner table, toward the end of three months after Pop's passing, Seth spoke up, "Claire and I wanted to talk to all of you."

Owen cracked a smile. "This sounds serious. Do we need t' break out the coldies first?"

Seth chuckled. "No. No beer needed." Nervously clearing his throat, he wouldn't make eye contact with anyone while he said, "We've been grateful for all every one of you have done for us over the last several years."

Nico gulped. "Why does this sound like y'er leavin'?"

"We are…sort of."

Dropping her head into her hands, Nana groaned. "Please, not now."

"We're only going across the street," Claire explained. "We bought Akoonah Station."

Kit gasped. "You did *what*?"

"Relax. We talked to Ethan and Hawk first," Seth explained.

"When?"

"We met them yesterday in town," Ethan confirmed. "They wanted to talk t' us before they made a move."

"That place burned completely t' the ground two months ago," Nico reminded him. "That was *after* it was possessed for *years*. How can you *seriously* be thinkin' of movin' over there?"

"It's a brilliant idea," Ethan started, but Nico cut him off.

"Brilliant? On what planet? You can't be serious!"

"We're very serious," Ethan defended their position. "If they buy the station, bein' Christians *on that land*, they will be in the best position t' stop the take over again."

"Is that land *ready* t' be taken over yet? Will that put them or their children in jeopardy?"

"What are we missin'?" Jarrah asked. "Why would it be dangerous for them t' own it?"

"Because of who owned it before."

"Haskell?"

"Haskell Stephens, an' before that was Jacki Monroe." Nico looked toward Heaven for some sense of direction. Taking a deep cleansing breath, he said, "I'll support it, as long as it doesn't get them hurt or exposed t' the evil that was there."

"My people are already over there right now prayin' over the land, an' for Seth, Claire, *an'* their family," Ethan acknowledged Nico's concerns. "Hawk'll help them hire men. He'll also teach them t' know what they're lookin' for when they hire them. They'll need Kit, though, t' do so."

"Me? Why?" Kit asked, stunned.

"Because you can tell by lookin' at someone whether they are one of His or not."

Crossing his arms in a huff, Aaron asked, "What does *that* mean? Why do I feel like y'er all talkin' over us, usin' some kinda code?"

"Is he?" Ethan asked Kit.

Looking at Aaron for a moment, Kit saw the darkness still in him. Even though he had been asking questions, she could still see the dark and knew he was not one of the Lord's yet. "No," Kit responded.

"No, *what*?" Aaron asked.

Kit sighed. "No, you are not a Christian."

"How do you know?"

"You're searching, but you're not His yet."

"How do you know I haven't done it? Who says I haven't prayed, just not in front a' you?" he challenged.

"Because there is still a darkness in you. Pete has a light inside him. So does Owen, Kendall, Barwon, Steve, Ed, Adoni, and Jarrah, just t' name a few," Kit pointed out. "But you? No, not yet."

"Is this true?" Ethan asked those she mentioned. After they all nodded, Ethan went on, "When we first met, I told you that you had a gift. This is a gift that will serve you well. Do you remember that? We were all at Paige an' Zack's house in Cairns."

"Yes. I remember," she confirmed.

"That's only one of a couple gifts you have. Yer dreams are another."

"Those are a curse!" she snapped, getting irritated with the direction of the conversation. "Don't you have something better t' talk about than my personal life?"

"I didn't think we had secrets," Barwon objected.

"We don't, but still. This is *me* we're talking about here."

"Technically, it's *us* we're talking about," Claire pointed out. "We need your gift to help us make the new station successful. You told me once that 'Akoonah' meant flowing water. You said the reason it was a bad station was because of the evil flowing from it. If we're on it, and are surrounded by the right ranch hands, then the evil will be replaced by the refreshing waters of the Heavenly Father."

With Claire's words churning through Kit's mind, she dropped her head into her hands in prayer. *Could she really do what they were asking? Would Seth and Claire taking over Akoonah's Station turn it for the better?* After a tense few moments, Kit agreed, "Fine. I'll do it."

"Good. We'll need you in order t' make this work," Ethan said, encouraged. "With the papers gettin' signed tomorrow –"

"Wait! *What?*" Nico said, getting annoyed. "Y'er signin' the papers *tomorrow*? This is too fast."

"Nico, we've been here for going on eleven years. Don't you think it's time we moved to our own station?" Seth asked, resting his hand on Nico's shoulder. "You guys have taught us a lot. We want to do this. You have this station to pass down to your children. We want something to pass down to *ours*. We want to be able to give them a future as well."

"I understand." Nico sighed. "It just seems so fast. I also feel a bit left out of this whole thing."

"You have a station t' run," Ethan pointed out. "One of the bigger ones in the territory."

"An' Kit has children t' raise," Nico countered. "The timin' of this –"

"Is God's," Ethan finished. "Does He really need t' show you again Who's in control?"

"No," he groaned. "I just…I get it."

"Look at the bright side," Claire said, unable to hide her excitement. "We're only across the street."

Kit slowly exhaled. "Another season of change."

"It's another step," Ethan added. "Look, we all have a purpose here on this earth. We need t' go through certain things t' make us strong enough for the next step. When we rely on, an' focus on God, it strengthens us even more."

"So, those bad things we go through aren't necessarily bad?" Aaron asked. "They're supposed t' make us stronger?"

Almost forgetting they were in a room with twenty-some people, Ethan was taken by surprise by Aaron's question. Quickly recovering, he responded, "What Satan at times tries t' use for evil, God can use for good. Romans 8:28 tells us, 'An' we know that in all things God works for the good of those who love Him, who have been called accordin' t' His purpose.' He can take the darkness an' make it good if we only trust in Him an' focus on Him until we get back into the light. Psalm 46:1 tells us, 'God is our refuge an' strength, a very present help in trouble.' Who do you go t' when you are in trouble, Aaron? Where is *your* refuge?"

"I don't – I don't know," he admitted.

"Proverbs 3:5 an' 6 tell us to, 'Trust in the LORD with all yer heart, an' lean not on yer own understandin'; in all yer ways acknowledge Him, an' He shall direct yer paths.' Who do you trust? Who directs yer paths?"

"I don't know."

"You've been searchin' for months. Matthew 7:7 says, 'Ask, an' it will be given t' you; seek, an' you will find; knock, an' it will be opened t' you.' You've been askin', an' He has been pleadin' for you t' come t' Him, but you continue t' choose t' resist. Why?"

"Because I don't like t' be told how t' live my life," he said, irritation evident in his voice.

"Who gave you that life?"

"My parents."

"God did. He created life from the very beginnin'," Ethan countered. "Jesus said in John 10:10, 'The thief comes only t' steal an' kill an' destroy; I have come that they may have life, an' have it t' the full.' Are you livin' yer life t' the fullest, Aaron?"

"I enjoy my life."

"That's not what I asked. Are you livin' yer life t' the fullest?"

"I don't – I don't know," he admitted.

"What are you searchin' for?"

Sitting there in silence for a few moments, Aaron finally asked, "Can we go take a walk? I'd like t' talk t' you. I think you have the answers I've been lookin' for."

"Yep," Ethan said, and they got up and left. Walking out into the station, they left a room full of stunned people. Ethan's concern was for Aaron, not those left in the house. After an hour of conversation, Aaron prayed by the light of the full moon to accept Jesus as His Savior.

*   *   *

Taking a few moments to recover from the directions of the whiplash conversations that happened around the table that night after Ethan and Aaron left, Nico turned to Seth and said, "You stood by me when you had every right t' be furious with me. I'll do whatever you need."

"Me too," Kit agreed, taking Claire's hand into hers. "I know we would've been fine, but the gift God gave me in your friendship over the years has made *fine* that much better."

"You and I had a rough start," Claire admitted, "but I'm glad you hung on until I came to my senses."

"Y'all are gonna make me cry," Kit said, wiping the tears off her cheeks.

"Do ya reckon we'll still see y'all each day?" Josh asked. The children had grown up with a blend of Aussie and Southern lingo, creating an interesting mix in their terminology.

Seth's son Scott shrugged. "Buggered if I know."

Looking at Scott in shock, their seven-year-old daughter Caitlyn objected, "I *will not* leave Leah an' Rachel!" Taking each girl by the hand, she insisted, "I'm gonna stay here if you say we can't see them every day!"

"Calm yer brumbies," their youngest, Sam, grumbled. "All you do is whinge!"

"I'm not whingin'. I'm tellin' it like it is."

Shaking his head, Sam just sighed.

"Well?" Caitlyn asked. "Are we gonna see 'em?"

"Of course you will!" Rachel said. "Why not?"

"Y'er only across the street," Caleb pointed out, while chewing on his biscuit. "Do yer legs not work?"

"I still have this cast on for another week," Rachel said, upset. "I won't be able t' come over until it's off."

"We won't be moving until at the very least our house is built," Claire pointed out. "We're not going to be camping. We go to sign the papers tomorrow, but we're still going to be here for quite some time. We were *hoping* Nana would help us with advice in building," she said, glancing at Nana, hopeful. "Your experience and expertise can never be surpassed."

"Flattery will get you everywhere," Nana said with a smirk. "And the only thing it'll cost ya is visitation rights t' yer little ones."

"You're their grandmother as far as they're concerned," Seth pointed out.

"She's not?" Scott asked, genuinely stunned. "I thought Nico was yer brother an' Nana was our grandmum. Are you sayin' that's not true?"

"That's completely true, on all assumptions," Nana corrected him. "Family is not always made only of blood. Look around this table. Each man an' woman surroundin' you is yer family."

"Even me, little man," Barwon said, messing with Scott's hair.

"Okay. Y'all are messin' with me," Scott objected.

"No we're not," Nana said with all seriousness. "If anyone comes onto this station t' potentially hurt you, I promise you that ever person around this table would put their lives on the line for you. *That* means family."

Still confused, Scott asked, "Is *anyone* around this table our blood family?"

"Outside of me, you're Mom, and you're brother and sister, no. No one around this table is related by blood. Having said that, Nana is one hundred percent correct, we *are* all family. The only thing that can potentially pull us apart is if someone chooses to leave this family or God takes them."

"We'll still see ya," Jarrah pointed out. "You'll only be on the other side of the north field fence. No worries."

"Good," Scott said relieved. "All y'all mean the world t' me."

"An' you t' us," Barwon agreed.

Chapter 12

Golden Days of Fall

Through the next year, both stations, along with Koala Pass, joined forces to set Akoonah Station up for success. Moving day was easier for Kit than she thought it would be. She was thrilled for Seth and Claire that things were working out for them, yet they weren't that far away.

As the next few years passed, while the children grew, the three stations continued to work together and bond as a group. Along with the daily adventures of owning and operating a station, Kit and Nico continued to mentor new groups of young men that would come through for a two-week stint on the station. Their first group was their most challenging, but also their most rewarding. Quinton graduated with honors before going to college. Afterward, he assumed his position with a better understanding of the human condition, and after a couple more two-week stints, he had a better understanding of what the value of hard work really meant. The other nine young men also fulfilled the rolls their families were hoping they would. It was a blessing to Kit and Nico to have played a part in helping them discover their mission in life.

During that time, life finally seemed to be working out for Kit. As Ethan, Nico, and Kit worked with the kids, Nana would periodically come up behind them and add her expertise, making them stronger each day in the physical as well as the spiritual aspects of life.

While she was thrilled to know her children had such a wonderful upbringing, she longed to talk to her father and her friends from college and Oklahoma. At times, she felt like part of her was missing.

"Of course part of you is missin'," Paige said, sitting with Kit on a bench overlooking the station one night while they were visiting. Paige's cancer continued to stay in remission, and she prayed it would stay that way.

"I don't know what to do about it."

"There's nothin' you *can* do. That was part of the deal you made when you left all those years ago."

Propping her chin on her hand, as she braced her elbow on her knee, she sighed. "That doesn't help."

Resting her hand on Kit's shoulder, Paige explained, "Despite the fact that you feel alone, know y're not. You may not have yer father here, but you have more family than you've ever dreamed of."

"I know."

"We often miss what we don't have. The problem is when we do that, we tend t' overlook what we *do* have."

"What does that mean?"

"We're so focused on what was taken from us, such as yer friends and yer mum, an' in a way yer dad, that yer missin' what's right in front of you. You have a sister in Claire. You have a grandmum in Nana, and a mum in me. You have a loving husband in Nico, an' four beautiful, healthy children. Y'er livin' what many people can only dream of."

"I get that, but –"

"But nothin', love. Life is t' be lived t' the fullest. God doesn't want ya livin' in the past, or ya may miss the good that's right in front of ya."

"How did you get so smart?"

"When you meet death face-to-face like I did through cancer, you tend t' look at things a different way. Yer dad is livin' where he's supposed to, just as you are livin' where yer supposed to. You've raised four strong children for the Lord, an' He'll bless them in many ways. You an' I both know that He wouldn't have brought ya this far just t' leave you. Now, yer feelings are yer feelings, an' yer entitled t' those. When those come, an' know there'll be more, remind them that y'er covered by the blood of Jesus an' that He has a plan for you."

"What are you saying?"

"If yer too busy lookin' back, you'll miss the attacks comin' at you from the front."

Kit sighed. "So, you're saying those are attacks?"

"Yep. If yer focused on the past, you won't look t' the Lord. Y'er distracted from yer *real* mission."

"I have a feeling you're right."

"You *know* I'm right."

"Unfortunately, I do."

"Then go, knowing that you are covered by the blood of Jesus."

"Yes, ma'am."

"An' know that y'er loved an' prayed for by yer family here."

"I know."

"Go live yer life t' the fullest, love. That's what we're created t' do."

"And to do it for the glory of the Lord."

"Amen, Kit. Amen."

*   *   *

"Mum," now eighteen-year-old Leah came downstairs for breakfast, "I can't get Nana t' get up. Can you come give me a hand? I know she wasn't feeling good last night before bed."

"Really?" Nico raised an eyebrow. "I'll go check it out. She's a mornin' person. That doesn't sound like Nana."

Getting up from the table, Nico made his way upstairs. With a feeling of foreboding in his core, he prayed with each step. When he didn't get an answer from knocking on the door, he walked into the room. The silence was deafening.

Sitting on the side of the bed, he touched her neck for a pulse. Dropping his head, he forced the feelings that wanted to overflow, down. Choking the tears back, he called for Pete.

"His voice was shaky," Kit said to Pete. Without another word, they raced up the stairs. "Nico? What's happened?"

"She's, uh…she's gone," he admitted, tears overflowing onto his cheeks as he hung his head in his hands, unable to control it any longer. "Nana was the strong one in the family. I don't know what I'm goin' t' do without her."

"I'll leave you two, an' go call this in," Pete said, and left the room.

"Thank you," Kit said, as she went over to Nico. He wrapped his arms around her as he rested his head on her abdomen. Rubbing his back, she sighed. "She looks peaceful. She probably went in her sleep."

"Still hurts. She was the matriarch of the family."

"I know," Kit said, leaning down, kissing his head. "I'm sorry. She may have been strong, but you are stronger. She had a faith in you, that you now need to have in yourself."

"Can I do this without her? Am I ready?"

"She wouldn't have given you the station so long ago if that were even in question." Lifting him by his chin, she rubbed the tears away as she reminded him, "Even if we doubt ourselves, we have learned where our true strength is. Isaiah 41:10 says, 'Fear not, for I am with you; be not dismayed for I am your God; I will strengthen you, I will help you, I will uphold you with my righteous right hand.' He is where your strength is founded. Lean on Him when you don't think you can stand anymore."

"I don't think I can do this."

"I do. Let it out now, so you can do what you need to do."

Sobbing, Nico clung to Kit, letting all of his feelings over the last few years pour out in the form of tears. When he finished, they prayed for the family and their friends, knowing how hard this was going to hit them all.

*   *   *

For the day of Nana's funeral, heaviness hung all over the territory. The clouds were even sad, as they blocked the sun from coming through. While her family and friends stood around the casket at the family burial ground, the tears never ceased.

Knowing the numbers would reach above fifty who would want to speak, Pastor limited it to family only. After the family other members spoke, Nico got up for his turn.

Resting his hand on her casket, tears continued to slowly crawl down his cheeks. "Nana was a strong woman who did what had t' be done. I pray I can run this station in a way that will make her proud of me. When she entrusted the family legacy t' me, I was humbled, yet proud. She had faith in my abilities an' me, when I lost all hope." Sighing, he shook his head. Looking toward Heaven for the words, he continued, "There are days I pretend I'm okay, but in reality I'm not. She was like a second mum t' me. I don't know what I have done had she not been there for me. I see her everywhere I look on the station. There was still so much for her t' do. There's so much she had yet t' share. I am happy she was able t' pass down her wisdom t' my children, an' I have the confidence of knowin' that they'll pass her spirit down t' the generations after them. In the still of the night, as I walk around the station, I hear her voice. I see evidence of her everywhere I look. I hear her laughter in the children. At times, I can't figure out whether t' be happy for her bein' in Heaven with the Lord, or cry because I miss her so much." Sniffing, he wiped his eyes. "Ohhh, Nana. You will never be forgotten. We love you an' pray y'er enjoyin' Heaven with the Father an' Jesus."

As he sat down, Pastor got up to close. "Life has a way of throwin' us into directions we don't feel we're prepared for. I believe everyone here would agree that Charlotte was one in a million. I do know, though, that she accepted the Lord as her Savior. When she did, it made a change in her that started in her core an' overflowed into those she came in contact with. It's always our hope as one of His t' have a legacy like Charlotte's. Let us join together in carryin' this family through their difficult time."

*   *   *

"Mumsy!" Rachel called, running up the stairs to Kit and Nico's room a month after Nana's funeral. "We're hoo-oome!"

"I hear that." Kit smirked, as her two daughters came bounding into the room. Their blond hair was halfway down their backs, and their sapphire-blue eyes sparkled. Kit was amazed at how well rounded the pair were.

"Is Willow with y'all?" Caleb ran up the stairs behind them. The now twenty-year-old boys were strapping young men, taking after their father after growing and working on the station all their lives. While they strongly resembled Nico, they had Kit's jet-black hair, which perfectly set off their sky-blue eyes. While they earned money for their work on the station, they often said they enjoyed it and wouldn't have it any other way.

"No. She said she would catch up with you later. She had a doctor appointment," Leah explained. "She left about lunch time. Kind of concerned that we didn't see her afterward."

"Yeah. Caitlyn couldn't get a hold of her either," Rachel pointed out.

"I knew about the doctor's appointment. That's why I was hoping she was with you," Caleb said, shoving his hands in his pockets.

"What's wrong?" Kit asked, noticing the shift in Caleb's disposition. "Are you two in a lover's quarrel?"

"No, I –"

"Caleb James Sullivan!" Nico roared, as he came into the house, slamming the door behind him. "Where are you?"

Wide-eyed, Kit quietly asked, "What did you do?"

Caleb dropped his head, not wanting to answer her.

Running over to him, Kit lifted his chin so he would look at her. When she did, she saw the fear in his eyes as a tear crawled down his cheek. "What happened?"

"I have a bad feelin' Willow's pregnant."

Kit had to catch her breath. "*What?*"

"You got Willow pregnant?" Rachel asked, appalled. "Have you lost yer mind? Have you not listened t' Mum an' Dad all these years?"

"What were you thinkin'?" Leah growled.

"I love her. We didn't mean for it t' happen. One thing led t' another an'…" Caleb's voice trailed off as he did his best to get his emotions under control. Looking to heaven for help, he said a prayer in his head for mercy.

When Nico stormed up the staircase, Caleb moved closer to his sisters, fearing his father for the first time in his life. "I'm sorry, Dad."

"Sorry isn't gonna cut it this time!" Nico growled, as Kit jumped between the two, pushing Nico back.

"Calm down!" Kit shouted.

"Calm down? He got Willow pregnant, an' I'm supposed t' just calm down? Tommy called, an' he's madder than a cut snake! An' I don't blame him! If someone got one a' the girls pregnant I would –"

"*Look at me*!" Kit yelled. When he looked at her, stunned that she actually yelled at him, Kit said, "Think about what we told Anna's parents when she got pregnant."

"Anna was pregnant?" Leah shook her head, confused. "Anna doesn't have any kids."

"Mind yer own," Nico snapped.

"Ease off!" Caleb snapped back in defense of his sister, as he stepped in front of them in a protective stance.

"You back off *now*!" Nico snarled. His face flushed when his blood pressure skyrocketed. Y'er only twenty years old. What are you gonna do now?"

"I'm gonna marry her!"

"Y'er gonna *what*?"

Standing tall, Caleb said, "She an' I talked. She's graduatin' this year. It only happened the one time. We asked the Lord for forgiveness, an' have been careful ever since. We really didn't mean for it t' happen. But, Dad, we've been t'gether for four years. It was wrong. I admit it. But it was only the one time in four years."

"SHE-GOT-PREGNANT!"

"I know! Realistically, though, you knew we were talkin' about marriage. We did it wrong, but we're goin' t' make it right. We already planned on gettin' married once she graduated."

"Y'er serious? What about Uni?" Nico asked, referring to college.

"You've been trainin' me an' Josh t' take over the station. Do you not know by now that one of us will be takin' over the station, while the other will be goin' out once Hawk sends Charlie for us?"

"Is that yer game? Y'er gamblin' with a young woman's heart an' life. What will you do if *you* are the one called t' be an A.N.G.E.L.? Do you not understand what that callin' means?"

"Oh yeah. It's been drilled into us since we were ten."

"Then *why* would you potentially place Willow in a position t' get her heart broken?"

"What do you mean? I would *never* break her heart!"

"What do *you* think will happen when *you* get called t' be an A.N.G.E.L.? What is she gonna do when you go out on missions? What is she gonna do when ya don't come back one day?"

As soon as he asked that, everyone in the room froze.

"Why wouldn't he come back?" Rachel asked, a tear crawling down her cheek. As she wiped it away, she reminded them, "One of *us* is supposed t' go too."

"Not necessarily," Caleb pointed out. "They only said two. They didn't say *which* two."

"So," Leah gulped, finally understanding the full implications of what being an A.N.G.E.L. could mean. "In reality, it could be both of *us*?" she asked, pointing to her and Rachel.

"It could be any of you," Kit clarified. "That's why we've been training you. We want all y'all to be safe."

"Then, why do we feel like you gave us up?" Leah asked, her bottom lip trembling.

"Why in the world would you think that?" Kit asked, horrified. "You have a choice. You have *always* had a choice."

"Then I choose t' marry Willow an' stay on the station," Caleb said. "I love the Lord an' would do anythin' for Him, but I want Willow. I don't think He would make me do somethin' I don't want t' do."

"What if *we* don't want t' do it?" Rachel asked. "What if *we* decide t' not go?"

"No one says you *have* to," Nico said, understanding their feelings for the first time. "Look, whatever plan God has for you, you will always be our children. God doesn't want t' force you t' do anythin'. That's the reason He sent Jesus. He wants you t' *choose* t' follow Him."

"What if I choose t' follow Him as the husband of Willow an' father of our child while workin' on this station?" Caleb challenged.

"That's between the three of you. If you, God, an' Willow are okay with it…" Nico looked from Caleb to Kit, who nodded before he turned back to Caleb, and said, "Then yer Mum an' I are okay with it too. Y'er right. Y'er an adult. Willow's an adult. If that's the choice the two a' you want, then that's yer decision. You two," he pointed toward Rachel and Leah, "had better not make the same mistake."

"An' risk seein' you look the way you just did again?" Leah huffed. "No thank you!"

Rachel shook her head as she crossed her arms. "I agree. I don't ever want t' cause ya t' look like that."

"There's one more person who missed this episode," Kit pointed out.

"Y'er right. I should go talk t' Josh. *You* need t' go talk t' Willow an' her parents." Nico pointed to Caleb. "They *are not* happy with you at the moment."

"Here." Kit ran over to her jewelry box and pulled out a ring Nico bought her after the birth of the boys. He bought one for her after the girls were born as well, but she insisted on only wearing Nana's wedding ring. That ring to her, held her heart the strongest. Nana was protective, strong, and carried the family. She hoped to leave a legacy as strong as Nana did. "This will help you if you get permission from Tommy an' Andi," she said, giving him the ring.

Hugging his mom, he whispered, "Thank you."

"Go make her an honest woman," Kit said, shoving him toward Nico.

As the two men stood toe-to-toe, Nico took a good look at his grown son, who, outside of his hair color, was the spitting image of Nico. Placing his hands on Caleb's shoulders, he said, "You all have made us proud since the day you were born. T'day is no different. While I wish you would have married her first, you *are* an adult, an' it seems y'er ready t' make adult decisions. If this is yer choice, an' if you obtain permission from her parents, I'll hire you t' work on the station. Once the two a' you are married, y'er welcome t' clean up Seth an' Claire's old house an' move in there. You'll be payin' yer own bills. An' while you'll be on the station, yer Mum is *not* a built-in babysitter. She may volunteer t' help, but you two are on yer own, only under the umbrella of the station. The benefit t' this is that we're here t' ask any questions, t' get any advice, an' in the event of an emergency there are plenty a' people around t' help. Also, her parents are just down the road. Please remember these things when you talk t' Tommy an' Andi. They will serve you well."

"Thank you," Caleb squeaked out, doing his best to keep his emotions under control.

"This is a tremendous step," Nico said, resting his hands on Caleb's arms, for the first time realizing how much Caleb was shaking. Taking a deep breath, and praying for strength, Nico finished, "But if you have both have prayed an' have a peace about yer decision, then we'll support you."

"Yes, sir."

"Please let us know as soon as possible. Preferably before it's plastered all over social media?" Kit asked.

"Definitely," he said, giving her another hug before he hugged his dad and left out the door for the barn to grab his horse.

"Well, that was interestin'," Rachel commented when the door slammed behind him.

"That was only a portion of the conversation," Nico pointed out. "Kit, you got this?"

"Yeah. You have another conversation you have to handle," Kit agreed. After he kissed her on the cheek, Nico disappeared down the stairs. "Have a seat, ladies," Kit said, gesturing toward the bed. As they sat down, Kit took a hand of each of them, and said, "Girls, you brought up an interesting comment that I think we should discuss a little further."

"Which one?" Leah asked.

"About the fact that you feel we're giving you away."

"When I think about it, I sometimes feel that way," Rachel admitted. "It's like you didn't even fight it. You just accepted it an' signed us up."

Kit took a deep breath to clear her mind, as she said a prayer in her head for wisdom. "While it may feel like that, I promise you it couldn't be further from the truth. We love y'all with all our hearts. I pray you have a full understanding of that."

"I do," Leah said cautiously. "Do you understand where we're comin' from? I mean, you an' Dad taught us a lot of self-defense, an' taught us how t' study God's Word. Nana passed down all she could, which was a lot, but what Ethan taught us was a lot different – even somewhat scary."

"Right. He taught you to see what is not there, to feel what you cannot see, and to anticipate the enemy's movement before he even makes them."

"Those were some hard lessons," Rachel said under her breath.

"But you succeeded. I'm grateful to Ethan for sharing his training with you. That's something we couldn't teach you. But, back to what we were addressing. Your life is just that. It's your life. If you choose to not go, you don't have to go. God doesn't want to force you to do anything. He doesn't sit up there and pull strings like we're marionettes. He wants you to choose Him."

"We did," Rachel said, confused.

"I know. And just like when you chose to follow Him, He'll lay on your heart if He wants you to be an A.N.G.E.L., and then He'll leave it up to you. That's part of free will. Ya see, He has a plan, and an idea of who would be perfect for that plan. But, make no mistake, He already knows who will do it if you say no. The only thing it'll do is take the blessing from you."

"What if it doesn't seem like a blessing?" Leah asked.

"Doing anything for the Lord will always be a blessing to *someone*. He doesn't do things just t' do them," Kit explained. "Whether He blesses you or the other person, or maybe even someone you've never met and your story blesses them, you *will* be a blessing."

"I get that. I'm strugglin' with the whole 'may not come back' thing," Rachel said, making quotes with her hands.

"Before you were born, there was an A.N.G.E.L. who lived here on the station named Shawn O'Brien. He and his girlfriend, Victoria Stanton, went on a mission one time and didn't come back. About a year or so afterward, Charlie came and explained what happened. Ya see, they went in to be a distraction in order to save an American A.N.G.E.L. and an innocent lady who got kidnapped. They may not have known that in rescuing those two, just how much was added to the kingdom. That girl may not even know the sacrifice was made. But know this, what they did was a tremendous blessing to those two people."

"A life for a life? That doesn't make sense," Leah said, following Kit's story.

"Well, what you don't know, that was explained to me just before I returned with them shortly before your training started, was that those two, the American A.N.G.E.L. and the woman with him, got married. They now have three children – twin boys and a girl. They have been training their children, just as you've been trained. Who knows? You may see them in the field one day."

"Interestin'," Rachel said, considering her words. "So, you're sayin' that other people are bein' trained right now for the same thing?"

"Yes. They're all over the earth. There are angels even among us right now. The Bible says that we may entertain angels unaware. You know Charlie's one of them, right?"

"Yes. What we didn't know is that there were others training who are our age."

"Does it matter?"

"What do ya mean?"

"If God calls you, are you gonna go?"

"Not sure," Rachel admitted.

"Then, my dear, you have some praying to do," Kit pointed out. "When He calls, you have to be sure of what you'll say."

"Looks like I have some prayin' t' do as well," Leah confessed.

"Sounds like a good idea. I love you both."

"Love you too," the girls both said before giving Kit a hug.

"In the meantime, also be in prayer for your brothers." Kit pointed out, "They may not be one-hundred percent sure either."

* * *

"You'd *better* be jokin'!" Josh growled at Nico.

"Nope."

"He got Willow preggers! I know a ton a' guys who'll get in line t' take him out for that one!"

"You knew they were gonna get married. He needs you t' back him up on this."

"You serious?" Josh asked, stunned. "What he did was wrong!"

"What *they* did was wrong," Nico corrected. "But, that's between them an' God. You need t' stand by yer brother."

"How can you be so calm about this?"

"Trust me, I wasn't earlier. Yer mum thought I was gonna have a heart attack."

"I'll bet!"

"After a rather heated conversation, we've come t' an agreement. What I need is for you t' stand by him."

After a few moments of consideration, Josh agreed, "Fair enough."

"An' *please* don't do the same thing. I don't know if I can do this again."

"No chance. I don't know what Caleb was thinkin' in this one, but I'll stand by him."

"Thanks." Nico patted his shoulder. "Now for the second thing I need t' talk t' you about."

"Really? Two bombshells? Please don't tell me one of the girls is preggers too?"

Nico chuckled nervously. "No. They said they never wanted t' see me look the way I did earlier."

"I would imagine. Then, what is it?"

"The girls brought up an interestin' point that I wanted t' talk t' you about."

"What's that?"

"They said they felt like we gave you guys up when it comes t' workin' with the A.N.G.E.L.s."

"Well, t' be honest, that thought *has* crossed my mind," he said, hopping onto the fence.

"Well," Nico leaned on the fence, crossing his arms while watching the sunset as they talked, "I'd like t' clear that up."

"No need."

"I don't want ya thinkin' like that."

"I love ya, Dad, but I know better. You both love us with all yer hearts. I also know we have a choice when it comes t' God. I've learned a lot over the years."

"Obviously," Nico said, impressed. "So, what will you do if y'er one of the two?"

He shrugged. "Then I'm one a' the two. If God calls me, I'm not gonna say no. That didn't work so well for Jonah."

"Too true."

"You don't need t' worry about me. If I don't end up bein' an A.N.G.E.L., then I'm gonna work here."

"Okay. What about a lady? I haven't heard ya say anythin' about a young lady lately."

"Probably because I can feel what direction God is leadin', an' I don't wanna start somethin' I can't finish."

"What do ya mean?"

"I already got the call," Josh admitted.

"What? When? Why didn't you tell me?"

"A couple weeks ago…an' I just know. I'm just waitin' for Charlie t' come an' get me."

"Y'er serious?"

"Very."

"An' y'er okay with that?"

"I am."

"Impressive."

"Nothin' t' be impressed about." He shrugged. "People get called every day."

"Did yer Mum tell ya what happened t' Shawn an' Victoria?"

"No. Ethan did."

"Was Caleb with you?"

"Yep. It was the three of us."

"What did Caleb say?"

"He was a little shaken. He an' Willow had been t'gether for about a year an' a half at that point. It's been weighin' on him every since."

"I can see how he would be torn."

"He's not goin'. It's one a' the girls."

"How do you know?"

"I know," he said with certainty.

"Did ya tell them?"

"Nope. Gonna let 'em figure it out for themselves."

"Probably a smart idea."

"That's what I thought. They'll know when the time comes."

"You are wise beyond yer years, my son."

"That's because I have wise parents." He smirked. "They made sure we were well prepared. Also, watchin' all those camps come through of the boys, seein' the ramifications of their choices an' actions, an' Nana's influence, along with Ethan's trainin'…we were destined t' soak up some type of wisdom. Learnin' t' feel what I cannot see, I think, was the biggest an' most valuable of the traits taught me."

"An', y'er okay with it?"

"Yep."

"Have t' admit I'm a bit taken aback. I knew it would come one day, but knowin' an' *knowin'* are two different things. An', you say it's one a' the girls?"

"Yep."

"Do ya know which one?"

"Yep."

"Interestin'. Well, it's not gonna change how we pray for you, but it does put an element of nerves back into the situation."

"I can see that," Josh said with a sigh, as the sun continued to drop in the distance. "But I know what I'll be doin' is very important. I also know I'll be helpin' people for the Lord, so I'm okay with that."

"Mind if I share this with Kit?"

"Honestly?"

"I would expect no less."

"I would rather not tell her until Charlie comes for us. I don't want t' deal with the emotions."

"Fair enough. Thank you for tellin' me."

"Y'er my dad. How could I not?"

"I appreciate it."

Hopping off the rail, Josh gave Nico a hug before he took off into the station. Watching the sun finish the final portion of it's decent, surrounded by stunning colors of pink, yellow, blue, and burnt orange, he was amazed at the beauty it held. Fall sunsets brought about a different hue of coloring that he appreciated.

Astounded by all God had done for them over the years in keeping them safe, granting them the gift of the children and the peaceful life on the station, he thanked the Lord, and asked only for continued support and courage to face the upcoming days.

Chapter 13

Forever Fall

Thankfully, Tommy and Andi had immense understanding regarding Willow and Caleb. With their wedding set for two weeks after they found out she was pregnant, it brought an element of chaos to the already bustling stations. Pastor was to marry them on Koala Pass Station, and a lot had to be done to pull it off. Between Koala Pass, Serenity Well, and Akoonah's stations, they had confidence they could do it.

On the morning of the wedding, things were insane as Andi, Kit, and Claire organized and delegated how to set things up. To Kit's surprise, Andi was excited about the upcoming nuptials, and gaining Nico and Kit as in-laws. "From what we can tell, she's due around Christmas," Andy said, as they draped netting over the archway Caleb and Willow were to be married under, while Kit tucked fresh flowers around the archway, and Claire directed the guys to set up chairs.

"Should be interesting to say the least. Tell me, how are you *really* doing? We haven't had an in-depth conversation about it yet," Kit pointed out.

"To be honest, I'm okay with it. I'm already a grandmother, technically more so than some people remember," she reminded her.

"This is true."

"I'm glad it's Caleb. He's sweet, an' treats her with the utmost respect an' kindness. We couldn't ask for anythin' more. Ya know, I don't know if I've ever thanked you for talking us into keepin' Willow t' begin with. I feel Anna's a better young lady for it. With her now a doctor an' datin' a great guy, I couldn't imagine the mess it could have been had we done what we were plannin' on doin'."

"I understand."

"I don't think you do. I couldn't imagine life without Willow in it. Yes, it was challenge since we were older, but I wouldn't change a thing. She's been a blessin' beyond what I could ever imagine. It breaks my heart t' think what we almost made Anna do."

"Things happen for a reason."

"An', I remember you sayin' that. When Caleb came over, the conversation we had on the day we found out Anna was pregnant flashed through my mind. You an' Nico stood by yer words…an' yer boy."

"Right. I *did* have to remind Nico of that conversation as well. In his defense, he did better than I thought he would."

"An' you guys takin' care in hirin' him, an' givin' them a home t' start in is a relief."

"Well, y'all handled the wedding. That was the least we could do."

"We appreciate it nonetheless."

"Look forward to seeing what the little one looks like," Kit admitted.

"Me too. They're beautiful children."

"I've seen Willow's dress. It's stunning!"

"Ladies, there are some young ladies lookin' for the two a' you," Nico yelled from the porch with Tommy, as they were resting after finishing their work for the ceremony.

"Coming," Kit called back. Quieter, she said, "The two of them are getting along unusually well."

"See that. Pretty sure that's a good thing."

"I'll take it any day," Kit said before the two of them headed upstairs to the awaiting young ladies.

When they got up there, they found Rachel (maid-of-honor), Caitlyn, and Leah (the bridesmaids), dressed in flowing peach dresses. While Willow's white dressed resembled theirs in the off-the-shoulder style, hers had beading and lace throughout.

"Beautiful! My son's a lucky man," Kit said, giving her a hug. On the male side, Josh was Caleb's best man, with Scott Simmons and Willow's brother Andrew (who was the closest of the brothers to Willow), were the groomsmen.

"Pretty sure *I'm* the lucky one," Willow pointed out.

"Just continue to take care of him, an' I'll be a happy mom."

"With those three watchin' my every move, I wouldn't dare mistreat him," Willow said with a smile, gesturing toward Caitlyn, Leah, and Rachel.

"You two are perfect for each other," Rachel remarked. "That's all we can ask for him."

"Thank you."

"Are you nervous?" Leah asked.

"More like sick t' my stomach. Whose idea was it t' get married in the mornin'?"

"I *do* believe that was yers, little one," Andi pointed out.

"Remind me of this at a later date," she grumbled, before turning back toward the mirror.

"This is a day you'll never forget," Andi comforted her daughter. "This will be the first of many more happy days t' follow. We love you. You know that?"

"Yes."

"Mom? May I come in?" Anna asked, poking her head into the room.

"Sure, hon."

She went right over to Willow and hugged her, with tears streaming down her cheeks.

"Y'er not supposed t' be the one cryin'," Willow said, brushing the tears away as fast as she could. "I'm gettin' married. This is supposed t' be happy."

Anna glanced at her mother, who nodded in reference to an earlier conversation they had. "May I have a word with her?" she asked the others.

"Sure. C'mon, girls," Kit said, ushering the girls toward the door.

"Kit? Can you stay? Please?" Anna asked. Then she added, "Moral support."

Having a feeling of what the conversation was about, Kit only nodded as she closed the door behind the others, and then took a seat on the bed.

Taking Willow's hands into hers, Anna took a deep breath to keep her emotions under control before she started.

"Y'er scarin' me," Willow warned.

"Willow, there's somethin' I need t' tell you, an' I know the timin' probably isn't the best, but Mom an' I talked and decided now is as good a time as any."

"About?"

Nervously clearing her throat before she continued, Anna confessed, "When I was seventeen there was a young man named Alec that I fell for, head-over-heels."

"Right. Our brothers don't care for him. Whenever his name is mentioned, I only hear grumblin' an' complainin'."

"That's because he an' I got t'gether, an' I got pregnant at seventeen."

"You *what*? What did Mum an' Dad do?" Willow asked in wide-eyed shock, still not yet connecting what Anna was trying to tell her.

"They allowed me t' have the baby, an' then they adopted her an' raised her as their own."

"I don't –" Willow stopped short, as she gulped. "Crikey! Are you tellin' me what I *think* y'er tellin' me?"

"We all make mistakes, but God in His grace an' mercy, can change a mess into a message. Through that, He taught me the value of life an' usin' my brain. I learned what t' look for, an' t' rely more on Him than I ever dreamed. An', even though it wasn't easy, after I had you, I returned t' school an' continued my education. In the meantime, Mum an' Dad were given the blessin' of gettin' t' raise you," Anna said, tucking a piece of Willow's hair behind her ear. "Ya see, Kit an' Nico talked Mum an' Dad into not makin' me have an abortion. Now, before you go off, know that they have never regretted that decision. The reason Andrew looks after you so closely is because he knows an' understands everythin' around yer birth. The others weren't quite so understanin'. Not t' fault them though. They all love you, as do I. I don't know what I would have done, had they made me go through with it. The reason I'm tellin' you this is so you know the truth. You also now know that I understand yer condition, an' the stress you've been under these last few weeks."

"I'm not sure what t' say," Willow said, in shock. "I mean, it makes sense, an' I appreciate you finally tellin' me, but it won't change anythin'. Mum an' Dad are the ones who raised me."

"As intended. I wanted t' let you know that I do understand what you've been through, *an'* what y'er goin' through. If you need someone t' talk to, I'm here," she offered. "Also, it makes it clear between us that you know what happened so long ago, so I don't feel like I'm lyin' t' you anymore."

"I appreciate it," Willow said, with the stress evident in her voice. "Just not sure what you want me t' do about it, especially when I'm gettin' married in less than an hour. Really? You wait until *now* t' tell me?"

"Mum wanted t' wait."

"May I say somethin'?" Kit spoke up.

Willow crossed her arms. "Please do."

Standing between the pair, she took a hand of each of them. "We make choices every day. Through this whole time, you've only known Anna as the successful young lady and older sister, right?"

"Right. It was kinda hard t' live up to," Willow admitted.

"What she's trying to tell you in a not so successful way, is that she messed up. She's just as human as you are."

"But, I feel as if everyone has lied t' me my entire life."

"Would it have made a difference if you knew sooner?"

"Probably not," Willow admitted.

"I know you've been worried this whole time of what other people may think," Kit said, resting her hand on Willow's shoulder. "Does it not make you feel a little better to know that your sister is not so perfect?"

"It does, but do ya see my point?"

"I do. But, can you imagine what she has gone through all these years? Watching you, knowing she couldn't comfort you or tell you, but stood by their agreement to let your Mum and Dad do it? You are part of her."

"A part I do *not* regret bringin' into this world, by the way," Anna added.

"An', I appreciate it, but I don't know what t' do with it."

"Do you love her?" Kit asked.

"Yes."

"Do you still respect her?"

"Knowin' she didn't kill me, yes."

"That wasn't what I wanted t' do. That's why I called Kit an' Nico," Anna said in her defense.

"And, once we explained the reality of the situation to Andi and Tommy, they agreed it would be a huge mistake to abort," Kit explained. "Now," she said, taking both of Willow's hands into hers, "Imagine, if you will, that you were seventeen and pregnant. Imagine also, that the guy is *not* Caleb."

"I can't."

"That was Anna's position, though. Now, imagine *your* child is around seventeen and pregnant. Would you want her to give up the rest of her life for one moment?"

"No."

"Those were the positions people were in. Anna was sworn to secrecy about telling you she was your mum. She didn't have a choice. If she did, then you would have been given up for adoption."

"Oh!"

"She had to wait, per their agreement, to tell you until Andi gave her permission. Now, since you're starting your own life with a new little one on the way, I'm thinking Andi and Tommy were okay with letting you know. Also know that neither Andi nor Tommy would change a thing. As a matter of fact, before we came up here your Mum was just saying what a blessing you have been."

"I guess I understand. It's just not what I wanted t' hear on my wedding day."

"Would you rather not know at all?"

"No." Facing Anna, Willow rested her hands on Anna's arms. "Thank you for always being there. I can't imagine what you went through all these years."

"The other option was unimaginable," Anna said, wiping the tears from her face. "At least I was able t' watch you grow an' get t' be here on this day. That's not *even* mentionin' gettin' t' see yer little one when it's born."

"Okay." Willow stood straighter, her body language spelling out that she reached a decision. "Here's what we're goin' t' do. As far as anyone else is concerned, y'er still my sister. Of course I'll tell Caleb, but it's up t' you if you want t' tell anyone else."

"I wouldn't want you t' keep anythin' from him."

"As far as everyone else, that's up t' you. As far as *yer* grandchild, we'll still keep it between us, but know this little one is yer grandchild as well, but will have t' call you Aunt. I don't want yer reputation tarnished after you worked so hard t' clean it."

"Thank you," Anna said with a smile.

As Willow gave her a hug, she said, "Thank you for finally tellin' me the truth. I appreciate yer honesty."

"I love you, Willow."

"I love you too."

"And for the record," Anna said, pulling away. "I got t' pick yer first name, as long as it wasn't too out there."

"I like my name. Thank you for pickin' a good one."

"Okay. Enough sappiness. You have to get married," Kit reminded her. "And, now you need to redo your makeup. I'll send Caitlyn back in for that. You only have about ten minutes before it's time."

Willow stopped her. "Kit?"

"Yes."

"Thank you for lookin' out for me, even before I was born."

Giving her a hug, Kit told her, "You are a true joy and blessing from the Lord."

"I only hope t' be as good a mum t' my little ones as you have been."

"You have some good examples of your own to follow. Also, if you let God guide you, and continue to rely on Him, you won't go wrong."

"Here's prayin'."

*   *   *

Stunning was a mild term for their wedding. As the three stations, and just about everyone from their area and church were in attendance, Caleb and Willow pledged their lives to God and each other.

As she watched her son make his vows to his wife, Kit couldn't help but to reflect on God's grace, mercy, and love…

Starting with her father. She thought of the way she grew up and the way she was treated. Even though she lost Jax and Anna, God used it for good, in order to bring her father and Ty to the accepting knowledge of Jesus Christ. The Lord even blessed Kit with allowing her the opportunity to forgive her father, giving her a peace about what she experienced before she had to go into hiding.

In regards to Ryan Darcy, the Lord allowed them to begin repairing their ruptured friendship through that horrible night of the F5 tornado, and then consequently him driving her to college allowed them to do a restart in their friendship. In doing so, she could release the bitterness she felt about the way he treated her in high school.

In allowing her to return to Oklahoma so long ago, the Lord gave her an amazing opportunity to get closure from all that she ran away from to go to college. Allowing her to work through the death of Jax, Anna, and her mother was a priceless gift. In the process, she was also able to give Jax's parents and Officer Williams some peace about the accident as well.

When she went to college, the Lord surrounded her with some amazing people. Her friends through college meant a lot to her, and helped guide her through the next four years. Stacey Spencer (now Schmidt) was a godsend. She helped Kit navigate the experiences she had in Oklahoma, as well as the loss of

Aaron and Jillian. She was her confidant, and one of the many people Kit often found herself thinking about, and longed to contact. While Seb and Ethan were also a major support, Seb turned out to be a better friend than a boyfriend, and she was grateful that the Lord showed her that so quickly. Praying for peace and happiness for all of her college friends, allowed her to still stay spiritually connected with them, without having direct contact.

Even though Joey and Lucca Rossi's antics were life threatening, the end result allowed Kit and Nico to have a life of peace together away from the chaos of the city. That relationship allowed Giovanni the opportunity to get out of the family business, and live his life freely.

The Rossi situation also brought about the grace restored to Dominic, who was still dating Charlene, much to her dismay. Charlene continued to state that she would wait for him, and that he was worth it, but Kit often wondered if Dom was holding back due to his past. Was he afraid to take that next step in fear that he would lose it all? Praying for clarity of mind for him, her thoughts drifted to Jillian.

Through Jillian's death, God allowed Nico into her life. Nico completely turned her life upside down – in a good way. He was her strength when she didn't even know she needed it. He protected her and looked after her, training her to protect herself. Nico was a blessing that she could never thank the Lord enough for! They were soul mates, and she was blessed to have him.

Also, without Nico, their children may not be there, and they never ceased to amaze her as well. While some had trouble telling the two sets of twins apart from their counterpart, Kit knew which was which before they even opened their mouth.

The differences were subtle if you didn't know them, blaring if you did. Cherishing each day she had with them, she continued to bathe them in prayer as frequently as possible.

For all the Lord gave her through life, His grace and mercy were the biggest gift. Without it, she would be a mess. She couldn't wait to see what else He had in store for her. Having said that, she knew it would be a blessing regardless, and she looked forward to each day granted to her.

*   *   *

Over the next five years, Kit and Nico's family not only expanded, but also progressed in life. Caleb and Willow had a baby boy, who they named Jasper Dylan Sullivan. Three years after Jasper was born, they had a set of boy/girl twins, named, Benjamin Alexander and Lilly Kathryn. In the meantime, Joshua graduated college with the double majors of: Modern Language and Criminology, while Rachel got her nursing degree, and Leah's degree was in Veterinary medicine.

About a week after the girl's graduated, the family was sitting on the porch one Sunday afternoon talking about church, when Josh suddenly stood, looking out toward the road.

"Who is it?" Nico asked, getting up, standing next to Josh.

Glancing over his shoulder to Kit nervously, who had little two-year-old Lilly on her lap, Josh quietly said, "Charlie an' Ethan."

"Now?"

"They probably waited until the girls graduated."

Nico shook his head and sighed. "Too early. I don't want t' give you up yet."

"Let's just see what they have t' say," Josh said, as he and Nico walked off the porch, meeting them part way down the road. They wanted to meet them out of earshot of the others. "G'day, Ethan an' Charlie," Josh said, shaking hands with them.

As Nico shook their hands in greeting, he asked, "What can we do for ya t'day?"

"Just wanted t' bring graduation congratulations," Ethan said, putting the men at ease. "No worries. We're not the ones comin'."

"Who's comin', then?" Josh asked, confused. "I figured it would be one a' you blokes."

"Oh, you'll know." Ethan chuckled, knowing exactly who was coming. "You may find yourself tongue-tied by the young lady of the group."

"What's that mean?"

Snickering, Charlie said, "She's just yer type."

"What type is that *exactly*?" Josh asked, slightly put off by the exchange. He knew these men knew things, and what they told him often concerned him.

"You'll see," Ethan assured him. "In the meantime, I believe there are some young ladies we need t' congratulate."

"They're on the porch." Nico gestured toward the porch before they headed back that way. "They're graduation party is tomorrow."

"I see. An' do they know yet which one is goin'?" Ethan asked.

"Neither has said. Do *you* know?" Josh asked.

"Yes."

"Mind sharin' with the rest a' us?" Nico asked.

"Nope. She'll let you know. In the meantime," Ethan started before stepping up onto the porch, "congratulations are in order for you ladies." Passing an envelope to both Rachel and Leah, he then turned toward Willow and added, "T' you as well."

Stunned, Willow asked, "How did you know?"

"Know *what*?" Caleb looked at her in surprise.

"I was goin' t' tell you later, but I'm pregnant again."

Josh rolled his eyes. "Hasn't anyone explained t' y'all how that happens?"

"No one *had* t' explain that one," Caleb said with a sly smile.

Blushing, Nico said, "Easy. Parents still in the area."

"Oh, like *you two* don't know." Caleb rolled his eyes. "Y'all had four as well."

"How many are ya plannin' on havin'?" Leah asked.

"Well, we figure with at least two a' ya bein' A.N.G.E.L.s, an' at this point neither a' the girls even have a boyfriend, that yer only hope a' havin' grandchildren are comin' from us."

"Point well taken," Kit agreed. "However, you're about t' max that house out."

"We're goin' t' get fixed after this," Willow said to ease their minds. "We only wanted four."

"What will ya do if they're twins?" Rachel challenged.

"Just be thrilled if they're happy an' healthy. Whatever amount God decides t' bless us with, we're fine with that amount," Willow explained, resting her hand on her stomach. "At this point, we're just addin' t' our blessings."

"True."

"An', just because I haven't told ya, doesn't mean I don't have a boyfriend," Leah quietly added.

"Meanin'?" Rachel looked over at her, stunned by the possibility of Leah having a secret she didn't know.

"Meanin', do ya know Finn Walker?"

"The one in yer veterinarian classes?"

"Yep."

"I thought y'all were just study-buddies."

"Nope," Leah said, proud of herself for keeping a secret for so long.

"How long are we talkin' here?" Josh asked.

"Six months."

"*Six months*?" Caleb's jaw dropped. "How could you do that for six months an' no one know."

"I never said *no one* knew," Leah corrected him, as she glanced toward Kit.

"*You* knew?" Rachel asked.

"Of course. There's not much that goes on around here that I *don't* know," Kit said with a satisfied smile. "Much the same as I know Josh is going to be an A.N.G.E.L. when they come for him."

"How do you know *that*?" Josh asked, glancing at Nico, upset.

"The signs are there," Kit explained. "You are also a lot brighter than your brother."

"I see. So, Dad didn't tell you?"

"Nope."

"But we have an uncanny way of knowin' things without havin' t' tell each other," Nico pointed out.

"Okay. So, if *Mum* knew about the boyfriend," Josh started, and then pointed toward Nico, "Then, did *you* know?"

Nodding, Nico agreed, "Of course."

"How come no one said anythin'?" Caleb asked. Turing toward Rachel, he asked, "An' how did *you not* know?"

"Because her mind has been elsewhere for the last six months," Ethan jumped into the conversation.

"Yeah. You've been a bit spacey. What's going on?" Leah asked. "Wait!" She put her hands up to stop everyone from talking. "Let me take a guess at this. Since, *you* know that she's been distracted," she said to Ethan, "I'm gonna guess it's because *you* got the call?" she asked Rachel.

"I did," Rachel admitted.

"Why didn't *you* say anything?"

"That's rich comin' from *you*," Caleb snapped, crossing his arms.

"Look, all y'all have secrets, and they are yours to reveal when *you* deem necessary to *whom* you deem necessary," Kit said, to put a stop to the bickering. "Those who needed to know, knew, and those who found out now, know as well. It's all good."

"Too true," Caleb agreed. "Speakin' a' which, I need t' take my pregnant wife home so she can get some rest," he said, pulling Willow up with him. The three little ones gave everyone hugs and kisses before they departed for their home.

When they were gone, Leah stood. "This looks like it's gonna be a deep conversation, so I'm gonna go call Finn. Night all!" she said before giving everyone a hug good night.

When the screen door closed and Leah headed upstairs, Ethan and Charlie settled into a more comfortable seat.

"What's goin' on?" Nico asked.

"Plans have been set in motion that will affect the two a' you," Ethan explained to Josh and Rachel. "Are you both ready?"

"Ready an' waitin'," Josh confirmed.

"Any day, anytime. Been waitin' for a while," Rachel agreed.

"Then know the time is near."

"How will we know?" Rachel asked.

"When they get here, you'll know," Charlie said, confidently.

"Do you know their names?"

"Yes."

"Do we get to know?"

"Not yet. We don't know if they'll bring others. But know this, there won't be any doubt in yer mind," Charlie assured them.

"All right." Josh stood, brushing his pants off from the ground. "Gonna assume that's it for us?"

"Yes," Ethan said. "The rest is for Kit an' Nico."

"Night," Rachel and Josh said, giving them all a hug before going into the house.

"This looks even more serious than the last conversation." Nico sighed. "Y'all need t' come by just for a visit once an' a while."

"Wish we could." Ethan smirked. "Unfortunately, this is *not* one a' those times."

"All right. Out with it," Kit said, impatiently.

"Do ya want the blunt version or the around the bush version?" Charlie asked.

"Is that a serious question with me?"

Snickering, Charlie shook his head. "No. Okay, we come with some good news, an' some not so good. Which do ya want first?"

Letting out a slow breath of air, Kit said, "Let's go with the good."

"Well, Lucca Rossi had a heart attack in jail last year," Ethan started. "Then Joey Rossi was taken out by a Rodchenko Family member just last month."

"Interestin'," Nico said, sitting back in his chair.

"Did you know?" Kit asked, stunned.

"Nope. I would have told you. That allows us t' breathe a bit more. Maybe now we can sneak in a visit t' yer dad."

Charlie cringed. "That brings us t' the bad."

Sitting up in her seat in alarm, Kit asked, "Is he okay?"

"Afraid not." Ethan shook his head. "An F-3 hit yer hometown yesterday, an' unfortunately he was in the wrong place at the wrong time. There were forty-three killed, an' he was among them. I'm so sorry, Kit."

Swallowing her tears, Kit took deep breaths to keep her emotions under control. "I know this is all in His plan," she said purposefully. "I know He gave me the opportunity t' mend things with my dad, an' for that, I'm grateful. Did he suffer?"

"Not much."

"Thank you for tellin' me."

Once Nico put his arms around Kit, she lost the fight for her emotions and burst into tears. "Spring is rough over there," Nico reminded her.

"I know," she sniffed, wiping the tears off her face. "It doesn't make it any easier."

"I'm sorry. We've had a lot of loss in our lives," Nico explained.

"Know that you are never far from His sight," Charlie encouraged.

"I know. Thank you for coming and telling us," Kit said, sitting back in her seat. "Is there more?"

"No. Just know that after all these years, you are now free from the Rossi's," Ethan said, resting his hand on her knee.

"I know. I also know our children are growing rapidly. We're grandparents, which is something I *never* thought we would make it to. I know God has blessed us beyond measure, and that He will continue to take care of us, as well as the kids. They're willing and ready for His service. Please take extra care in watchin' out for them?"

"Always," Ethan assured her. "We've watched them grow, an' I've had the privilege of trainin' them since Josh an' Caleb were ten. I'll look after them as one a' my own."

"That's all we can ask," Nico said, appreciatively.

"If you recall, our adventures often started in the fall, whether here or in the States," Kit pointed out. "It seems appropriate that we get this news in the fall."

"Forever fall," Nico sighed.

*   *   *

A couple of days later, Dominic sat down on the porch with Kit and Nico. "Thank you for taking some time out of your day to meet with me," Dom started. As he was talking, Seth and Claire rode up on their horses and tied them to the railing before they took a seat on the porch with them.

"While y'all are always welcome, what are you doing here?" Kit asked, nervously looking from Seth and Claire to Dom. "Why do I feel like I'm about to get another bombshell. I've already had an eventful week."

"Afraid it's not over yet," Dom admitted. "I called you all here for a reason."

"Do you know what's going on?" Nico asked.

"Yes," Seth said, holding up two plane tickets.

"What's going on?" Nico asked, visibly agitated that he had no idea, but Seth obviously did.

"I cannot thank the two of you enough for all you have done for me through the years," Dom said, and then sighed.

"This isn't one of *those* conversations, is it?" Kit asked, tucking a portion of her hair behind her ear.

"Shhh," he said, resting his hand on hers. Shaking his head, he sighed again. "To have been able to see you happy, to see your children grow up and marry, and have children of their own has been a pleasure. More importantly, though, was to have been given the chance to discover the wonderful gift of grace and salvation. I was even able to find a woman who loved me for me."

"Are you getting married?" Kit asked, with a smile.

"The fact that the idea of that makes you happy, warms my heart. Please let me finish, or I may not get it all out," Dom asked. Looking toward the sky for a moment of encouragement, he saw a bird soar through the air. Nodding, he continued, "The Spirit and I had a rough few years, until I finally gave in a couple of days ago, after Charlie and Ethan's visit. Ya see, Charlene and I broke up, because I'm going back to The States…with Seth."

"What? Why?" Kit asked, confused. "I'm lost."

"You both have given me many gifts, but I have to face what I did many years ago. Seth is taking me back to face my past."

Kit objected, "But –"

"No. You have given me the option, and I appreciate it, but this is something I have to do. You're safe now, according to Ethan and Charlie. Your children have children. I released Charlene from our relationship. I confessed to her and Pastor what I've done, with Seth by my side. He has agreed to go back with me. That way I don't feel alone…or chicken out."

"You *knew*?" Kit asked, wide-eyed.

"Kit…*Katie*, you have been a wonderful friend. Your forgiveness has meant the world to me, but it's now time for me to face my past," Dom explained. "You could have turned me in long ago, but you didn't. Nick, you could have done it as well, but you gave me a chance. I appreciate the opportunity you gave me to find the Lord's grace and mercy, but this is something I have to do."

"I understand," Nico said.

"But, they could put you on death row!" Kit objected.

"Then so be it. I took the lives of two young people. I violated young ladies. I kidnapped you and almost killed you. I have made my choice. At least I go with the saving knowledge and love of Jesus, my Savior. For that, I can never thank you enough."

"Are you going to tell them where you've been?"

"No. They can ask, but I won't answer." Dom shook his head. "Seth will tell the truth, that I came to him here to turn myself in. That's all they need to know. Thank you for all you have done for me," he said, a single tear crawling down his cheek. "Nick, please continue to take care of Katie. I need to go before I change my mind. Stay here, though. Seth will tell you what happens to me. Stay here. I don't want to undo everything you've worked for over all these years."

"Thank you."

"You've given me the gift of spiritual freedom, and I will continue to keep your secrets."

Giving him a hug, Kit ran into the house without another word. "Thank you for giving us the consideration of letting us know," Nico said, standing to shake his hand. Surprising him with a hug, Nico returned it, knowing it would probably be the last time he would ever see him. Then Dom and Seth got on the horses and took off for Akoonah Station before heading to the airport.

As they rode off, Claire turned to Nico, and said, "This actually stinks. He turned out to be a good man."

"But he still has to face his past. I give him credit. It takes a big man to do that. With the power of the Spirit, I believe he will face it with strength. The Lord took him down this path for a reason. I'm just glad to see the final ending of this story."

"You know, I initially thought you were crazy, but after seeing the plan play out, I can see the steps. I'm just sorry Charlene got hurt in this."

"Me too, but I'm relieved he made the final choice he did. It restores my faith in the humanity I knew it was in him. Now I need to go restore the faith Kit has in her. She's lost a lot, and has given a lot. She will still have to give up two of our own for the Kingdom. She's a strong woman, but I feel that I may need to let her know that I'm still here and I'm not going anywhere."

"Mind if I come with you?" Claire asked, wiping the few tears that fell. "Dom grew on me too, but she was friends with him before this all happened. I can't imagine this is easy. He may very well be going back to face death row."

"But he's ready."

"Then I pray he goes in the faith and strength that God will go with him."

* * *

A week after Charlie and Ethan came for the girl's graduation, Rachel and Josh both walked out of the house after getting a snack. They looked toward the road to see a jeep bouncing down the drive toward them.

"Interestin'," Rachel commented before she glanced toward Josh to see his reaction.

"It's time," Josh simply said. Taking his radio off his belt, he said into it, "Mum, Dad, they're here."

"Who's here?" Nico asked.

"*Them*," he enunciated.

"Got it. We're helpin' Willow with the little ones while she feeds the baby," Nico said, referring to their final little one, Zachary Jacob.

"Get here as soon as ya can. Not sure how much more time we got."

"Be there as soon as possible."

"Copy that," Josh said, and replaced the radio on his belt as the jeep pulled up to the house. Three young people got out of the vehicle. Stunned by the beauty of the young lady, who had a thin build, sparkling green eyes, and chestnut brown hair that hung to her mid-back in loose waves, Josh had to catch his breath at the sight of her. He knew in an instant what Charlie and Ethan were talking about. "Welcome t' Serenity Wells Station."

"Thank you," the young lady said, shaking his hand. "My name is Angel English, and these are my brothers, Jesse and Jonathon," she introduced them.

"I'm Josh Sullivan, an' this is my blood-n-blister, Rachel," Josh said, as everyone shook hands in greeting. "How can we help you?"

"Pretty sure you know why we're here," Jonathon pointed out.

"We do. How did you find us?"

"That's the interesting part." Angel smiled. "Well, we were basically led here."

"What do ya mean?" Josh asked, leaning against the porch post, crossing his arms.

"We could show you, if you'd like?" she offered.

Struck by her demeanor and her laid-back nature, Josh felt himself instantly attracted to her. "Sure. Curious t' see how you came about findin' us."

As they made their way to the back of the jeep, Nico and Kit came out of Caleb and Willow's house to see the group. "We're losing them, aren't we?" Kit asked.

"No. They're just movin' on t' another season in their life," Nico corrected her. "By the looks a' the tanks with the young lady, they'll be pretty well protected."

"Let's hope they had good trainin," Kit said, walking up to the group.

After introductions were made, with a twinkle in her eyes and a smile on her face, Angel pulled the tarp off a metal box three-foot in length.

Glancing into the back of the jeep, Rachel asked, "What's in the box?"

Joel 1:3

Tell it to your children, and let your children tell it to their children, and their children to the next generation.

Hebrews 13:2

Do not forget to show hospitality to strangers, for some who have done this have entertained angels without realizing it!

See what the other A.N.G.E.L.s have been assigned in

The Holy Flame Trilogy.

| Book 1 | Book 2 | Book 3 |

Summary

Courageous. Brave. Fearless. Valiant. These synonyms are often used to describe firefighters/paramedics, police officers, and military personnel. They face danger and lay their lives on the line when they leave for work. What are their struggles? Could that hinder their job proficiency? Who is taking care of those who are taking care of the citizens of this country?

Casey Carter is a 'newbie' to the firefighting family of Engine Company 15. Not only does she have to prove herself as a probationary firefighter, but she also has to battle misconceptions of females within her newly chosen profession. As situations begin to arise, can she count on the firefighter brotherhood to have her back? Will she be able to pass the tests placed before her, or are there aspects that she was not even aware existed?

Often in life there are two realms in play. There is the physical realm - what is right before you; the other is the spiritual realm - what is unseen. Each can directly affect you, whether you believe they exist or not. Can Casey keep them in balance when she is not exactly sure what she is fighting? Can a group of men help her see what cannot be readily seen, hear what cannot be readily heard, and be able to overcome what she never knew existed? Will they be able to show Casey her true Call To Duty?

The next generation is taking over. In the Award-Winning
Divine Legacy Series.

Summary

As two of the children of Nico and Kit Sullivan, along with Mark and Casey English's, make up the new members of the A.N.G.E.L.s, their job is to gather their remaining teammates. In the process of acquiring the two members listed in the United States, they run across a situation that isn't on their agenda. Amber Jones was in need of miraculous intervention, and God answered her call with the next generation of A.N.G.E.L.s. The A.N.G.E.L.s find some unique help along the way and learn valuable lessons that will change how they function and see the world from that point forward. Read along as the next generation picks up the torch, claiming their Divine Legacy.

Connect with C.J. at CJPetersonWrites.com